A Pursuit of Madness

A Twisted Princess Collection

AMBER BUNCH

HELLO,

Little Rabbit

No part of this publication may be reproduced, distributed, or transmitted in any form or by any means, including photocopying, recording, or other electronic or mechanical methods, without the prior written permission of the publisher, except as permitted by U.S. copyright law. For permission requests, contact [Amber Bunch – abunch0615@gmail.com].

The story, all names, characters, and incidents portrayed in this production are fictitious. No identification with actual persons (living or deceased), places, buildings, and products is intended or should be inferred.

Book Cover: Getcovers

For all inquiries, please contact:

Abunch0615@gmail.com

Or visit: https://www.amberbunchauthor.com

Paperback ISBN: 979-8-9865255-6-3

E-Book ASIN: B0C9NY1NKY

All rights reserved.

No portion of this book may be reproduced in any form without written permission from the publisher or author, except as permitted by U.S. copyright law.

Contents

Trigger Warnings	X
Dedication	XIII
Map	XIV
Map	XV
1. Alice	1
2. Rose	13
3. Dean	22
4. Hatter	30
5. Alice	39
6. Dom	46
7. Rose	56
8. Alice	64

9.	Hatter	74
10.	Alice	82
11.	Alice	91
12.	Rose	103
13.	Dom	112
14.	Hatter	119
15.	Dean	129
16.	Alice	139
17.	Rose	152
18.	Dom	161
19.	Alice	167
20.	Dean	176
21.	Alice	184
22.	Dean	193
23.	Hatter	203
24.	Dom	212
25.	Alice	218
26.	Dean	227
27.	Alice	237
28.	Alice	243
29.	Rose	253

30.	Hatter	263
31.	Alice	270
32.	Alice	280
33.	Alice	288
34.	Hatter	295
35.	Alice	301
36.	Alice	306
37.	Alice	317
38.	Dom	323
39.	Dean	330
40.	Rose	338
41.	Hatter	349
42.	Rose	362
43.	Rose	375
44.	Alice	385
The Letter		398
Epilogue		399
Chapter		409
Also By		410
Acknowledgements		415
About the Author		417

| Chapter | 418 |
| Chapter | 419 |

Trigger Warnings

This book is not for the faint of heart. Please read all warnings before you continue.

- ~ Dubcon
- ~ Light Blood Play
- ~ Bully
- ~ Child Abuse (Physical and Sexual Assault)
- ~ Gore
- ~ Loved One's Death
- ~ Mention of Child Death
- ~ Pew Pew Play
- ~ Torture
- ~ Sexual Content
- ~ Adult Language
- ~ BDSM

~ If I'm missing anything, please let me know by visiting https://www.amberbunchauthor.com

For the ones living vicariously through their books.
Why Choose?

Pink Flamigo Country Club

Hatter's Mansion

Henry H[a] Tea Sho[p]

Black Spade Territory

The Red Queen's Castle

Jabberwocky Lagoon

Singing Siren"s Meadow

WONDERLAND

Chapter One

Alice

"You're a crazy fucking bitch!" The man beneath me screams, struggling against his restraints, drawing a shrill giggle from my throat as I watch a big fat tear roll down the sharp hollow of his cheek.

Pussy.

"Now, now. . .Is that any way to speak to your date?" I muse, adrenaline racing through my veins as I prop my elbows on his chest, resting my chin in my palms, my legs dangling on either side of the table from where I sit straddled across his lap.

It took me almost an hour to drag his unconscious, naked body in here, hoist him up on the table, and set him up to be a proper patient, fit with a gown that doesn't quite cover his pale ass.

His arms and legs have been secured to the surgical table with cuffs around his elbows and wrists. His lower body is bound tightly by leather straps to either side of the cold metal table.

Don't get me wrong, by no means is this guy of small stature, being a former football player and an avid health junkie...had I not slipped the drugs in his drink before we left the bar tonight, he could have easily overpowered me.

But it's ok. He won't be getting away from me now.

With a surge of rage, I rip the rest of the duct tape off his skin, tearing it hastily and making him flinch as I rip away tiny bits of his flesh.

Who would have thought after the amount of Ketamine I slipped him, he would wake up in the back seat of my car on the way here, and I would wind up having to waste two rolls of my tape to keep him still?

Then, I had to remove every last bit just to get him prepared for surgery.

Preposterous!

Normally it doesn't take nearly as much. Shit, it doesn't take any at all if I get the opportunity to break their legs and dislocate their shoulders first.

Using the fact that he can still lift his head as an advantage, he spits in my face, "I'm going to kill you, you dumb ass cunt!" He screeches, veins popping up from his scrunched forehead. "Do you realize who the fuck I am?"

I do, in fact, know who the fuck he is, and I can't say that I give a damn either way.

The infamous Tyler Mason—Husband to one of London's most popular fashionistas and also the son of the city mayor. He's a nasty sadistic fuck that thinks he can take whoever and whatever he wants without consequences.

But tonight, he made the mistake of picking me up.

I absolutely adore the odds of it all. And now, the thrill of having one of the most vile human beings under my thumb is such a delight!

Tyler has his hands in everything. Drugs, prostitution, sex trafficking, money embezzlement—you name it, and Tyler has done it.

Like father, like son.

Their wives are no better, though, if I'm being honest.

They all look the other way just so they can continue living their lavish lifestyles of diamonds and caviar. Such simple-minded women, though. I truly feel like they don't even care about what their husbands do.

They don't even question their whereabouts when they stumble through the front door coming home in their blood and semen-stained trousers.

Then, there are the women like my mother—the most wretched of them all.

They're the ones who enjoy the money and power for themselves, so they groom young women and children before selling them to the highest bidder. Some of the girls they receive are kidnapped, whereas others are promised a better life than the one they have living on the streets—only to find one way worse than they could have ever imagined.

I just so happened to be lucky enough to be born into it myself.

How fucking thoughtful of you, mother.

I was her most prized possession, after all...Her precious little money maker.

"It will only hurt for a little while, Alice." She whispered in my ear as I cried beneath the weight of her holding down my shoulders—quelling my struggles as the large, burly man above me wrinkled his forehead in concentration, sweat beading in the crease right above his eye as he thrust into me, destroying my innocence and my body all at once with his disgusting selfish desires.

I closed my eyes so I didn't have to see his face, showing little emotion once my small body became numb to the pain being thrust upon me—or rather, into me.

The alcohol on his breath made my stomach sour, and his chest heaved with every harsh pump of his hips, releasing the toxic smell in my nostrils, so I turned my head away, only to be met with the suffocating smoke coming from the red-hot cherry on the tip of my mother's cigarette, her favorite tool to punish me with.

The fur on the cuffs of her robe are soft against my face, "Easy, Sully, don't ruin her on the very first go. Save some of her for later." She laughs, bringing the ivory tip of her opera-length cigarette holder to her plump lips, drawing a puff before releasing it right in my nose. I cough loudly, choking on the smoke, and the man grins, revealing the two broken and rotting teeth in the front of his mouth.

He grunts in response to my mother's request and finishes up soon after.

When it was all over, my mother left me lying on the bed in my blood-soaked nighty, bruises covering the entire portion of my inner thighs from being assaulted by a man ten times my size. I could hear her in our living room asking him if he enjoyed his time, as it isn't every day you get to take a fresh virgin piece of ass.

I hope the twenty thousand she received for my sanity was worth it.

Her final words to me that night had been when she came into my room again after Sully went back home to his wife and family. She tucks a loose strand of blonde hair behind her ear—the only part of her that came unraveled during her wicked deeds—and throws a tattered old bath towel and a blue and white petticoat dress on the foot of my bed, "Get cleaned up and get rid of this mess before your father gets home, and don't you dare speak a word of this to him." She smiles, an evil even the devil should fear. "I would hate for you to lose what love he has for you if he finds out what a nasty little whore his treasured little girl has become. You wouldn't want him to hate you, would you, Alice?"

My trusty stuffed elephant is held tightly in my arms as I rock back and forth, biting my bottom lip to hold back the tears that threaten to spill from my tired eyes and scoop the items off my bed, shaking my head, "No, Mother. Of course not."

"Good. Now, hurry, or you'll be late for supper."

Tyler squirms again, bringing me back to the fun moment we were just having together.

"Don't be such a silly goose. I know *exactly* who you are." I tell him, playfully swirling my finger in the patch of chest hair poking out from the neck of his gown. "It's because of who you are that made me decide to bring you here."

A couple of years ago, when he was still in college, he was charged with multiple cases of rape, but before his trial, the charges were suddenly dropped, and the three girls that accused him disappeared about two months later.

Of course, no one looked into their disappearances. Instead, rumors were spread about them being money-hungry whores that lied about being raped just so they could get a payout and skip town.

I know the truth.

Those girls are never coming back because they're dead. And while Tyler may not have committed the murders himself, he is the one who has their blood staining his hands. He is the one responsible for the closure their families will never get the chance to have because the judicial system is helping to keep it covered up.

I wonder if he's going to scream the way those poor women who he forced his cock on did when I begin performing his surgery.

Will he bleed the same way they did?

Will he beg me to stop, to show him mercy even though he wouldn't do the same in return if it were me in his place?

I doubt mercy and soft sensual sex are the reasons he picks up prostitutes in the first place.

I've heard the stories, and I've witnessed the damage he can cause firsthand. Once he picks a girl and leaves with her, she never comes back as the same person she was before he inflicted his horrors on her.

"I—I don't even fucking know you!" He stutters, his pearly whites sounding like fragile teacups clinking together as fear begins to creep into the back of his mind.

Now things are starting to get exciting.

It's the fear that gets me off the most, I think, or perhaps it's the screams that follow shortly after.

I've never been able to fully decide.

"I'm your judge, jury, and executioner, Tyler—a beautiful nightmare that you will never forget," I reply, grinding my pussy against him. The thrill and anticipation of what's to come is becoming almost too much to bear.

"What are you going to do to me?" His green eyes are bloodshot now from crying.

Good.

He should be frightened. He has no idea of the type of pain he's about to endure, the blood that will be spilled once I begin.

I really shouldn't be so messy, but I just can't help myself.

Not that it matters anyway. No one ever comes out this way. Why would they?

My hospital is located in the middle of nowhere—long forgotten by society and hidden within the depths of tightly woven, thorned trees—making it almost impossible to leave once you get here.

There's only one way in and one way out—a singular path that leads to and from the massive space, with the rest of the ten acres being fortressed by sharp razor wire fencing. It had been designed that way so if any of the criminally insane, that were once homed here, escaped, they would have been easy to track down.

Most people believe it to be haunted after the fire that claimed so many lives almost a century ago. The old newspapers said one of the convicts escaped, locking everyone else inside, including the doctors and the guards.

Then, she doused the outside with Kerosene and burnt the place to ash; the screams of those trapped inside are said to have been heard from miles away in a nearby town. Some people even now go as far as to say that they can still hear the screams, and those brave enough to venture inside my Asylum have sworn they've seen her wandering the hall, not realizing it's just me.

It always makes me laugh watching them run away, pissing on themselves from the fear they instill in their own minds by overthinking something as trivial as ghosts.

Besides, the ghosts have way better things to do than to fuck around with the frightened townspeople. Especially since the rebuild of this place. There's a garden courtyard, an indoor putting green, and a large game room filled with an array of things to do. With so many delightful wonders, why would they waste their time trying to scare people?

They leave that part to me.

Even still, the place became abandoned because the doctors and guards were too afraid to stay and keep up with the place. Now, they have a new hospital in town that they use. It's not as lovely, in my opinion. I've been there once, and I much rather prefer my own.

This place has a history for me.

My father used to bring me here when I was a little girl, becoming our temporary reprieve from my mother's cold words and harsh hands. One day when we were walking through the woods, we found a massive, old, twisted tree trunk in a small opening. It looked as though it had grown around an old gold-framed mirror, and the large trunk had swallowed it—the mirror becoming one with the tree, splitting its middle into a reflective oval shape big enough for a grown man to walk through.

There was nothing else surrounding it except for bright green grass that was speckled with small colorful mushrooms and wildflowers. I'd gone near it to pick some of the flowers when I tripped, falling into the tree. My father tried to catch me, but we both were sucked into the mirror and, as a result, were thrust into a magical land filled with wonder, where we were greeted by the most beautiful woman I had ever seen—one my father would soon fall madly in love with.

My father was a good man. He was loving, hardworking, and loyal to those he loved. He loved me with fierce unconditional love, even after he had found out about my darkest kept secrets. I was still the most important thing to him, and it would be that weakness that would eventually lead to his death.

Looking down at Tyler, a lightbulb goes off in my head, and a bright smile spreads across my face at my newfound idea.

"Ohhh, Tyyyyler!" I sing, hopping down to the cold tile floor, my bare feet not making an ounce of sound as my toes connect with the hard surface. I walk over to the small metal table holding all of my tools, picking up a crimson-stained set of pliers.

Naughty, Alice.

How very unsanitary of you to not have cleaned up properly when you have all the equipment you need at your disposal. No, no...This won't do at all.

I set them over on the counter to deal with later, this time picking up a pair of needle nose pliers, waving them at Tyler, "These look like good fun! What would you like me to rip off first, fingernails, nipples, or should I pull your eyes from their sockets?" I grin.

"You're gonna fucking die, bitch. My men will be coming through those doors any minute, and when they do, I'm going to shut you up with my dick, and then I'm going to beat you to a bloody pulp before I skull fuck you and leave you here to FUCKING ROT!" He screams the last part, laughing hysterically—his eyes wild and crazed.

I let out a drawn-out sigh, shaking my head, almost feeling sorry for the lad. All my patients go through the motions. Fear, denial, anger, acceptance—It's always the same.

Every. Single. Time.

I don't expect this time to be any different, but I'm just giving them a taste of their own medicine, a bitter spoonful of the same poison they inflict on the world.

Reaching into the small pouch of my dress, I retrieve an old, tarnished pocket watch glancing down at the time.

I'm late.

"Tell you what. . .I'll give you thirty seconds to decide. Fair?" I ask, tipping up my chin to meet his gaze.

"Please, lady! Please don't—don't do this!"

"Twenty-five seconds, Tyler. Better hurry."

The pounding of our hearts is the only thing I hear. His from fear, and mine from the addicting thrill of ridding the world of these special kinds of bastards, one by one.

"I—I can give you money! Whatever you want, just name it. You don't have to do this. You don't have to kill me!" He pleads, but why would I want his money?

Money can't give me what I want. . .What I *need*.

"Fifteen seconds."

"FUCK!" He yells, struggling against his bindings.

The watch's tiny hands reach towards the twelve on its cracked face, and I flip it over, showing Tyler as the last second of his free will ticks by, I watch eagerly as all the sense of hope he had drains from his eyes, "Times up, love." I whisper in his ear before plunging the sharp tip of the needle nose pliers into the cavity of his left eye, gripping the soft ball of tissue and yanking it from his head. He writhes beneath me on the table, his screams bouncing off the pristine white walls of my operating room and straight to my core.

My blue gloves are now splattered from the blood gushing from the small open hole in his head, and I can't help but to giggle at the poetic justice I find in my choice.

Talk about an eye for an eye—am I right?

Chapter Two

Rose

My face burns with the imprint of my queen's hand. Well deserved, I suppose, as her tea hadn't been at the correct temperature when she sat down to it.

How could I have been so careless?

I should know better by now, yet it seems I'm always making mistakes of sorts.

"I'm so sorry, Your Majesty. I'm ashamed of serving you such rubbish," I squeak, scrambling to the polished floor to clean up the broken bits of glass before I enrage the Queen further.

"You insolent girl! Get this mess cleaned up at once, or I'll have your head!"

Not that she didn't just slap the porcelain cup out of my hand or anything.

Stupid old wench.

Smiling at the insult rattling around in my head, the porcelain I've been collecting clinks together in my apron as I shift on my feet so I can reach a little farther to snatch up a larger piece that had bounced away when the cup clattered to the floor.

"Did I say something amusing to you?" The Queen questions, raising her perfectly arched brow.

"No, Your Majesty."

"Then fix your face before I fix it for you!" She demands.

"Of course. My apologies." I say hastily, standing up and making my way over to the trash bin under my gold-trimmed crystal tea cart, disposing of the shards of glass.

Then swiveling around, I reach for the pot-belly teapot in order to fill another cup. This time I carefully test the temperature before making my way over to the Queen's side.

She takes the cup from my hands, taking a small sip, nodding her head to let me know I hadn't failed her once again and that this time it would do.

After taking another drink, she places the small teacup on the glass-topped table next to her throne and pinches the bridge of her nose, letting out a resigned sigh, "Three of my guards were killed today," She begins, her voice dripping with a sickening sweetness I know to be fake. "They were killed by unregulated magic, and as you know, this kind of behavior will not be tolerated in my kingdom."

I nod my agreement and then she continues, "Those who cross me need to be put in their place."

No! Please, not again!

A twisted smile spreads across the Queen's face like a snake slithering out of its pit, her voice booming across the court, a whip cracking against silence, "The Hatter thinks he can turn my kingdom against me?" She bares her teeth in a rictus of fury, her skin flushed with rage as both her hands slam down on the chair arms on either side of her.

"He will soon discover why Wonderland is solely under my control. All of Wonderland will learn why *I* am the Queen and why they are nothing in comparison to me." Her eyes flicker with madness, meeting my own as she raises her hand and clenches it into a fist, promising destruction to anyone who dares to challenge her authority, "I will squash him under my heel like the pathetic bug he is, making a lesson out of him for all of my subjects to see, a warning to anyone who dares to challenge my reign."

My heart sinks in my chest, a heavy burden crushing down on me from the weight of all her evil.

I know what this means, and I hate it.

I hate her.

But I can't show it, not when my life hangs in the balance.

Instead, I merely nod my head, keeping my eyes lowered to the red and black checkered floor, praying to any deity who would listen to help me escape this nightmare.

"Of course, Your Majesty, as you should," I whisper, my thumbs and middle fingers tapping together rapidly at my sides in an attempt to calm myself.

The use of Wonderland magic was banned once the Queen began her reign of terror, and she's been using me and her minions to keep it that way.

Ever since I was a little girl, she has been manipulating and abusing my power. Of course, back then, I had no idea it would be used against my own people.

And now most folks don't want to risk getting caught using their own magic, so they've been buying unregulated magic from Hatter and the Black Spades.

The Queen's snarl turns into a twisted smirk that makes my skin crawl, "I'm glad you agree because there have also been reports that the same village the incident occurred in is harboring a couple of the Black Spades men," She informs me, lifting from her seat and slowly making her way to where I stand.

"I see," I reply, still tapping my fingers together.

She reaches her hand out to stroke the angry red mark on my cheek she had placed there only moments before, "So, you know what's expected of you then, my beautiful Rose?"

I can feel my own anger boiling inside of me, a typhoon of rage threatening to consume me whole as I struggle to keep my emotions in check.

I take a step back, crossing my arms over my chest, trying to hide and disappear into the shadows of her guardsmen lining either side of the room, but her eyes seem to follow me, piercing through my very soul.

I know what she wants from me, and I can't bear the thought of it, but I have no other choice than to obey her commands and find the men she speaks of.

I shift on my feet, lifting my gaze to meet her own, and finally give her the answer she's looking for, "Ye—yes. I know."

"Delightful!" She exclaims as she picks through the small pastries on the tray on top of the tea cart.

She knows I'll easily be able to sense their magic and point them out to Absinthe and Yelana, sealing those men's fate with no chance of escape.

I had been born with my mother's gift of sensing and absorbing nearby magic.

However, thanks to the Queen, I can no longer absorb magic since she placed an enchanted necklace around my neck whilst I slept, keeping me leashed to her like a fucking dog on a chain.

Her face is drawn tight from the perfectly secured bun on the top of her head right below her ruby-adorned crown when she looks back at me, and her mouth is drawn in a thin line while she scans my face.

The long sleek black dress wrapped tightly around her curves skims the floor as she creeps closer to me, stopping only once her porcelain face is mere inches away from my own.

"You look nervous, dear. Is something wrong?" She asks, her eyes narrowed.

How can she even ask me that?

She acts all calm, pretending to be concerned and innocent. . .It's absolutely disgusting.

She took *everything* from me.

My father, my childhood, my dignity—my life.

I try to keep my focus on the Queen's face, but all I can see in my mind is the image of her kneeling in front of me when I was still a small child. Holding my hand and comforting me as she faked tears regarding my father's untimely disappearance. Hatter's father was eventually taken into custody for my father's murder, but I'm certain the Queen had something to do with it.

She never loved me or my father. All she wanted was power.

Once she convinced me to give up the throne and to let her rule over the Kingdom because I was too young for all the responsibilities and hardships, she began my torment.

She acts all high and mighty, but the truth is without her guardsmen. . .Without her executioners, and without the Jabberwocky at her disposal, she would be nothing—A powerless shit stain in the crack of my ass that I could simply wipe from existence.

The old memory threatens to send me over the edge, but I take a deep breath to compose myself and force a smile, shaking my head. "No, Your Majesty. I'm fine, really." I lie through my teeth, refusing to let her see the truth behind my words.

This has become a talent of mine throughout the years of her implacable ruthlessness and cruelty, a gift I'm sure many others wish they'd possessed prior to losing their heads.

The thing is...The Queen craves perfection, and I realize this.

She prefers to have it her way or no way at all. And she doesn't care for any kind of chaos that she doesn't devise herself.

No, not at all.

She won't tolerate even the slightest bit of defiance from her subjects.

I've learned that the hard way.

However, with time, I've learned to manipulate my emotions and words to meld into the perfect image of what she thinks a good little servant girl should be.

Walking slowly in a circle around me, she reaches out, picking a tiny piece of fuzz from the shoulder of my blouse with her face turned up in disgust, "Good." she smiles, tilting her head slightly, "I trust that you will take care of this matter, then?" She questions.

"Consider it done, My Queen," I almost wince at the words but quickly steel myself.

Her head nods in satisfaction, "Absinthe and his wife will be awaiting your arrival in the morning. I'll have a carriage ready for your departure no later than dawn."

I can feel a cold sweat running down my spine.

If they are coming, that means this will only end with someone's death.

But this is just like the Queen—keeping her henchmen and beautifully manicured hands dipped in everyone else's business.

For now, there is nothing I can do about it, so I turn and begin walking towards the black steel-plated doors leading out of the throne room and into the hall.

"Oh, and Rose," She calls out from behind me, malice exuding from her words.

Freezing in my tracks, my heart leaps painfully into my throat, and I choke on my words, Ye—Yes?"

"I expect you to leave no stone unturned when it comes to finding these men. And once you do, I have a special task for you."

"A task, Your Majesty?" I question, turning back around to face her, the blood running cold in my veins.

"Yes," She answers. "I want you to bring me the hearts of the men they are hiding. Their treason cannot go unpunished."

I've never been asked to kill before.

I'm meant to monitor and track down the individuals who use Wonderland magic...But not *kill* them.

"If I may ask, why me and not one of the executioners?"

"Because I'm losing faith in where your loyalties lie, and I want you to prove yourself to me. Consider this—a test. I need to know that you are committed to the Kingdom, Rose. So, I am offering you that chance. Do you not want or appreciate that?" Her voice is harsh, and her eyes are void of any sentiment.

We both know this has nothing to do with the Kingdom and all to do with her fear of being overthrown by the Hatter, along with her sick obsession with controlling people.

With a deep breath, I force a nod, knowing that I have no way out of this, "As you wish, Your Majesty."

"Do not fail me, Rose. You know the consequences will be dire."

With that, I turn, pushing through the doors quickly, with my heart pounding in my chest as I make my way through the twisted halls of the palace, the Queen's words echoing in my mind.

It's not like I haven't been asked to do unpalatable tasks before, but this is different.

This is murder.

I finally make it to my bedroom and fling open the door, only to slam it shut behind me.

I then stomp across the tiny room and throw myself onto the hard mattress of the bed, burying my face in the pillow and screaming as loud as I can.

When I can no longer scream, I flip onto my back, looking out the small window of my room, tugging at the necklace wrapped around my throat.

I swear...one day, I *will* break free from this castle, and once I do, I'm never turning back.

CHAPTER THREE

Dean

"Boss says it's time for you to pay up, kitty cat." I grin, putting my cigar out on the back of Chester's hand where Dom has it held in place on the black wooden desk in front of him.

Not smiling much now—are you fucker?

One of our shipments is missing, and my brother and I have been sent to find out why. This is the second one this month to vanish without a trace, and both have been on Chesters's watch.

A cat jumps down from where it's sunbathing on the ledge of the large open bay window inside Chester's office and stretches out its front paws. Its tail is held high as it yawns, licking its lips. The tiny animal's purr softly vibrates against my leg as she rubs her body against the material of my suit.

I kneel down to pet the cat and stroke its soft, black fur, scratching her behind the ear when she nudges her head into my hand, emitting a contented meow.

"What a lovely feline you have here, Chester," I say, looking up to him with a malicious grin. "It would be a shame if anything were to happen to her. You know how much Dom hates cats."

Especially Chesters cats.

The cute kitty facade doesn't work when you know all too well that it can turn into an invisible razor-toothed monster that can shred the flesh right from your bones in a matter of seconds.

Chester's dark brown eyes dart between me and Dom, flicking over to the cat now curled up next to my leg. "I don't know anything, I—I swear," he stutters, his voice strung high with tension, but he doesn't flinch away from the cherry of my cigar.

I must admit, Chester is one tough son of a bitch. Which is why we brought him into the Black Spades, to begin with. With his smarts and his ability to control his feline demon spawns, he's been a huge asset to our cause.

But while he may be one of us, and he may want to get rid of the Queen just as much as we do, even our own need to be taught a lesson from time to time.

"I'm going to need you to give me a little more than that, Chester. That's an awful lot of pixie dust to go missing without a trace, and it was *your* men that were last seen with it. Now, tell me their fucking names." I almost growl the words.

"Rupert and Jeremiah were the ones doing the pick-up. Pan's boys, who were supposed to be handling the drop last night, were found dead by the docks by a couple of fishermen before Jeremiah got there." He complies, sweat dripping down the tip of his curved nose. "Jeremiah says Rupert never showed up for the drop, and according to the logbooks, he didn't show up for work today either."

I stare at Chester, contemplating his words. Something doesn't add up, and I can sense that there's more to this story than what we know. Rupert was one of our best men, and he would never miss a job.

I guess it's possible that he could have simply taken off with the pixie dust, but my gut is telling me that that's not the case.

I'm certain of it.

Someone's done their homework. And they somehow knew exactly when the exchange was taking place.

But how did they get passed our systems and inside the docks to take out Pans boys?

Very few people know about the entrance that's hidden within the rocky cliffs of Reaper Island, and those who have accidentally found out about it didn't live long enough to tell anyone else. Not to mention it's secured by a passcode that changes on a weekly basis.

Additionally, the Black Spades have been refining our security measures for years, so it's not as if we're flying blind.

And yet, the pixie dust is gone, and we have absolutely jack shit to go on.

The Queen has been sending her guards after us for years, and every single one she's sent has either been sent back her beaten half to death as a taunt, or they're dead. So, I seriously doubt it's one of hers stealing our shipments.

They wouldn't have the balls anyway.

Well, her executioners might, but she wouldn't dare risk them for something this trivial.

This means that either someone on our side has betrayed us or someone is putting in a lot of time and effort to find out our little secrets.

I clench my jaw, sucking in a breath through my nose as I think further into things, signaling my twin brother to release Chester from the death grip he has him in.

Chester sits back in the dark leather chair, folding his hands on the desk in front of him. "Fucking hell, Dean. Was all that necessary?"

I shoot him a dark look, and Dom cackles loudly from the other side of the room, where he's rummaging through Chesters's liquor cabinet.

"Nuff said, boys. I get it. Business is business. No hard feelings." Chester laughs.

And I know he understands.

Crazy fuck.

Dom saunters over with three glasses filled with a light amber hue of liquor, "Where can we find Jeremiah?" He asks, passing a glass to each of us before plopping in the chair next to me, his one green eye and one blue eye locked on Chester.

"Knowing him, he'll be at the pub just a couple of towns over. He went and got himself pussy whooped by one of the girls that works there." Chester replies, shaking his head in disapproval.

"Do you know anything about her?" I ask, my curiosity now peaked.

Chester shrugs, leaning forward to pour more of the amber liquid into his glass. He takes a long swig before he answers, "Just that the kid said she was a good lay, and she's definitely a looker. I think she moved her a few months ago from one of the towns further north, up by the Queen's castle."

"Did he mention her name?" I ask, leaning forward to place my elbows on my knees, letting my hands fall between them.

She can be involved in this somehow.

"I think he said her name is Nova. I believe he called her his *little star* if I remember correctly." He chuckles.

Nova.

Why does that name sound so damn familiar?

Dom perks up at the mention of the girl's name too. We meet each other's gaze, both of us confused but determined to find out more.

I sit back in my chair, my mind going a million miles a minute. "Thanks for the information, my friend. I think we'll going to go pay them a little visit now."

Dom stands up first, stretching his knuckles out in front of him before placing a hand on Chester's shoulder, "Well, it's been fun, Chester, ole boy."

"Fuck you, Dom!" Chester spits, swiping away his hand as Dom doubles over, laughing hysterically.

"I really am sorry our visit wasn't under better circumstances," I say, slamming back the rest of my drink and placing my empty glass on Chester's desk. "I hope next time it won't be so unpleasant. I'll let you know what we find out about Rupert. In the meantime, I don't want any new hires. It's too risky."

Chester gets up and walks us over to the door, "Eh, like I said—no hard feelings. I would have done the same thing if I were in your shoes."

He shakes my hand, and Dom and I head out the door, the lock clicking softly behind it.

It's clear Chester doesn't even trust his own men right now.

Smart man.

It takes us maybe three minutes to get back to our car. Once we get in and I start the engine, Dom turns to me with a deadly gleam in his eye.

"What is it?" I ask, knowing full well what's going on in the back of his mind.

I know my brother better than I know myself sometimes. He's all I had after our entire pack was slaughtered by the Queen's executioners, Absinthe and his wife, for using our moon magic.

We were just kids when it happened. We'd been out all day in the forest, playing and hunting for food, when we heard all the commotion and fighting. We ran as fast as we could but when we got there, all we could do was watch as they murdered everyone we knew, our parents, our sister...everyone.

Then, they burned our town and homes to ash, leaving us with nowhere to go.

We trekked for weeks out in the woods, sleeping in caves and scrounging for food.

Eventually, we ran into Hatter.

He was alone, too, after his father had been accused of and executed for the King's murder.

The Queen had thus seized control of Wonderland, leaving it in her wicked clutches.

It didn't take her long after to begin her slaughter fest. So many had been locked away or even executed just for wielding their magical abilities.

We still haven't found out exactly how yet, but the Queen has a way of knowing when the people of Wonderland use magic. She then sends her executioners with an offer, or if it's someone who's a repeated offender, they are beheaded on the spot without so much as a bat of the eye.

The car hits a pothole causing the steering wheel to jerk sharply to the right, and I swerve slightly from the impact.

"Damn it, Dean! Get control of your ungodly wagon of death!" Dom shouts in my ear, his blonde hair wild from the wind.

"I hit a rut in the road. Get over it." I sigh, rolling my eyes.

"This is why I'd rather just run," Dom mutters under his breath.

His words bring a dull ache to my chest, "You know we can only run in the forest, brother. At least for now."

Dom nods, his jaw hardening and the muscles twitching in it as he chews on the inside of his cheek, fighting to keep his wolf at bay.

"This Nova bitch just showing up out of nowhere can't be a coincidence." He eventually says, tapping his fingers on the knee of his dark blue jeans.

"I agree. She is a loose end we'll need to tie up before another drop is sabotaged. However, before we can scare her off, we need to talk to Hatter and see if he knows anything about her or where she's from."

"Ok, but I call dibs on getting to torture her first." Dom grins, mischief swirling in his mismatched eyes.

"I knew you would, brother," I say, pulling the black car off the main road and onto the dirt trail that leads the backway into Hatter's mansion.

Dom can be a bit twisted when it comes to his methods of getting people to talk, but he does always get them to talk.

One way or another.

So, for her sake. . .I hope we're wrong.

CHAPTER FOUR

Hatter

My finger taps against the cold, icy glass of bourbon settled in my hand, my eyes scanning over the paperwork piled neatly on the top of the dark green desk I'm seated at.

It had once belonged to my father, the original Hatter, back when he was a haberdasher, making and selling hats before the Queen had him framed and beheaded for the King's murder.

Now, it sits as a quiet reminder in the center of my study, a symbol of my family's past, and a testament to the corruption that still festers within the kingdom, never allowing me to forget how I came to run this twisted world I now live in.

I've sat here for hours going over the files of every single member of the Black Spades, and I still don't know who the double-dealing rat bastard is.

It just doesn't make any damn sense.

This is a pretty tight-knit crew, consisting of only a small number of members, all of whom I can count on both of my hands.

I've trusted very few to work for me, and there are only two I consider to be like my brothers and trust fully, even with my own life.

I swirl the amber liquid in my glass, taking another sip, before sitting it down on the coaster next to the gun on my desk.

Leaning back in my chair, I let out a resigned sigh. I need to take a break from this before I lose it.

Losing control now could ruin everything I've built, and I've come too close to chance making any more mistakes.

Whoever it is will be dealt with accordingly. Dom will have his fun, and we *will* get some fucking answers.

No one fucks me and my brothers over and lives to tell about it.

My hands tremble from the rage coursing through me as I pour myself another drink, the stress of the day taking its toll on me.

Luckily, I hear the roar of an engine pulling in. That means Dean and Dom will be bursting through the front door any second now.

Standing up, I straighten my black tailored suit jacket before making my way out of my office and into the den to meet them.

As usual, I can hear them before I see them, and they're arguing about the damn car again.

Dom bitches anytime he has to travel any other way than running.

He really enjoyed the time we spent in Neverland when we were boys. He would stay in his wolf form most of the time.

Always pissed me off too.

But only because he and Dean could communicate telepathically when they shifted, and I had always felt left out.

It wasn't until we met one of the lost boys of Pan's, who was a young warlock that I was able to communicate with them as well. He conducted an ancient lunar ritual, binding us in a mutual brotherhood—blood brothers, in other words.

It was a grueling ceremony, and all of us bear the matching scars to attest to the intensity of the bond we now share.

As I step into the dimly lit den, the scent of smoke and whiskey fills my nostrils. Dean and Dom are already there, seated on the plush black leather couches and smoking their cigars like they own the place. Their eyes meet mine, and I can sense the tension immediately.

Something's wrong.

"What's going on, boys?" I ask, keeping my voice low and not like I almost tipped over the edge again tonight.

It's been so long since I last lost control. And I vowed after that dreadful night to never unleash that side of me again, to keep it hidden in the deepest depths of my soul.

Dean gets straight to the point, pulling me back from the wretched memory, "Rupert's missing. Two of Pan's men are dead, and the dust is gone. All of it."

Fuck.

"Does Pan know yet?"

"Not sure." Dom grunts. "We wanted to discuss Chester's newest hire and the little lady he has been spending his time with."

I turn to Dean with a raised brow, my voice barely human, "Explain."

He takes a long drag from his cigar before exhaling a cloud of smoke, then butts it out in the glass tray on top of the coffee table in front of him, "Chester said Rupert was supposed to meet Jeremiah at the docks but never showed up." He pauses, waiting for my response, but I wave him on.

Glancing over at Dom, he continues, "Jeremiah has been seeing this girl for a few months now that seemed to just randomly show up out of nowhere, and she's from one of the towns up north near the Queen's territory. My guess is she might be working with the Queen to take us down from the inside."

I feel my heart rate increase as Dean's words sink in. The Queen is always looking for ways to destroy us, and having someone on the inside would be a perfect opportunity for her to do so.

That doesn't feel quite right, though.

Does it?

There is something else, but I can't put my finger on it.

"What's the girl's name?" I ask them.

"Chester said her name is Nova," Dean replies. "Do you know anything about her?"

My mind races with all the possible ways I might know her, but I don't have the slightest clue as to who the fuck she is.

That's about to change.

I take out my cell and type up a message to Henry, requesting that he search for whatever information he can find out about her.

He's known to be the go-to guy for any kind of information or the one you see if you need to disappear for a while, especially if you're willing to pay the hefty price tag the crafty old bastard throws at you.

Henry runs a teashop in a small town about three hours from here--his way of staying under the Queen's radar.

"No, but I'm hoping to soon."

Dean and Dome exchange uneasy glances while I sit there, lost in my own thoughts for the next few moments.

My phone rings, and Henry's crackly voice fills the other line as I press the device to my ear, *"Fuck you, Hatter! Not even a "Hey, how the fuck you doing" before you start barking orders? I'm gonna be fucking dead before you bring your rotten ass back to see me!"*

A smirk forms on my lips, so feisty for such a frail old man.

I can picture the permanent scowl on his face as he curses me through the phone, his wispy white hair spilling out of the hat my father made him back when we visited the tea shop together when I was a young boy.

"Alright. Alright. Take it easy old man." I laugh. "I'll be coming to see you within the week."

"I'll believe it when I see it." He mumbles.

"So, what can you tell me?"

"All I could find on her without doing a deeper search—which I'll get to in a minute, so don't start your bitching—is she appears to be an orphan. Her family was killed during the initial restructuring of the kingdom when the Queen took the throne. She was left to die amongst the carnage of her mutilated family after her tongue was cut from her mouth and she was beaten to the edge of death.

Among the dead were her mother, father, older brother, and her sister, who was just an infant at the time."

"Fucking hell, Henry," I whisper as my stomach churns and my chest squeezes, my heart plummeting to what feels like a dead stop.

The twins glance over at me, their expressions mirroring one another's as they listen to our conversation, soaking up every detail.

"Can you find out where she is living now?"

"Let's see..." Henry says, and I can hear the tapping of a keyboard coming in loud and clear from his end of the phone line. *"Yes. I have her last known address here. I'll send it over."*

"Thanks, Henry. Keep digging. See if there's anything else you can pull up on her."

"Will do. You boys try to stay out of trouble." He says, laughing as he hangs up the phone.

He's all too aware that we are the very source of disaster, a terror that has others running with fear if they so much as cross our path.

I prefer it that way, and when I get my hands on the motherfucker that stole from me, my brothers and I will make him suffer, and I will enjoy every second of his pain before I slowly squeeze the fucking life from him.

Dean smiles, looking up from his phone to meet my gaze, "We going for a ride now?" He asks.

I don't miss the exasperated look on Dom's face at the mention of being in a vehicle again, but he gets up off the couch, muttering something about how we're trying to kill him, and heads towards the door anyway.

I nod before going to my study and grab my pistol off the desk, shoving it in the holster beneath my jacket. Then I casually make my way back out to the living room, where the twins are patiently awaiting my order.

Let's go." I say, grabbing a set of keys from the hook by the front door, "But we're taking my car."

"Thank fuck. I can handle your driving a hell of a lot better than his." Dom groans, pointing at our brother, earning himself a punch from Dean as he walks past him.

They are literally yin and yang.

In contrast to Dom's light blond hair, Dean has black. Dom hates cars and prefers running as a wolf, and Dean gets off on driving anything he can get his hands on, as fast as he can. They have mismatched eyes. One green and one blue. Where Dom's right eye is blue, Dean's right eye is green, and vice versa with their left eye.

I laugh at their carefree banter, shaking my head, then push through them and out to the garage, where we keep all the vehicles we wind up smuggling in from the Topside.

Slipping into the driver's seat of the sleek black *Escalade* I recently came across, I place my hand on the steering wheel, the leather cool against my palm, and push the button on the dash. The large SUV starts right up, and its engine purrs, gently vibrating my seat. It's a work of art; every inch of the car screams luxury, from the supple black leather interior and beautifully lacquered wood that is splashed throughout to the curved OLED touch screen that sits center on the dash. It has all the bells and whistles.

"I call shotgun!" Dom yells, jerking open the passenger door with unnecessary force and jumping into the seat next to me.

"Whatever," Dean replies as he scoots into the back seat, leaning his head back against the headrest, and lights up a cigar.

The garage door groans behind us as it closes. I press the gas pedal, and the tires squeal when the car lurches forward out onto the road behind the house. A few minutes later, we're on our way to the address Henry sent over.

Time to get some real fucking answers.

CHAPTER FIVE

Alice

Tyler is a sight for sore eyes. He's a bloody mess and must have peed himself three or four times now.

That's the part I hate having to clean up the most—when my patients can no longer control their bodily functions.

It grosses me out.

He passed out again from the pain, so now I'm just waiting for him to wake back up to inform him of the next and final step.

His remaining eye is still intact, so he will be able to observe the surgery I'm about to perform, a decision that was easy to make, and fortunately, it's almost time for me to begin.

I rub my gloved hands together, feeling the thrill of excitement coursing through my veins as I prepare for the procedure. I don't get to perform such delicate and intricate work as often as I'd like to, but when I do, it fills me with a sense of purpose and pride.

Tyler stirs on the table, groaning softly, as drool tinted pink from blood drips from his mouth.

"Well, hey there, sleepy head. I was wondering when you were going to join me again." I say, smiling widely.

Tyler blinks a few times with his remaining eye, trying to gather his bearings, and then moans as the anguish sets in again. He tries to move, but the restraints keep him firmly in place.

"Wh—why?" His chapped lips manage to ask.

His plea is pathetic.

"I already told you. You're a bad man, Tyler, and this world has no place for people like you." I reply sweetly.

"Please. You can let me go," He whines, his voice ragged and slurred from the loss of fluid and blood.

"I could, yes." I sigh, knowing some patients can get a little emotional at this point. "But I'm not going to."

He barely has the strength to glare at me and starts to sputter, struggling with his words as he tries to bluff his way out of the predicament he's gotten himself into.

Not that his empty words will persuade me any. I'm doing my due diligence by getting rid of the demons much like him.

Why won't he understand that?

"You have to be a saint in this world, Tyler. A saint." I say firmly.

"You can't do this to me," He pleads, his voice getting thick with tears and probably blood.

"I believe we've already established that I can," I reply softly.

Reaching for the scalpel, I remove it from the tray where I left it and pull my mask over my nose.

Tyler's naked body trembles on the table before me as I grab the apex between his legs and place the tip on the scalpel flush against his pubic bone, preparing to make the first incision.

I've already cast a mold of the appendage to add to my growing collection, a souvenir to relive the pleasure of our time together.

Just as I go to cut, I hear a loud clanging down the hall and the sound of muffled voices.

It's Halloween, so kids sometimes get off on breaking into my hospital to frighten themselves, make messes they never clean up, and destroy equipment that they can't replace.

It makes me so damn angry.

Not this time, you little fuckers.

I don't bother gagging Tyler before I leave the room. They'll only mistake his groans for the ghosts anyway.

The lights flicker softly, making the shadows jump between the white walls of the long hallway; it's as if they are quietly dancing in a macabre ballet.

Cautiously, I round the next corner, where the only lighting is from the moon peeking through the broken window to my left.

I hear mumbling, so I slow down, slipping into one of the empty rooms. The cobwebs hanging from the ceiling tickle my nose, making me giggle out loud, and the pitter-patter of the intruder's footsteps comes to a halt.

They should be scared.

My hospital isn't precisely a crystal castle with windows made from stained glass to show its majesty, but it's mine, and I hate when others think it's okay to invade my home—my place of commiseration.

It's not fair.

My blood-stained face remains obscured by the shadows and the dusty old curtain as I watch the two figures rumble through the paperwork at the nurse's station about five rooms down from the room I'm hidden in.

First, they broke into my home, and now they're going through my things, how very rude!

I quietly sneak past the slightly ajar door and back into the dark hall. Their backs are turned away from me, so I keep to the wall, making myself less noticeable in case they do turn around.

It looks to be two boys no older than sixteen or seventeen.

One is dressed as a character from a popular horror movie I once watched, and the other is dressed as a witch. His face is done in pretty makeup, and he has natural dark hair grown past his shoulders, tying the look together nicely.

Halloween really is the perfect time for looking all sorts of different.

Even with the blood streaking my pale blue dress and white apron, mascara streaked down my face with smudged red lipstick to match; I fit in quite nicely.

The slasher and the witch don't seem to notice me as I creep up behind them, shuffling as quietly as possible. I must look unthreatening as I stare at their backs, only because they've yet to see me.

"I've been waiting for you," I whisper softly as I grab the witch by the arm.

Wide-eyed, he turns to meet my wild, devilish stare, a blood-curdling scream leaving his thin, pale lips.

Terrified, he pushes me away like I'm some monster.

I fall to the floor in silence, my brain rattling in my skull from the impact. He trips as he backs away, falling only a few short feet away from me.

I shake my head slightly as I crawl towards him on my knees coming to a stop only inches away from the toes of the white shoes he's wearing—and yes, painful as it is, it's so worth it to see the terrified look on his face when an evil smile cracks my face.

They're scared shitless, making me shake with laughter as the witch scrambles to grab the slasher's arms and pull him up off the floor.

They stare at me in horror, and low and behold, dear Tyler chimes in just at the right moment, wailing like a stuck pig, frightening the boys even further.

Trembling and falling all over the place, they scream like babies in their cribs, calling to their mommies for a bottle of milk.

Alas, my work here is done, and I can finally finish what I have been trying to do all fucking night.

I storm back to my operating room, clean up, and prepare for surgery once more.

Time's ticking, and I have little time to work with before Tia notices I haven't shown up for her party yet.

Oh well.

Fun is fun, but work is work, and I have to play both sides to survive this fucked up world.

It's time to put my mask back on and do my thing, "Are you ready, Tyler?" I ask, grabbing a clean scalpel from my tray.

I lift the scalpel, and an inhuman shriek rips through the air. I steady my arm and bring it across, splitting the skin of his dick, the sharp instrument easily tearing through the soft tissue and muscle.

Tyler's entire body convulses as his guttural cries fill my ears, "There, there now. It's alright. You won't be needing this anymore where you're going. Besides, it's hurt too many people for me to let you keep it, even in hell."

Blood spills from the wound, down his hips and thighs, and drips to the floor. The cut is large, gaping, and gory, with bits of flesh trailing from it, like little threads on a ragged cloth; it won't be long before he dies.

Not my best work, but I may have been a bit hasty after being interrupted with such belligerence.

I smack his face, gaining his attention, what little he has left anyway, "Oh, one last thing before you perish. . .For my last judgment, I want you to feel what you've made so many others feel—what I was forced to feel for too many toilsome years. Now, pay close attention." I tell him before shoving the severed appendage in his ass with only his blood available for lubrication.

His face twists, contorts, and crunches up in extreme pain—the same pain he inflicted for years while he took pleasure in causing it.

Choking on his cries, he makes his last fighting effort to escape the binds holding him without success, the light in his unexpended eye dulling as his trembles stop and he deeply inhales his last breath.

Releasing a content sigh, I rub the hair back from his face and put my lips close to his ear, "Sleep tight, darling."

Chapter Six

Dom

We roll into town just as darkness starts to descend. The skyline is painted orange and purple as the sun sinks behind the horizon.

There are a few lights on in homes, but not much of anything else is lit up. It's a small town that could easily be missed if you were driving by and not paying any attention.

"Let me do the talking," Hatter says from the front seat as we pull up to a small cottage-style house, and he cuts the engine.

Everything is quiet.

It's hard to tell if anyone is even home. Not that it matters anyway. We'll be waiting for them whenever they finally do show up.

And then it's my turn to have a little fun.

Watching people bleed is probably one of my favorite things to do to pass the time.

I'll be the first to admit that a sick, perverse pleasure washes over me every time I stare at the crimson river of life spilling from my victims. It's even more exhilarating for me than it is to shove my cock down a girl's throat and hear her choke and beg for mercy before I break her beyond repair.

My dick begins to swell against my jeans as I think of all the ways I'm going to torture Jeremiah while I make his little girlfriend watch.

Maybe I'll start by cutting off a finger or two and watch them both squirm under the pressure of being forced to listen to every agonizing scream he has to offer me.

I can hear the roar of a motorcycle from the distance, and it sounds like it's still about three miles out. Even when I'm not in my wolf form, my ears can hear more than any human ever could.

Wolf shifters have exceptional hearing and can hear sounds from miles away, even if there are loud noises in the background. We also have a very keen sense of smell, which enables us to smell objects that are far off in the distance that others can't pick up on.

Dean hears it, too, because he perks up in the backseat, flicking his cigar into the cupholder ashtray in his door, "Think it's them?" He asks.

"Not sure," I reply, tilting my nose to the sky out the open car window, trying to catch their scent; they're uphill, however, so it's useless at the moment.

We all get out of the car as the hum of the bike draws nearer, Hatter going around to the front end, propping his foot up against the fender as we wait.

Sure enough, I catch Jeremiah's scent. It's the same nauseating, overly musky cologne that singed my nose hairs at the docks.

One that he uses way too much of, if you ask me.

"It's them," I growl, curling my upper lip.

"Good," Dean says, cracking his neck. "Let's get this over with."

The knot in my stomach tightens as the engine winds down, and the sound of it comes to a halt down the hill.

Why the fuck is he stopping?

"Damn it," I murmur, glancing at Dean.

And I was ready to make his head pop like a fucking watermelon.

Obviously, he knows we're up here. I glance over at Hatter, furrowing my eyebrows together in confusion.

Hatter shrugs his shoulders, takes off his jacket, places it back in the car, and takes a step towards the trailhead, "I guess we're going to him then."

I flex my fists next to me, my heart rate speeding up as we walk down the trail.

As soon as we round the bend, Jeremiah sits up, his lip curled in a sneer. A small female with black hair, tattoos, and a pixie cut is sitting behind him.

He's got his leather vest on and a pair of dark blue fitted jeans, his oily mop of ashy brown hair pushed back in an unkempt mess.

"I figured I would be seeing the lot of you. To what do I owe the pleasure, gentleman?" Jeremiah asks, leaning back and placing his hands on the gas tank of the sleek midnight blue bike.

He's trying to play it cool, but I can sense the fear festering beneath his skin.

He's nervous.

Dean's eyes are narrowed, his focus on the petite girl perched on the back of Jeremiah's bike.

I strain my ears, but I can't hear the soft thump of her heart or sense anything from her. It's as if she doesn't exist at all.

Even though she can't speak, she watches me and my brothers intently, almost like she's studying us, her icy blue eyes darting back and forth between us, hanging on to every move we make.

"Cut the shit, Jeremiah. You know damn well why we are here, so don't play fucking coy," Dean snaps, flicking his cigar, hitting the toe of Jeremiah's boot.

Jeremiah throws the helmet in his hands to the ground and spits at Deans's feet as he kicks out the stand, dismounting his bike.

I launch towards him, my teeth bared.

"Disrespect my brother again, and I'll pull that pretty tongue from your mouth so you can match your little bitch."

Apparently, she's his sweet spot because he pulls a gun out from the back of his pants and points it at my head with a shaky hand, "I'll kill you all if you lay one fucking finger on her. Do you understand me?"

I laugh, pressing my forehead even harder against the steel barrel of the gun, the coldness of the metal like a soothing balm to my hot flesh.

"Try me." I dare.

Hatter's eyes flash red as he steps between us, his arms up in a gesture meant to de-escalate the tension that's gaining momentum by the second.

Jeremiah might not be afraid to duke it out with me, but the moment he spots a glimpse of the beast that's within Hatter, he instantly begins to back away from me and towards his motorcycle.

Everyone in Wonderland has either experienced or heard about the horrors he's capable of if he ever loses control.

Our brother has fought for as long as I can remember to not go off the deep end.

It's something he struggles with every single day, and it's only become harder over the years, ensuring the other part of him he tries so desperately to hide doesn't escape his grip.

I can see the bloodlust he possesses in his eyes, and it's only a matter of time before his darkness breaks free from the containment that holds back the hate and rage that swims under the surface of his composed demeanor.

Hatter's mouth is pressed into a hard line, and his eyes could burn holes in the cocky motherfucker's skull with the intensity of his glare.

"Last warning, " He snarls, pointing his tattooed hand in Jeremiah's face. "One more disrespectful move from you, and I will tear your head off and feed it to the hermit crabs that live in your mother's cunt."

I make eye contact with my brother, and a goofy smirk tugs at his lips.

Nice.

Leave it to Hatter to threaten the most diabolical things with the finesse of a fucking God.

Slowly, Jeremiah puts the gun back in his holster and runs his fingers through his hair before linking them together with Nova's.

Nova sits expressionless, still watching like a hawk, her knuckles white from how hard she's squeezing Jeremiah's hand.

"Alright. Let's get on with it." Jeremiah says, crossing his arms.

I let out a short chuckle, amused with the kid's attitude, "So sassy! It looks like this one actually grew a set of balls."

Almost makes me sad that I'm going to have to kill him before we leave.

Hatter rolls his eyes at me, the small scar slicing through his eyebrow rising with the motion before he turns his attention back to Jeremiah.

"I'd really love for us to do this without trouble," Hatter tells him, fixing the fedora atop his head. "So, if you tell me where I can find my product, we can all leave here tonight."

"I'm going to tell you the same thing I told Chester. I don't know where it is. When I got to the drop, Pan's boys were dead already, both decapitated. Whoever killed them and took the dust was already long gone. Rupert was supposed to meet me there, and as you all already have heard, he didn't show up."

"Do you think it was him?" Hatter asks.

Jeremiah rubs his jaw, contemplating the question, "No, I don't think it was him either." He finally replies.

"Who else did you think it could be?"

"My first thought was Absinthe got to them, but when I took a closer look at the wounds, the cuts were way too jagged--Absinthe would have never left such sloppy work."

Absinthe is a lethal assassin, the Queen's right hand, and Jeremiah is right about one thing—he's not sloppy. His work is quick and clean.

"I can send you over the pictures I took." Jeremiah offers.

"And we're supposed to fucking believe that you had absolutely nothing to do with this?" I spit.

I am so fed up with this asshole and his lies. I should shift right now and sink my fangs in his jugular, let his blood warm my mouth as he bleeds out on the fucking ground.

The stench of his anxiety almost makes me want to curl over and puke. He's hiding something. That much is clear.

"Do you think I give a fuck if you believe me or not—"His phone beeps, and then I notice a slight shift in his expression.

"Who is it?" Hatter asks.

"They just found Rupert's body—or I guess I should say what's left of it." He says, turning the screen to show us a picture of Rupert's mangled form tied to the front of the boat that carried the Pixie Dust here from Neverland.

"Damn it." Hatter curses to himself.

Chunks of his face are missing, as are most of his fingers and toes. His guts are hanging loosely from the massive cut going down the center of his stomach, and it looks as though someone tried to pop his head like a piece of fucking bubblegum from the way his eyes are bulging from their sockets.

Whoever did this wanted to send us a message.

"The girl." Dean inquires, his gaze darkening as he nods over at Nova. "What have you told her about our business together?"

"Listen, man, all she knows is that I work for Chester, and I deal in illegal magic," Jeremiah replies, quickly glancing over at the girl in question. "She doesn't have anything to do with any of this, so please, just leave her out of it."

"I'm afraid we can't do that," Hatter says calmly.

A cold grin cracks my lips. It's about damn time I get to play. I was starting to get worried there for a minute.

Jeremiah eyes the key in the ignition and slides the girl further down on the seat so she can attempt an escape, thinking none of us would notice what he's trying to do.

"Go ahead. Have her try, but I promise you, she won't make it far before I drag her back here and let Dom have his way with her," Hatter laughs.

"You son of a—"

Nova hops down from where she's sitting and taps Jeremiah in the chest, cutting off his sentence before signing something to him. He shakes his head and uses his hands to speak back to her in a language my brothers and I can't comprehend.

Her tiny body takes a defiant stance. She places her hands on her hips and glares at him before she huffs and forms a fist, moving it up and down at the wrist.

He touches his forehead to hers, nestling her face in the palm of his hand, "I never meant for you to get you mixed up in this shit."

She nods, a tear slipping from her eye and down to the dimple on her chin.

How fucking sweet.

"Ok. I haven't been completely honest with you, fellas." Jeremiah admits, rubbing the back of his neck.

"You don't say," Dean smirks.

"Let him speak," Hatter interjects, shooting Dean a look.

He grabs Nova's hand, placing a kiss on the back of it. "I only got into this business to get closer to the product, but not in the way you all think. Go ahead, babe. Show them." He says, and the raven-haired girl comes forward, dropping to her knees before us.

When the sound of breaking bones radiates through the night air, it hits me as hard as a three-ton rock to the head, and Dom is just as dumbfounded as I am when the realization dawns on the both of us.

She's a fucking wolf shifter, and she's from our pack.

CHAPTER SEVEN

Rose

My eyes scan the outer rim of the wood line, drawn to the beauty of nature as I pull my soft curly red hair away from my face, securing it behind my head with the band that's around my wrist.

Every now and again I'll catch glimpses of Wonderland's smallest of creatures scuttling across the forest floor or rustling through the trees.

The wonder and awe of the forest captivates me, pushing away the dread that has settled in the pit of my stomach from the task I have ahead of me; ripping away the hearts of two living beings whom I don't even know.

We've been traveling most of the day now to the town where the two men from the Black Spade clan are believed to be hiding. I stink, and Phantom, my horse, is growing weary, panting beneath me as she stumbles across the ragged stones that have fallen from the Jabberwocky's mountains.

As the sun begins to set, I finally spot the town in the distance. It's a tiny village made up of a few thatched-roof houses and a single tavern at the center of it all.

"Our targets are there." Absinthe stops, pointing to the tavern and telling Yelana, his wife. "Once I execute the traitors, burn this disgusting town and its filth to the fucking ground."

"With pleasure, my love." She purrs, then turns to me with glaring eyes and a smug smirk on her perfectly carved face. "You think the Queen's little pet will do as she's been told, or do you think we'll finally get to kill her?" She questions.

My stomach churns at the thought of what I must do here, but I steel myself and edge my horse forward, putting a cork in my bottled-up emotions.

"If she fails, you can have all the fun you desire with her. If you wish to melt the flesh from her bones, I will ensure you can fulfill that fantasy."

A giggle escapes her lips as she glances back at me, taking in my expression of shock and fear. My face likely mirrors the hue of my fiery red tresses.

I force myself to swallow the lump in my throat, my fingers tightening on Phantom's reins, but I stay quiet, moving forward, cursing them both in my head.

If my magic weren't imprisoned by this damn necklace, I would murder them right where they stand. I'm not a killer by nature, but I have endured so much pain by their hands and the Queen's that I would happily end their lives without a single fuck given.

As we approach the town, the scent of ale and smoked shadowfinch fills my nostrils, and my stomach growls, hungry from the lack of food during our trip.

The bird-like animals are a delicacy, and they are known for their inky black feathers, haunting songs, and shimmering purple eyes. The meat from the small animal tastes quite unique, though some may find the intense flavor a bit unsettling.

I dismount, stretching deeply, my bones protesting from the long ride, and lead my horse through the crowded streets. Gazes from the townspeople meet my own, the air growing thick with tension and desperation as they watch me and the Queen's well-known assassins march through their village, their fear evident because they know what's about to come.

Absinthe stalks next to me, his massive executioner's blade dragging the ground, reflecting the last rays of the sinking sun.

He towers above me, his muscular arms extending from the brown leather vest hugging his torso, his face concealed behind a matching leather mask that fits snugly against his skin—the only visible facial features are his soulless eyes, which burn as intensely as the fire that shoots from Yelana's hands.

She skips beside him, twirling her long ash-colored braid, popping the piece of gum she's been chewing on for the last hour.

Yelana is a tall and slender woman whose being radiates pure evil. She revels in the sick thrill of burning people alive—no matter the gender or age of her victims, the smell of charred flesh and death is the only thing that matters to her.

I often wonder how the two even came to be married with all the malice and hate they carry inside of them.

The men from the Black Spades are nowhere to be seen, but I can sense their magic close by, so they can't be too far.

My heart races as we walk along the dimly lit cobblestone streets to the tavern—the moment I've dreaded drawing nearer with each agonizing second that ticks by.

Pushing past the curious onlookers, I try to ignore their whispers and hushed tones, yet I'm utterly aware of the countless eyes following our every move. We reach the tavern entrance, and I take a deep breath, clenching my fists inside my gloves to steady my nerves.

The door creaks as Absinthe pushes it open, revealing groups of men and women mostly sitting around wooden tables with cold mugs of beer in their hands. Their murmurs fade into silence as they catch sight of Absinthe, Yelana, and me looming in the doorway.

I straighten my posture, trying to appear calm and collected before the potential enemies, not wanting to let my demeanor slip in front of the Queen's executioners.

Yelana strides in, her grin widening, "Well, look what we have here." She asks, walking over to the table in the back righthand corner of the room where a group of three men are shuffling to gather the tiny bottles of potions and bite-sized confections that litter the table, undoubtedly Hatter's product that gives its consumers temporary magic.

I watch their eyes dull when Absinthe walks towards them, the muscle in his jaw twitching as he cracks his neck, his blade screeching on the stone floor of the tavern.

The three men cower, their shaking hands betraying their fear. Yelana's laughter fills the room, echoing off the walls and sending chills down my spine. I've always hated her laugh—it sounds like death itself, cold and terrifying.

She sits in one of their chairs, kicking the heel of her boots onto the table, gesturing for me to join her, her demeanor too carefree for the depth of the situation.

I reluctantly oblige, keeping my eyes trained on the floor instead of the three petrified men.

Suddenly, one of them speaks up, his voice shaking, "We're not afraid of you."

This time, Absinthe laughs, "Is that so?" He muses.

The man nods, trying to feign confidence, but his eyes dart nervously to the blade in Absinthe's hand.

The other two men back away as Absinthe takes another step closer, invading the small, mousy-looking man's space, his eyes narrowed through the small holes in his mask, "You should be." He growls, swinging his executioner's blade with a force that cuts through the man's neck like butter, the blade so sharp that it takes a few moments before his head falls to the ground, his body following quickly behind.

I stare at the lifeless body, a wave of nausea rolling through my stomach, seeing Absinthe wiping his blade on the dead man's shirt before flicking the excess blood onto the floor.

Screams roll through the tavern while people scramble for the exit, tripping over one another as they flee, hoping to escape with their lives.

Yelana throws her head back, cackling and clapping her hands in delight, relishing in the chaos, her doe eyes twinkling as she watches the destruction unfolding before us.

The remaining two men are backed against a wall. The taller one makes a break for it, wings sprouting from his back in an attempt to take flight.

Blood splashes my face, his wings crumpling to the floor, a mangled mess of feathers and gore. Defeated, he drops to his knees, accepting his fate. Absinthe swings his axe, the man's head falling with a soft thud to the floor.

Out of the corner of my eye, I notice the bartender ushering two figures out the back door. I have sensed their magic since our arrival, knowing they were hiding somewhere in the tavern.

Yelana notices, too, because she turns to me, a challenge in her voice, "You're up, Red. Unless you're too soft to handle the job." She mocks, reminding me of her and Absinthe's earlier conversation.

She's never been shy about wanting to kill me, and I've never understood what I did to make her hate me so much unless it's just a part of her sick personality.

Grabbing the small glass of whiskey still sitting on the table, I bring it to my lips, tilting my head back and downing the liquid courage before I set off after the two members of the Black Spades.

I don't get a chance to move due to the heavy hand on my shoulder halting me. "Bring back their hearts," Absinthe warns, the look on his face cruel. "Or I'll be forced to dismember you."

I nod and gulp down the lump forming in the back of my throat. "I know what to do!" I snap, jerking my shoulder away from him.

I run out the back exit door, stepping into the night air. The cool breeze hits my skin immediately, pricking my clammy flesh with a chill.

Outback is an alleyway dimly lit by streetlamps and lined with dumpsters. I squint my eyes against the darkness, searching for signs of where they may have gone but finding nothing.

I sprint ahead leaving the alley behind, emerging into the small cobblestone street. To my right is a row of shopping carts closing down for the day, and to my left is another alley lined with homes.

I hear the crunching of what sounds like glass underfoot and freeze, pulling my sword from its sheath around my waist, "You can't hide forever." I say. "I can sense your magic."

Slowing my breathing, I wait for a response or another sound. Nothing.

My knuckles have turned white from my death grip on the sword's hilt, and my boots echo down the dark, vacant lane with each step I take.

Suddenly, a hand grabs my wrist from behind, and I spin around, pulling my arm free and aiming my sword at the stranger's neck.

I expected two grown men from the Black Spades to be standing in the place where kids not much older than I was when I lost my father stand. A girl in a ragged torn dress with all her hair shaved off and a younger boy who looks like he might be her brother.

I stare at their pleading faces, uncertain of what to do next.

These aren't the savages the Queen swears them to be—they're children.

Fucking children!

And I'm the one that has to kill them.

Chapter Eight

Alice

My blonde hair is bunched up in high pigtails on either side of my head, still crunchy from Tyler's dried blood. The world is so illiterate about the things going on in it that no one even notices it's not stage blood; rather, they tell me how amazing my costume looks as I push my way through the hordes of people dancing in the center of Tia's enormous living room.

She had moved to London as a young girl with her mother after her father passed away in search of a new beginning.

We met in college during our studies, where she majored in culinary arts, and I majored in biological sciences.

Our connection was immediate, forged in the fire of our shared experiences of loss. The trauma we went through as children quickly became the foundation that brought us together, making us now the best of friends.

As I make my way towards the kitchen, I catch a glimpse of myself in one of the many mirrors adorning Tia's walls. The powder blue and white corset I'm wearing leaves little to the imagination, and the short, frilly white skirt barely covers my backside. It's a far cry from my usual attire, but tonight is a special occasion.

Tia's Voodoo Masquerade Ball.

The room is filled with guests who are dressed in extravagant costumes from various eras and fantasies, and the music is loud enough for me to feel the vibrations in my chest.

I look around, trying to spot Tia through the crowd, but I should have known better than to think she'd be in the crowd, so I make my way to the kitchen, where I'm sure she's making magic.

I bump into a couple tongue fucking in the middle of the hallway before finally making it to the large pristine kitchen of Tia's mansion.

At the stove stands Tia, her black waves pulled neatly behind her head with a light green ribbon that pops against her gorgeous dark brown skin. She's stirring a large pot of delicious-smelling stew when I sneak up behind her, "Smells yummy!" I declare, my mouth salivating as I lean over her shoulder to look inside the pot.

She whips around quickly, her hazel eyes lighting up when she catches sight of me, and a wide smile spreads across her face, revealing two rows of perfect white teeth, "Alice, you made it!" She squeals, her southern accent coming out to play. "I was beginning to think you weren't going to show, sugar."

"I wouldn't have missed it for the world." I grin, snagging a piece of raw pumpkin off the counter and popping it in my mouth. "Shouldn't you be out there enjoying your party instead of being stuck doing this?"

She'd carved out about fifty small pumpkins to use as serving bowls and placed them in rows along the counter on gold-trimmed plates. Hor devourers are spaced out evenly on white linens that top the rolling tables she has servers taking out to serve guests, along with countless trays of pink champagne.

I cannot fathom how she managed to keep her beautiful emerald dress with its delicate lace details clean.

I would have had it ruined.

Tia chuckles, shaking her head," Girl, you know I'm doing what I enjoy besides, I can't leave my guests hungry now, can I?" She takes a spoonful of the stew and offers it to me, "Try this. It was my daddy's special recipe."

I take the spoon from her, savoring the warm liquid on my tongue. It's rich and savory, with just the right amount of spices to make my taste buds dance. "This is amazing!" I moan, taking another spoonful.

She beams with pride, grabbing a spoonful for herself. Her eyes flutter shut as she shoves the spoon through her full lips and lets the flavors soak her palette, "Mmmhmm! Papa sure knew what he was doing when it came to cooking. He always dreamed of leaving New Orleans to come to a place like this so he could open a big restaurant with food so good everyone from around the world would travel there just to taste it." She sighs at the thought as she wipes a tear from the corner of her eye.

"He'd be so proud of you, T," I whisper, pulling her into my arms for a hug.

"Ugh! What would I do without you?" She smiles, squeezing me tight. "Okay, enough tears and sadness for the night.

She pulls away, smoothing the front of her dress, "Now, help me get this food plated." She playfully demands.

I snort, going to work with her on plating food until we have several servings set out on large silver trays ready to go.

Servers filter in and out of the kitchen until the last tray is gone, and there are only the two of us left standing in the kitchen.

Tia grabs a cloth from the oven, wiping down the light cream countertops, before plopping down on one of the breakfast bar stools.

I grab a pitcher of cold ice water from the fridge, pour us each a glass, and garnish the rim with a fresh-cut lemon.

"Thank you for your help tonight."

I wave it off, "No need to thank me; that's what friends are for, and it's not like I really even did anything. You're the one who did all the hard work."

"I'm going to miss this." She says.

"What's that supposed to mean?" I ask, bobbing my lemon up and down in the glass with my finger.

She grabs a breadstick from the basket on the counter, tearing a piece off, "I'm going back to the States after the holidays." She sighs. "I wanted to tell you, but you've been pretty scarce here lately."

My heart drops slightly as I continue to toss my finger around in my drink. She's right. I haven't been around much.

I wish I could tell her that I'm changing the world, that I'm protecting people because the monsters that make things go bump in the night are very fucking real, and they look just like everyone else, their true forms hidden behind the mask they choose to show society.

I can't tell her any of that, though she wouldn't understand. No one would.

My hand drifts down to my wrist, fingering the scars that still linger on my body, the revenants of my past that remind me of who I am, why I do what I do, and just how many demons I've faced and still survived.

"I'm sorry," I whisper. "I've been really distracted lately."

Tia notices my change in demeanor, her expression softening as she places a hand on mine, leaving the breadstick on the counter. "Is everything okay?"

I shake my head, "It's nothing. Just some personal stuff that I'm dealing with."

Personal stuff like how once she leaves, I'll be completely alone again.

"You know I'm a good listener if you want to talk, and I'll help with whatever you need, you hear?" She insists, standing up to clear our mess.

"I know. One of the many reasons I love you." I smile, taking the glasses from her. "You relax and enjoy the party. I'll clean up."

"You sure?"

"Yes, now go!" I laugh, shooing her out into the hall.

As Tia walks away, with her silhouette disappearing into the crowd of partygoers, I feel an overwhelming sensation of loneliness bearing down on me. I'm used to being alone; it's what comes with the job. But I never thought I would actually miss someone's presence as much as I'll miss hers.

She's the first person that I've cared for since the death of my father and my banishment from Wonderland.

Banishment.

More like I nearly met my own demise had the guards been able to catch me before I made it back through the looking glass.

I was quite young at the time and completely distraught upon returning to London with the news that my father wouldn't be coming back home.

My punishment that evening was the most brutal and vile of them all. The doctors were able to fix the internal bleeding and did so without a single question as to how it began in the first place then, sent me back home with my wretched mother.

The following night, I snuck into my mother's room while she was passed out from the countless bottles of wine she consumed, carefully taking my time tying her wrists and ankles to the four large posts on her bed before throwing a bucket of water on her face.

The look on her face was absolutely priceless when she saw me staring at her from the edge of the bed.

A server returning an empty tray full of empty plates loses his balance, crashing into me. I hiss from the sudden surprise but manage to help him steady the tray and regain his footing.

The idiot doesn't even turn around or look back to apologize; he just keeps on walking as if it never happened at all.

Fucking twat.

I sigh, leaning against the table and closing my eyes for a moment, my hands shaking with rage. I probably shouldn't be so annoyed at the guy, but I am, and it's taking every ounce of self-control I have not to rip his throat out.

Perhaps I should go find Tia and get my mind off killing the asshole. He doesn't deserve to die, after all. He just caught me in a bad state of mind and threw me off guard.

I spot Tia by the bar, chatting animatedly with a tall, husky fellow that I recognize as one of the local professors that I've been stalking for the last couple of weeks.

He's another monster that needs to be laid to rest.

A few nights ago, when I followed him to his favorite cafe, he was meeting with a student. She was crying because she was failing and she was going to lose her scholarship. I watched him slip something into her drink while she was in the bathroom after offering to give her private tutoring lessons after hours in his classroom.

Waiting by the bathroom exit, I caught the young girl and told her to call someone to pick her up and to tell the professor something had come up. She was shaken after I told her not to drink her coffee and that I would order her a new one. She must have felt something was off about him, too, because she didn't hesitate to take me up on the offer, nor did she say a word to him when she walked right by him to get in her boyfriend's car.

Arriving at the bar, I immediately notice that Tia's way out of her comfort zone by the look on her face, so I slide up next to her, forcing him to move back, "Hey, T. Who's your friend?" I ask.

She smiles, letting out a breath of relief upon seeing me, "Oh, Alice! I'm glad you're here. This is Professor—"

The hook-nosed man frowns slightly, trying to hide his displeasure that I'm interrupting his predatorial moment with my friend before he glances over at me, "You ladies can me, Joe." He eagerly grasps my hand, placing a kiss on the back of it, his attention never faltering to his fixation on my tits even as he straightens back up.

"It's so nice to make your acquaintance, Joe," I state, pulling my hand back, the corner of my lips curving into a wicked smile.

He looks taken aback, looking over at Tia for a moment as she excuses herself to check in with the other guests.

"Are you joining me, Alice? She asks, raising her perfectly arched brow.

"Do you mind if I sit this round out?"

Her eyes flash with concern, "Not at all. Let me know if you need anything." She nods to Joe, then turns and walks over to greet an older couple standing over by the spiked punch fountain.

"You're not like other girls," Joe remarks, his voice low and husky.

"And what makes you think that, Joe? I ask, my eyes widening innocently.

He chuckles, gesturing to the bartender for another round of drinks before his eyes return to me, "You're a bold one, aren't you, Alice?"

I lean in closer to his, pushing my breasts together so an ample amount of cleavage is right below his face, my lips brushing his ear as I whisper, "Oh, I can be quite bold when it comes to something I want."

"And what is you want?" His breath quickens, his cock straining against the tight blue fabric of his pants.

I have him eating out of the palm of my hand already, and I haven't even pulled out the big guns yet. Killing him tonight is going to be easier than I thought.

I can't risk him hurting Tia or anyone else for that fact.

I smile, my finger tracing his jawline, masking the disgust and hatred I feel, "Come back to my place and find out." I tease. "All you have to do is say yes."

He licks his finger and then runs it down my neck, leaving a trail of moisture to my cleavage, "Show me the way."

Chapter Nine

Hatter

*S*weat drips down my back as screams pierce through my skull, death, and carnage littering the ground around me. The head of a small child rests in my hands as blood drips from my teeth onto its tiny face. I stand there frozen, only beginning to realize what I had just done.

It's as if my soul has been ripped from my being, and it's being forced to watch helplessly on the sidelines as the demon possessing my body wreaks havoc and destruction.

My laugh is cavernous and dark, one I don't recognize, and my eyes are a bloodied red. My shirt is ripped, my hair matted to my head, and I have bits of flesh and bone all over me from the frenzy of the massacre.

The sharp metallic scent of blood hangs in the air, the stench of death thick, burning my throat with every breath.

"If only I could have saved him," I whisper through my clamped teeth, hurling the head toward the ground, watching as it bounces off the ground from pure force and splits into as it hits a large tree.

I stare at the ruined mess of a child's body in front of me, my insides twisting.

This demon inside of me longs for death. He thrives on the fear of others, and there is nothing I can do to stop him once he's been unleashed.

I can hear his voice in my head, whispering terrible things to me, and even though I try to fight him off, he still takes control, reminding me that I'm just its puppet.

I avert my gaze from the piles of corpses, looking down at my hands, the hands of a killer, the lifeless eyes of the people I've just killed still searing their way into my mind.

Bile rises in my throat as I try to force the demon back into its cage. After some effort, he recedes, and I can see through the red haze of rage again, but he doesn't let me forget what I have become, a beast with only one thing on his mind: blood.

My eyes spring open, and I sit up, gasping for air. My body is drenched in a cold sweat, my fingers trembling as I wipe my forehead with the back of my hand, and I take a deep, steady breath to calm my racing heart.

I race to the large window next to me, flinging the curtains open and staring at the dark sky and bright white moon. The stars are all twinkling brightly, but they can't distract me from the chaos running rampant in my mind.

A chilling breeze blows in through the open window, cooling my heated skin and calming my nerves.

This is why I don't sleep. This is why I've been meditating for years. *This* is why I've learned to control my emotions, but it's all in vain.

The darkness is always there, always calling to me ever since that day.

Ten.

I was only ten years old when I watched my father's head fall from his body, his dull eyes staring up at me when it came to a stop not too far in front of me.

It felt like I died there with him. The pain clawed at my insides, like a black shadow that crept up my sides, wrapping around my chest and constricting my lungs until I was left gasping for air.

My hands wander over the silky curtains, flapping in the wind, feeling the softness of the material on my fingertips help me regain a semblance of calm, allowing me to ignore the demon lurking in my head.

It's been a long fucking day, and my brothers and I just got the biggest shock of our lives when we found out about Nova's true identity.

My fist clashes with the wall, shaking the whole room, but I don't feel any pain—only rage.

The pounding of blood rushing through my veins is deafening, drowning out all my other senses.

I still need answers.

I make my way out to the kitchen, where my brothers are already waiting. I must have woken them up, too. At this point, they've become accustomed to my nightmares and sudden outbursts of destruction.

I examine the looks on their faces and realize that they're distraught by something, too.

Most likely from Jeremiah and Nova's presence in our home until we figure out what to do with them.

With Nova being one of the last shifters from my brother's extinct pack, we couldn't just kill her.

Well, we could have, but we decided against it.

Dom's temples are pinched between his thumb and finger as he paces back and forth in front of the sink, and Dean is sitting shirtless at the table, cigar in hand, smoke curling around his fingertips.

"Bourbon or tea?" Dean asks as I pull out the chair on the other side of the table directly across from him and sit down.

"Both," I reply, propping my elbows on the table and rubbing my palm against the stubble along my jaw.

Dom places water on the stove in the kettle Henry gifted us with a while back, and Dean goes to find a bottle of Bourbon, coming back with a full decanter and three crystal glasses, plopping a large ice cube into each of our cups before pouring the golden liquid nearly to the brim before handing them off.

I lift the glass to my lips, taking a hefty swig, savoring the burning sensation that the alcohol leaves on my tongue while it trickles down the back of my throat.

Bourbon is my drug of choice on the nights I can't sleep; it helps numb the pain, quelling the angst of my demons.

"We shouldn't have brought them here," Dean says suddenly.

"And what would you have suggested we done?" Dom growls.

I lean back in my chair, staring at the ceiling while the clock ticks an uneven rhythm in the silence that follows their outburst.

Taking another swig of bourbon, I let it swirl around my mouth, waiting for someone to speak. When no one does, I clear my throat. "We can't just let them go, and we can't just kill them. And It's no secret the girl has been through hell." I tell them.

The kettle whistles and Dom turns around moving it from the hot burner to the center of the stovetop. He places his palms on the edge of the counter, his head hung low between his shoulders, "She's one of us, Dean."

"No, she's not!" He snaps back instantly. "We don't know one fucking thing about her, nor do I care to. I say we throw them both out and let them fend for themselves. We're not running a Goddamn charity project, Dom."

I hate seeing my brothers like this. But they both handle their pasts differently, and I can see the turmoil written all over their faces.

Dom is a crazy fucker who enjoys killing a little too much, but when it comes to family and the loss of their pack, he's more sensitive about it than Dean.

And I'm willing to bet this has to do with Layla, the sister they lost when their pack was attacked. She and Dom had been extremely close as children and his grief at her passing has never gone away.

"Don't you think I fucking know that?! But I can't live with her death on my hands. If we send them back out there without the protection of our men, the Queen's guards will find her, and they will kill her. She's the last of our people, Dean. The very thing we are fighting for. The reason we do all of this." He gestures around to the empire we alone have built together.

I can feel the tension in the room start to dissipate as the power of Dom's words sinks in. Dean takes a step back, his eyes flickering with uncertainty.

"Fuck!" He screams, slamming his fist down on the table.

Dean is stubborn to the core and has a strong sense of pride. He hates to be proven wrong, especially when it's about himself.

But this time, I watch as an unmovable force bends with mercy. He knows how much this means to Dom.

They couldn't save their family back then, so Dom is even more determined to protect the only connection they have left to their pack—Nova.

"Perhaps," I begin, tracing the rim of my glass. "Jeremiah and Nova can find refuge in Neverland. Pan owes me a favor and they'd be safe until we have enough of the rebels to back us and we're strong enough to take our Kingdom back."

As I finish my sentence, the three of us fall into a heavy silence. The only sound comes from the crackling of the fire in the den and the distant howl of the wind outside.

I can see the worry etched on Dom's face, but he seems to be considering the idea as he fumbles with the tiny teacups he just pulled from the black oak cabinet above him. He places the teacups on the table, filling all three with Jasmine Dragon Pearl tea, a tea Henry brought with him from the topside when he first arrived in Wonderland over fifty years ago.

It's been my favorite ever since.

Dean's gaze meets mine. "Do you really think that's the best option?"

I nod, trying to appear more confident in my decision than I feel, "It's worth a shot. At least until we can figure out a safer plan. You're right. We can't chance keeping them here in the manor. It's too risky and people will talk. They will think we've grown soft and weak, and that is something my brothers, we cannot have."

Dom speaks up, his voice low and gruff but a slight grin on his face, "I can agree with that. It does seem like the best option we have right now. Dean, what do you think?" He questions, a glimpse of hope blossoming in his mismatched eyes.

Dean exhales and rakes his hand through his tousled hair. "Alright, we'll do it your way," he says. "But if this backfires on us, don't come running to me for sympathy because all you're gonna get is an—*I told you so.*"

With a nod, I rise to my feet and step away from the table. "Good, it's settled then. I'll speak to them both in the morning and tell Pan to expect their arrival by nightfall. If either of you needs me, I'll be in my study."

They nod and we say our goodnights before I turn and make my way down the dark hall and into my office, flicking on the lights.

I'm too on edge to sleep so I might as well start digging into the few leads Dean found earlier tonight. I have another shipment coming in two days and I'll be damned if these motherfuckers catch me off guard again.

This time I'll be ready and when we catch them, I'll hand them over to Dom so he can rip them apart--piece by agonizing piece and when he's done extracting information, I'll mail their body parts to their families and to whoever is running their pathetic operation.

Their actions will be repaid in kind—they will reap what they have sown, and we will make sure they know the day they decided to challenge us was their *biggest* mistake.

CHAPTER TEN

Alice

The windows of my small red car are fogged over, Joe's breath hot against my neck as his fingers search for the small clasps of my corset.

I nibble the soft flesh of his earlobe and he groans, his pants growing heavier and his eyes squeezing shut.

I lower one hand to the buckle of his pants, tugging at the belt until it falls to the floor.

His breathing grows ragged as I slide my hand into his boxers, my fingers wrapping around his hard length. He pulls away from my neck, his eyes dark and intense as he takes in my flushed face. His hand continues to fumble until finally, the clasps give way and he pulls the corset off my shoulders, leaving me in only my lace bra and panties.

He moans softly as I slowly stroke him, my movements growing quicker with each passing moment until his head falls back on the seat.

I take the opportunity to quickly pop open the small compartment above my head, snatching up a syringe full of tranquilizer I keep for moments like this, while carefully ensuring the latch doesn't make a sound when it clicks back into place.

Joe is completely lost in the moment, his eyes closed and his lips parted as my hand moves slowly on his dick. He leans in to kiss me, his hands roaming up my sides and to my breasts.

His eyes flutter open when he takes my nipples, rolling them between his fingers, and I push him back into the seat, taking control and climbing on top of him, making sure to keep the syringe hidden by my side.

He grabs my hips, dragging me closer to him until I can feel his heavy member rubbing against my thigh.

His mouth spreads into a wide grin before he kisses me roughly, his tongue harshly consuming me. My thighs tense up when he pulls me towards him, my nails digging into his shoulders as I struggle to keep the needle from falling out of my hand.

I hold back a groan of disgust when his fingers slip inside my damp underwear, the touch a little rougher than I would have liked.

It's not him making me wet, rather it's the thoughts of what I'm going to do to him when I get him to my hospital.

His fingers continue to rub painful circles not even hitting my clit, his type doesn't care if they hurt, they only care about themselves and what they can take from others.

I swallow hard, fighting the urge to vomit, "Do you want to fuck me, Joe? Do you want to feel how tight my pussy will be when you slide inside of me and I'm wrapped around your cock?"

He growls, his patience wearing thin with my teasing, "Fucking hell yes, now stop fucking around and let me enjoy this tight little body of yours." He groans, pulling off my panties.

"Don't you want to play first?" I ask, raking my nails down his bare chest.

He doesn't answer. Instead, he grunts in frustration lifting the straps of my bra off my shoulders, tearing it off of me, and tossing it to the side, "No. What I want is for you to shut the fuck up."

I smile to myself, my plan is coming together just as I had planned, better in fact. Poor guy doesn't know what he's getting himself into, does he?

"In that case. . .You shouldn't have let me talk," I whisper, rubbing my entrance against the tip of him, causing him to relax and shudder beneath me.

He still hasn't noticed the needle in my hand just waiting for the right moment to strike.

I bite my lip, grinding my hips harder on him, before finally reaching between my thighs and grabbing his cock. My hand shakes from the adrenaline pumping through me as I line him up at my entrance and descend down on top of him.

"God fucking damn it, you're so fucking tight," he curses, his eyes rolling back as he grips my hips with a bruising hold.

I press my lips into his neck before biting hard enough to break the skin, the coppery taste of blood slipping onto my lips.

"What the fuck!" He yelps, trying to pull away from me.

I smile innocently at him, "Didn't you like that? Isn't it why you're so rough with me?" I whisper into his ear, out of breath and sweating from the pleasure cascading down my spine.

My legs tighten around him as I continue to sink down until I'm fully seated and he's balls deep inside me, my pussy stretched tightly around him.

I grip the syringe in my hand, raising it up to his neck, taking aim. His eyes widen as a cold smile breaks my face and I plunge the needle into his flesh and push the plunger, releasing the serum into his jugular.

"What did you do," he accuses, as his muscles go still under me and his face becomes slack.

"Nothing you haven't done before." I press my fingers to his lips before he can say anything else, "Shhhh. Don't speak, it will be easier."

He's still inside me, but he has no idea what's going on anymore. He's caged inside his own mind.

His eyes grow heavy, slowly sinking shut and I place a kiss on his cheek. "See you soon."

I tip over the bottle of wine in my hand shaking it upside down over my waiting mouth—empty.

Well, this is bullshit.

Skipping down the hall, I make my way to the set of elevators near the large stairway that leads down to the main entrance of the hospital, and press the button, reeling on my heels as I wait for the elevator to ding.

I feel disappointed as I toss the empty container into a nearby trashcan, "Waste of fucking time if you ask me," I mutter to myself.

Joe still hasn't woken up so I've been bored and my patience is starting to grow thin.

I believe I still have a few bottles of wine stored in the basement, which is home to the old medical equipment, and the morgue.

My wine stays perfectly chilled in the body coolers, making them the perfect cellar to store all of my bottles.

Hey, a girl's got to have priorities, right?

The elevator dings and beeps at me, signaling that it's finally arrived and I eagerly step inside, quickly pressing the basement-level button.

First, I go to the equipment room and hook my extra phone up to the building speakers, turning on my favorite playlist, then dance my way to the mortuary, waving my arms above my head as I shimmy down the corridor.

I shout a greeting to Nico as I spin around the autopsy table and head for the back of the room, where the cold storage unit lines the wall. My feet move quickly in time with my music as I descend the flight of stairs.

Nico is one of the ghosts that lives in the basement. He died more than fifty years ago when he was only twenty-five.

He was on the volunteer fire department and met his demise when a barn caught on fire.

We got a merry little group down here.

Another ghost lives with him. His name is Roy and he's a creepy old bastard.

He and Nico love to get drunk and dance with me. Honestly, I think they're just happy to have someone who cares enough to pay them attention and who listens to their babbling.

I open up one of the cooler doors and pull out another bottle of wine. This one was a birthday gift from Tia.

I'd almost forgotten about it.

Nico and Roy appear, sitting across the table from me as I uncork the wine and begin to drink straight from the bottle.

I squish my face at them, sticking out my tongue and they laugh.

I grab their cups and pour them each a small glass.

They're lightweights.

I've been skeptical about this bottle, but I have to admit I am pleasantly surprised by the delicious flavor. It's a creamy, fruity blend that tastes of apples and berries, but with undertones of dark chocolate.

I spend the next twenty minutes jamming out and dancing with Nico and Roy before I head back upstairs to see if Joe is awake yet.

I'm sure you can imagine the look of shock on his face when he sees me walk in, suited up for surgery.

My muscles are screaming to be relieved from their exhaustion, but I still have one more task left to do before I can lose myself to sleep tonight, and I still need a shower.

I feel yucky.

It's not my normal routine to have multiple operations scheduled in a single day but there was no way I was leaving that creep at the party to make my best friend his newest victim.

Nah, fuck that. Not when I can make him and his vileness disappear from existence all together.

"Oh, goodie! You're awake." I state the obvious.

He must not grasp the gravity of the situation because the words that fall out of his mouth next are some of the stupidest I've ever heard.

"I suspected you were a freak but I didn't realize you would be this kinky, sweetheart."

I smile and pick up the craniotome, a special tool used in brain surgeries, from off my surgical tray, "Are you really that dense, Joe?" I ask, walking up behind him where he's strapped down to my operating table.

I stroke the tool in my hands before flipping the switch that turns it on, and it roars to life in my palms with a loud buzzing screech.

"Jesus fucking Christ! What are you going to do with that?!" He screams, straining to get off the table, but I shove his head back down, slamming it into the table where I then secure his skull with a three-point head clamp.

I wouldn't want him to go and hurt himself.

I eye the different attachments that I can screw on the end of the craniotome. I contemplate for a moment, trying to decide which would be the best for what I need to do, before deciding on a small blade attachment that will easily cut through bone, opting to make this fairly quick.

"I want to see what's inside that lovely head of yours, Joe. I want to see all your dirty little secrets. For instance, like the one I witnessed here recently, the one where you prey on young girls at coffee shops, offering them assistance with their studies, only to take advantage by drugging them to use for your own sick pleasures."

His face drops at my confession, "I—I wasn't going to hurt her, I swear! I just wanted—"

"I know exactly what you wanted!" I snap. "You're a disgusting excuse for a human being, Joe. I've heard all of the excuses perverts like you make for yourself, and I've seen how you think there's nothing wrong with your actions. But there is. And fortunately, I am here to save you from your debased indulgences, to see how you...*Tick*." I raise the blade above his head.

"Please! Wait! I'm sorry! Don't! Don't do this!" He pleads.

"Oh, it's too late for apologies, Joe."

He closes his eyes, his mouth whispering a silent prayer when the saw hums to life in my hands.

"Silly man. Your God can't save you." I laugh, bringing the blade down, blood splattering across me and the ceiling.

His cries send a thrill through me, making my pussy ache and my legs slick with my arousal.

This is what I live for, what I do best.

Cutting away the ugly parts of the world, one beast at a time.

CHAPTER ELEVEN

Alice

"Oh, come on!" I scream at the branch clawing at my clothes, tugging me back as I drag the large bag that still has Tyler's head and a few other body parts that I'm unsure of which man they belong to anymore.

After I find the perfect spot to bury the last of my surgical scraps, I drop the bag to the ground, plopping down next to it to catch my breath.

It's been a long fucking night.

As I sit there, panting, trying to catch my breath, I feel a sense of satisfaction, in the end, it had all been worth it.

The razors I feel inside my lungs with every breath I inhale, the sweat dripping down my forehead, stinging my eyes, the burning in my muscles that threatens to melt my bones. . .All of it.

I look around the dark, moonless night. The world seems so still.

Crickets chirp from a set of bushes to my left, and the wind rustles the leaves on the cold forest floor, granting me a chill that runs down the length of my spine.

I wish Father were here; he would have enjoyed a night like this.

I stand up, wiping my brow with the back of my hand, before grabbing my shovel and then shoving the dull edge into the hard crust of frozen earth.

My high of the night is beginning to fade and the minuscule amount of clothing I'm in does little to keep the harsh wind from nipping at my flesh.

As I dig deeper into the earth, the dirt and gravel fly up, covering my face and hair. But I don't care. The physical exertion is just what I need to distract myself from the chill in the air.

After the hole is large enough, I bury the rest of the two men, stroking my hand against Tyler's lifeless face before I toss it into its shallow grave.

I stand there for a moment, staring at the fresh mound of dirt, feeling nothing.

The only thing I have left to do now is to dispose of the bag and get rid of any other evidence before the sun comes up so no one can discover my deeds.

But as I prepare to leave the grave site, I hear a rustling in the nearby bushes. My hand instinctively goes to the knife I keep tucked in my boot, ready to defend myself if necessary.

But as the bush shakes and a small figure emerges, I relax slightly. It's just a rabbit.

I observe it as it quickly moves off toward the old tree that once held the entrance to Wonderland.

I decide to follow it, leaving a trail of footprints in the dirt behind me. The trees loom large and ominous, casting long shadows across the forest floor. The darkness seems to swallow me whole, but I press on, my determination fueling my every step as I stumble on roots and rocks chasing the tiny creature.

Finally, the rabbit halts right in front of the old dead tree, its pink nose twitching as it scratches at its ear, seemingly watching my every move.

How curious.

I step closer to the rabbit, studying it carefully. Its fur is white, slightly tinged by dirt and leaves, and its eyes are a bright red that appears to glow in the darkness.

I feel a sudden urge to reach out and touch it, to feel its soft delicate fur against my fingertips. But as I extend my hand, something strange happens. The looking glass reappears in the center of the tree and the rabbit darts straight into it, vanishing as it collides with the glass.

My eyes must be deceiving me because I can't even fathom what I'm seeing right now.

Is it a mirage born from exhaustion, or have I simply gone mad?

That must be it.

After all these years of looking for a way back—it can't be true.

But when my palm grazes the smooth surface of the mirror, it appears to absorb my skin. I jerk my hand away from the glass, feeling my heart hammering in my throat.

As I watch in disbelief, the mirror begins to shimmer and swirl, pulsating with a strange kind of energy. It's as if the very fabric of reality is melting away before my eyes.

Part of me wants to run away, to return to my home and drink another bottle of wine with Roy and Nico, but the strange pull in my stomach keeps my feet planted in place.

I take a step toward the mirror, stretching my arm out in front of me. Sucking in a deep breath, I hold it and leap forward.

The glass starts to twirl and twist around me, pulling me into its depths.

I feel like I'm falling, the world around me shifting and morphing, like a kaleidoscope in motion, colors blurring in a dizzying haze all around me.

I want to scream, but the air has been ripped from my lungs as I continue on my downward spiral until I come to a stop, my feet finding solace when they touch firm ground.

I find myself standing in a forest, much like the one I had just left, but it's no longer night and the sun plays hide and seek with the shadows when the breeze rustles the branches allowing it to occasionally filter through.

Wonderland.

I'm back.

I can finally get the chance to avenge my father and kill the bitch that took him from me.

My eyes adjust, taking in the scenery around me. It doesn't seem as bright and lovely as it once did when I was a little girl.

It's not the same kingdom that I once wanted to call my home, now it's just a reminder of the heartache and loss the Queen caused me, an oppressive memory that has festered in the back of my mind for the past thirteen years, rotting the last bit of good and sanity I had left.

The trees are taller and thicker than I remember and there's a light fog hovering between them. It's quiet, too, eerily so. No chirping birds or rustling leaves—just the sound of my erratic breathing.

As I take a few steps forward, I notice that the ground is covered in a layer of soft moss, and cute little colorful mushrooms sprinkle the ground. It's like walking on clouds, and it muffles the sound of my footsteps until a twig snaps beneath my foot almost making me jump clear out of my skin.

I laugh at how easily it startled me and continue forward, not knowing which way to go when I come up on a split path.

Hmmm. Which way to go, Alice?

I look to the path to my right where the forest seems to grow denser, then to the path on my left where I can spot flowers sprouting in the distance on either side of the path.

Falling to the ground, I cross my legs under me, placing my elbows on my thighs, and prop my chin up on the palms of my hands as I contemplate the best path to choose.

However, choices are like branches in a stream: sometimes, the way forward is hidden beneath the surface, and sometimes, there is no way to tell which direction will lead you astray.

Lost in my musings, I barely notice a faint noise coming from the bushes not too far away from where I'm sitting.

My head snaps in the direction of the noise and I see a rabbit hopping over to me, stopping a few feet away to stare at me with its beady red eyes.

"Oh, it's you again," I say, as though it will understand me. "Do you know which way leads to the Queen's castle?"

The rabbit stares at me for a moment, its nose twitching as it sniffs the air. Then, with a flick of its tail, it hops down the path to my left, disappearing into the underbrush.

I hesitate for a moment, wondering if I should follow it.

What's the worst that could happen?

I stand up and dust off my dress before making my way down the path to the left, my curiosity getting the better of me.

I stroll along the winding path, inhaling the pleasant aroma of blooming flowers. The further I head down the trail, the larger the array of florets become.

A beautiful melody drifts in the breeze, and my ears are captivated by its enchanting sound, beckoning me to come closer. As I approach the vast meadow, I notice that the flowers surrounding me have grown even larger, towering over me like giants, their petals soft and velvety to the touch as I brush my fingers over them.

With the quickness of light, one of the enormous daffodils transforms right before my eyes into a gorgeous woman, her green skin shimmering in the sunlight. She has large breasts, and flowy vines speckled with raspberry-colored blooms that cascade down her shoulders like human hair.

Her lips part as a captivating song spills from her mouth, her feet stepping in rhythm to her own tune. She sways around me, her hands tugging at the ends of my untamed pigtails.

For a moment, I am paralyzed, my body frozen in awe as the flower woman dances around me. Her touch is gentle, but forceful, pulling me into the rhythm of her movements. Her voice is soft and sweet, but also seductive, luring me deeper into the meadow, like a temptress in the night.

As we dance, she whispers sweet and alluring nothings in my ear, her breath hot against my skin. I can feel myself becoming intoxicated by her, my body responding to her every touch and movement.

Her movements become more intense, and I find myself losing control, my body swaying and gyrating along with hers.

I close my eyes, giving in to the pleasure of the moment, and when I open them again, I see rows of jagged teeth inches above my face.

The once attractive woman has now become a terrifying beast preparing to devour her prey. Her long claws reach for me, a low screechy growl emitting from deep within her throat.

My heart climbs in my chest, beating frantically as I stumble backward, trying to put as much distance between myself and the flower creature as possible.

I'd forgotten the unpredictable environments and perilous creatures that lurk within this topsy-turvy world.

Fear is quickly replaced by a burning desire, a hunger that I can't explain, the longing to feel her teeth on my skin, to be completely and utterly consumed by her.

I shake my head, trying to fight the feeling. She pounces on top of me, she's quick, pinning me down to the ground. I can feel her hot breath on my neck, her sharp teeth gnashing at my skin.

I scream, struggling against her hold, but her grip is strong, and I can't break free.

The cloud over my mind fades as the fear creeps in, and I remember the knife tucked away inside my boot. I grit my teeth, almost tasting the sweet satisfaction of her death.

I stretch my arm as far as I can, my fingers just touching the hilt of the blade.

Just a little farther.

Bringing my leg up as far as I can while trapped beneath a rabid monster, my hand finally wraps around the knife.

Fuck yeah.

I'm going to stab this cunt in her fucking face!

I pull the knife out of my boot with a swift motion, the blade glinting in the bright sunlight. The flower creature's eyes widen as she sees the weapon, but she doesn't release her grip on me. Instead, she snarls, and her claws sink into my arm. A burning pain sears up through my limb and into my shoulder causing stars to spin in my eyes.

The cut is deep.

Blood oozes from the wound, staining the ground beneath us. I scream again, this time in agony, as the flower creature digs her claws deeper into my flesh. I can feel her hot breath on my face, the stench of decay on her breath.

I hiss in pain and grit my teeth, but I refuse to give up. With the knife still gripped tightly in the hand of my uninjured arm, I bring it up and plunge it deep into her side. She lets out an ear-piercing shriek, as green goo bubbles from the wound.

The creature wails in agony, but still, she refuses to let go of me. I twist the knife in her side, trying to get her to release her grip, but she only digs her claws in deeper. Blood is pouring from my arm now, and I can feel myself growing weak. I need to get away from her.

I bring the knife up again, this time stabbing her in the head. I do it over and over again until the flesh of her face is shredded hanging loosely above me like spaghetti.

Her grip loosens and I take the opportunity to push her off of me, panting and gasping for air as I struggle to climb to my feet.

The wound in my arm throbs, but I ignore it as I watch her writhe on the ground. I can see the life fading from her eyes.

Serves her right.

With the last bit of strength I can find inside me, I start running back to the forest. I should have picked the other path.

I'm beginning to think that the rabbit wanted me to die. But of course, I know that's just crazy talk.

I reach the middle of the forest again, my energy spent. I collapse to the ground, holding my arm. I have to stop the bleeding somehow.

A wolf howls nearby, its call quickly answered by another.

Fuck me.

I take deep breaths trying to calm my erratic breathing, desperate to stay conscious. I glance around, frantically looking for a place to hide, my arm throbbing with each beat of my heart, sending waves of pain through my body.

The trees are thick, but I can hear the wolves getting closer, encroaching upon me.

There is nowhere left to run or hide. I am exhausted, wounded, and completely vulnerable. I let out a cry of frustration, knowing that I am cornered. The sound of their snarling jaws fills the air, and I brace myself for the inevitable attack.

My vision starts to blur as I place my good hand on the ground, trying to push myself up so I can fight. But when the wolves break through the trees, they don't attack right away.

Their bodies are huge, each twice the size of a normal wolf. Two pairs of mismatched eyes stare at me. The wolf on the left has jet black fur while the other is gorgeous golden hue. They're both so fucking majestic.

I'm in awe despite the terror pulsing through my veins, as I watch two powerful wolves staring me down, my heart still racing from the sheer magnitude of fear I feel.

The golden wolf steps cautiously towards me, it's nostrils quivering as it sniffs at the air around me, stopping only a couple of feet away.

It noses under my tattered sleeves and sniffs my wound, its rough warm tongue lapping at the blood that had dried on my skin. The wolf hesitates, taking a step back, its eyes darting between me and the other wolf. Its fur fades away and its features soften until a large muscular man stands in its place.

His dark blond hair is a devilish tousled mess, and he runs his fingers through it spilling some of the locks over his forehead. His distinct features are set off by a strong jawline and full lips that are curved into a mischievous smirk.

"Looky what I found, Dean. A scared little rabbit." He says speaking to the other wolf.

My breath hitches in my throat as he walks closer, crouching down next to me, his rock-hard cock bobbing dangerously close to my face.

He gazes at me, his different-colored eyes gleaming with amusement, "Hello, little rabbit."

Chapter Twelve

Rose

I fled.

I couldn't bring myself to do it. I couldn't kill those kids.

So, I left, watching the town burn over my shoulder, the flames a red and orange blur as I cried and ran away as fast as I could.

I'm sure Absinthe and Yelana aren't far behind me.

Forcing my legs to move faster, I sprint away from the destruction. Without me, they won't be able to track down those teenagers I helped escape, rather they will follow me because they know the Queen needs me—she needs my power.

I run blindly through the forest, my heart pounding in my chest. I don't know how long I've been running, but my legs ache and my lungs burn from exertion. Finally, I come to a stop, collapsing against a tree as I try to catch my breath. The scent of burning wood and flesh still lingers in the air, causing me to gag and cough. Tears stream down my face, hot against my skin.

I double over, gasping for breath as I try to process how I'm going to survive my betrayal. I don't know anyone outside of the castle and no one will be willing to help me because I'm a known accomplice to the Queen.

What the fuck am I going to do now?

I just want to be free.

I can hear the earth crunching under what sounds like heavy boots. They're here.

I frantically scan the darkness around me, trying to see who or what is stalking the dark shadowy terrain.

Squinting my eyes, I make out the silhouette of a tall, imposing figure moving with purpose in my direction. I dip behind a tree, trying to hide myself as best as I can.

Nausea swirls in my stomach, I'm scared shitless. I take a chance, peeking around the tree. My hand shoots up to cover my mouth to stifle the scream trying to escape from my lungs when I notice it's not human at all.

The Jabberwocky looms large, its wingspan blocking out the stars above. Its eyes are like twin fires, glowing an ethereal orange that seems to pierce right through your soul.

It has a long snarling snout, saliva dripping down its razor-sharp fangs, and a hard, spiked ridge that stretches from its head, down the entire length of its spine all the way down to the tip of its tail. Its white teeth glint dangerously in the pale light of the night sky—a stark contrast to the damn near impenetrable black leathery scales on its body.

Its breathing is a deep rumble like an approaching thunderstorm that echoes through the darkness around it, drowning out the pounding of my heart.

The Jabberwocky is one of the Queen's most feared and deadly creatures. It's not something that can be reasoned with or bargained with. It's a killing machine bred for one purpose only: to eliminate the Queen's threats.

And I've now become one of those threats.

I huddle close to the trunk of the tree, hoping its leaves and branches will conceal me. Unfortunately, my efforts are in vain as the creature's sharp vision can spot me from afar, not to mention its sensitive nose has already detected my presence.

I dip my face in my hands, my tears falling through the cracks of my fingers. I don't want to die before I've even had a chance to live.

Before I can attempt to make a break for it a blazing ball of fire comes barreling through the woods with Yelana and Absinthe following shortly after it.

"I swear when I get my hands on that stupid bitch—"I hear Yelana yell as she kicks at the small rocks in her path.

"The Queen said she is to be brought in alive, my love. We can't disobey her too."

"She said *alive*, Absinthe. She didn't say she had to be in one piece. She doesn't need her legs to find magic. I have better things to be doing with my time than chasing after some lame-brained girl who doesn't know how to follow orders." Yelana's voice is laced with venom, sending a cold chill through me.

Shit. Shit. Shit.

If they catch me, it's all over with.

I suck in a shaky breath, holding it in my chest, trying not to hyperventilate.

As they approach, the Jabberwocky lets out a deafening roar, its orange eyes trained on both executioners.

My mind races trying to find a way out of this, but the Jabberwocky is blocking my escape in one direction, and the two executioners are closing in on me from another.

The moonlight reflects on Absinthe's axe, making the blade glisten in the night sky. The sudden light hurts my eyes which have grown accustomed to the darkness and casts a harsh shadow over his face.

I hold my breath, praying they won't see me. I can hear their footsteps getting closer and closer until they sound like they're right in front of me. I peek back around the tree and see Yelana standing there, her eyes filled with pure hate.

"Oh, this is going to be fun." She smirks.

I take off in the only direction I can, which is towards the Jabberwocky. My heart is pounding in my chest, and I can feel a cold sweat breaking out all over my body. I don't know what I'm doing, but I know I have to do something—anything.

I run as fast as I can through the dark mountainside, my feet pounding against the hard earth below. The Jabberwocky snarls as I sprint towards it, and I half-expect it to take me down as soon as I get close. But to my surprise, it doesn't attack and lets me pass.

I glance back and see Yelana and Absinthe hot on my heels, their eyes burning with fury.

Yelana thrusts her arms out in front of her, sending a stream of fire at the ground near my feet but misses me.

I smile at her mishap.

My lungs burn with the effort of running, but I don't slow down. I can't. Not when death is nipping at my heels.

My heart is racing, adrenaline pumping through my veins, and the wind whips my hair around my face, making it difficult to see. I'm running blindly, following my instincts, and hoping that they will lead me to safety.

I hear the deep rumble of flapping wings above me, the Jabberwocky is following me too.

Up ahead, I see a small cave entrance and make a beeline for it. It's too small for the Jabberwocky to pass through, and hopefully, I can lose Absinthe and Yelana in the dark tunnels of the cave.

I'm almost there.

But right before I slip into the security of the cave, claws are digging into my flesh, and I'm being lifted into the air.

My heart drops as I realize that I'm now in the clutches of the Jabberwocky. Panic sets in, and I kick wildly, trying to break free. But its grip only tightens, and it starts to fly higher and higher, away from the safety of the ground and into the cloudy sky. My heart races as I look down, my eyes wide with fear. I can see Yelana and Absinthe shrinking smaller and smaller beneath me, their angry faces turning into dots in the distance.

"Let me go!" I scream at the massive beast.

The Jabberwocky's only response is a rumbling growl that reverberates through my entire body. I close my eyes tightly, fighting the fear that threatens to overwhelm me. I feel myself losing consciousness the higher we climb and I try to force my eyes to stay open, but the lack of oxygen is making it harder and harder to focus.

With a sudden stop, I'm thrown to the ground, shocked when I realize that the creature has taken me to the peak of its mountain.

Why didn't it take me back to the castle?

I sit up groggily, feeling dazed and disoriented. There's a sharp pain in my head, and I bring a hand up to touch the back of it.

"Ouch!" I wince when my hand hits the knot protruding from my skull.

I must have hit a rock when I was dropped.

As I assess my surroundings, I become aware that the Jabberwocky has brought me to its lair.

A shiver runs down my spine as I realize that I'm alone with the monster. The Jabberwocky circles around me, its massive wings creating a gust of wind that sends my hair flying.

It nudges me in the direction of the large entrance of its cave. The inside is vast and dark, the only light coming from the bioluminescent mushrooms growing on the walls.

The lair is filled with bones and remnants of past prey, reminding me of the fate that awaits me. The creature's massive body looms over me, menacing and powerful. I feel small and helpless in its presence.

My hand becomes my guide through the dark tunnel, feeling my way along the rough edges of the cave. I stumble as my foot hits a pile of bones, the sound echoing through the cavern, and I squeal when a mouse runs out of a skull and across the top of my foot.

The Jabberwocky nudges me again, guiding me further down the passageway until we reach an even larger cavern.

Silver picture frames line the wall holding photos of a family. I walk closer, squinting my eyes through the darkness to make out the people in the photos.

A fire roars to life when the beast blows a stream of flames into a makeshift fireplace centered in the room, allowing me to see the family.

My family.

"What in the hell?" I whisper, the Jabberwocky's blazing eyes boring into me as if it's waiting for a response.

It touches its snout to a photo of a man holding a small baby. It's my father and me when I must have only been days old. I'd never seen this picture before. He looks so happy.

As I stare at the photo, a feeling of longing and sadness starts to creep up my chest. I can't hold back the tears that begin pouring from my eyes, an ugly wail escaping my throat as I trace over the picture, recalling my father's face.

It's been so long since I lost him, I'd almost forgotten what he looked like. Though, I can still remember how his beard would tickle my face when he kissed my head after tucking me in at night.

The Jabberwocky exhales a low growl as if it's trying to communicate something to me.

I stare at him, bewilderment swirling in my mind as I utter, "What? What are you trying to say?"

It touches the photo again, then drags one of its long claws on the wall of the cave, emitting a loud screech as it does.

It's two letters. An M and an E.

Me.

My eyes grow wide, the blood in my veins turning to ice and I shake my head.

"No." Tears run down my cheeks. "That's not you. That's my father and he's dead. They killed a man for his murder. He's gone." I sniff.

The Jabberwocky narrows its eyes at me and lets out a snarl nodding its head back and forth and pounds its front foot on the ground.

It touches its nose to the word *me* then knocks the picture off the wall and it falls into my hands.

"You're trying to say you're him? I ask, pointing to the man in the photo. "You're my dad?"

The creature snorts, exhaling a plume of smoke from its nostrils, and bobs its head up and down.

I stand there, clutching the photo to my chest, in disbelief. Could it be possible that the Jabberwocky is actually my father? It sounds insane, but after everything I've experienced so far, nothing seems impossible anymore.

There's an intelligence in its eyes, a familiarity in the gentleness of its touch when it rests its head on mine as if it's trying to hug me. It makes me want to believe that it's truly him.

"But, how?" I ask, my voice barely above a whisper.

The Jabberwocky tilts its head slightly to one side, and I spot a stone embedded in the center of its chest. Instinctively, my hand moves to clasp the necklace that restricts part of my power. As I touch the necklace, and examine it closer, It's made from the same stone that's embedded in the Jabberwocky, realization dawns on my face, softening the beast's gaze.

"Don't worry," I clench my teeth together to escape the urge to scream. "We'll make fucking sure she pays for what she's done to us."

Chapter Thirteen

Dom

S he looks like shit.

Kind of.

A vivid crimson coats her clothing, what looks to be a once vibrant and detailed poofed skirt is now nothing more than tattered rags, fluttering in the light breeze, revealing the curve of her hips and an incredible ass that peeks out to taunt me.

My gaze lingers as I examine her, marveling at the beauty that's underneath all the caked blood and dirt, her pale blue eyes shining like diamonds in the bright midday sun.

She's frowning, her lips pulled into a pout that highlights the most adorable fucking dimples I've ever seen, making her even that much more attractive.

I smirk which to her probably looks like I'm baring my teeth, as she glares at me, her eyes narrowing when she crosses her arms in defiance.

I can see the fear in her gaze, but also a stubbornness that intrigues me. I take in every inch of her battered form with a mix of concern and desire. It's a sick combination, I know, but I can't help the way my body reacts to her.

She's like a wounded animal, and I'm finding it more difficult with each passing moment to deny myself the pleasure of tasting her—devouring her.

My brother and I have been tracking the strange girl ever since we caught her running through our woods. We thought she was a goner when one of the sirens from the singing meadows attacked her, but she wasn't about to go down without a fight, and in the end, she fucked that bitch's entire world up.

Granted, from the look of the gaping cuts on her arm, she didn't exactly come out unscathed from the battle herself, but she doesn't even show that she's in any pain.

My little rabbit is tough.

I step closer to her, noting how she flinches but doesn't back away. I can feel the pull of her energy, the way her body reacts to my presence. She's afraid, but there's a flicker of something—else.

As I tower over her, I can feel her heart racing beneath her chest. It's like music to my ears, and it takes all my self-control not to pounce on her right there. Instead, I press the tip of my nose to her face then slide my tongue across her cheek, licking off the layer of dried blood.

The sound of the sharp gasp that passes through her luscious pink lips makes me fucking feral. And just like that, I know she's going to be mine.

My own personal plaything to savor, ravish, and ultimately ruin.

I'm going to rip into her, tearing away at her until she's nothing but a hollow shell of her former self. I will savor every last morsel of her being until there is nothing left in her; no life, no soul, nothing but a corpse trapped in an eternal moment of emptiness.

Oh, but then...Then she's going to come alive for me—she's going to be so consumed by the savage hunger of lust and pleasure, that she will beg for me to break her more.

I shift back into my human form, crouching down beside her. My cock is painfully hard, aching with an intensity I've never felt before.

I'd already decided I was going to take her the moment we'd caught sight of her running through our woods, but now I'm positive that I'm going to fuck my little rabbit until she's screaming my name.

Dean shifts and hurries over next to me, his hand trying desperately to hide his swinging balls.

"Next time maybe you should let me speak first." He says.

I roll my eyes, "Stop being ridiculous. I think she likes me." I grin.

She glares at me, and oh man, if looks could kill.

"You both can go fuck off." She snaps, ripping off a piece of the frayed fabric of her blouse and wrapping it around the gashes in her arm.

She's trying to stop the bleeding, all while being a petty little smart-ass. She's gonna make this fun.

"Who are you?" Dean questions the girl, crossing his arms over his chest.

Her eyes lock on his cock, and his face turns three shades of red as he shoves his hands back down to cover up his groin.

"See something you like, little rabbit? I'm sure we can—"

"Knock it off, Dom." My brother growls causing me to wheeze out a high-pitched laugh, my eyes widening in mock fear.

"Alright. Alright." I put my hands up like an innocent child, causing his scowl to deepen the wrinkles between his eyes.

I glance back at the girl who has her eyes locked on mine.

"You want me. Admit it." I deadpan, a smirk growing on my lips at the blush creeping its way up her neck.

"Fuck you."

"Gladly."

"Ugh!" She shrieks, frustrated with my antics. "You're an infuriating prick!"

I've been called worse.

Fury bubbles under the smudged mascara on her face, and she's on her feet in an instant, hurling her fist at my face.

Moving at the last moment, I grab her wrists and pull her forward into me. Giving her a lopsided smirk, when I pull her hips into mine. Her eyes go wide and her body pushes back against me, a growl escaping from her lips.

"Let me go!" She struggles, trying to free herself from my grip as her small fists beat against my chest.

I can feel her heart beating rapidly under my hands, sending thrills straight to my already hard dick.

"Contentious little beast, aren't you?" I rasp in her ear, causing her nails to sink into my skin.

I can smell her arousal. My little rabbit is just as affected as me.

Her breasts bounce as her chest moves up and down with each heavy breath she takes.

I lick her neck, inhaling her scent—"Mmm. You smell like strawberries and sin."

"Dom, leave her alone." Dean sighs, pinching the bridge of his nose. Though, his erection doesn't evade my attention--he wants her too. "We need to take her to Hatter and see what he wants us to do with her."

I huff a breath, dropping my hands, and my grip, letting her fall directly on that round apple ass of hers, "Fine."

Her eyes narrow at me, but her cheeks flush a darker red, her breathing picking up in pace.

I look down at her, grinning, and wink. "We'll play more later.

"I'm not your fucking toy!" She huffs.

"You will be," I promise her.

Dean goes to pick her up and she screams her objection, scrambling away from him as fast as she can.

I rub my hands together and take a step toward her, "Oh no you don't."

She's pretty quick to be injured and quite strong for her size, before either of us can seize her she's running back at Dean, full speed with a damn knife in her hand and stabs him in the chest.

She laughs hysterically, bringing it down twice more, "DON'T FUCK WITH ME!" She screams, raising her arm to stab him again.

Holy Fuck. She just keeps on getting hotter and hotter.

Dean twists the knife from her hand and jerks her off the ground with an incredulous strength. Then, flips her upside down and hangs her by her ankles.

"Are you kidding me right now?" He asks sarcastically shaking his head at the tiny psychopath dangling from his hand.

Being a wolf shifter, his wounds have already begun to heal. Along with being able to heal quickly, and having good eyesight and smell, we're also stronger than most, which is why no one really messes with the Black Spades.

That is, until recently.

She kicks her legs and tries biting him, "PUT ME DOWN!"

Dean shakes his head in dismay. "You're a wild one."

I'm hunched over with laughter, admiring the spectacle unfolding in front of me.

"PUT ME DOWN YOU SON OF A BITCH!" She screams.

I walk over, kneeling down so my face is close to her, "We can do this the easy way or the hard way, little rabbit. The choice is yours."

She's deathly silent for a moment, her face pinched in thought, looking back and forth between me and Dean.

"Well?" I ask, quirking my brow.

She closes her big blue eyes, taking a deep breath before they open again, a sly smile forming across her lips, "Well in that case." Her velvet voice whispers, "I'll just make it easy on the both of us." She whips her head forward, cracking it into my nose, breaking it, then spits in my face.

She's chosen the hard way, it seems.

Honestly, I would have been disappointed had she not.

She's lively and absolutely vicious—I love it.

I swipe my finger through the spit on my face and place it on her lips, "I'm only a little sorry I have to do this." I say before knocking her unconscious.

Fuck.

We still didn't get her name.

CHAPTER FOURTEEN

Hatter

My brothers bust through my office door butt-ass naked and drop a lifeless girl on the floor at my feet.

"She dead?" I ask.

Dean shakes his head, "Just unconscious. Bitch stabbed me. . .Three fucking times." He responds, a loss of pride peeping through his gruff response.

I poke her with the point of my sleek black leather dress shoe, "She's just a tiny fucking thing."

"And mean." Dom laughs, pointing to his bloody nose, his toned muscles flexing as he leans against the wall.

I raise an eyebrow at them, "What the hell did you guys do? Her arm is going to need stitches."

"All we did was knock her crazy ass out. The arm wound was from a siren, not sure about anything else." Dean says, tossing a white t-shirt over his head.

I get out of my desk chair and squat down to get a closer look at the girl lying on the floor. The first thing I notice is her long golden hair and how it cascades down her petite frame, held up on either side of her head with silky ribbons.

Her skin is smooth and pale, and her lips are plump pink. She looks so vulnerable, lying there on the ground.

I reach out to touch her cheek, to see if she's still breathing, but then she stirs and my hand jerks back. Her eyelids flutter and then open, revealing wide, bright blue eyes. They stare up at me, uncomprehending at first, before she seems to realize where she is and what is going on.

She lashes out with both her feet, connecting hard with my chest. I feel the force of the blow pushing me back until I lose my balance and fall to the floor, stunned by her sudden attack.

"See?" Dom says, "Mean."

I slowly get up from the floor, brush the dust off the jacket of my suit, and fix my tie, not sure whether to feel admiration or rage.

There's no denying she's got spunk.

"What's your name?" I ask, trying to keep my tone calm and non-confrontational.

"That's really none of your business." She hisses, through her clenched teeth.

Her shoulders are hunched, her body trembling. She's trying to keep it under control, but it's evident she's terrified.

"I assure you; it is very much my business since you were apprehended on my property." I try a different approach, showing my authority, allowing her to see that I won't be putting up with her shit.

Her lips press into a thin line as she stares at me, and she raises herself up so she's in a sitting position, but she doesn't say another word.

"Ok. Where are you from?" I ask her.

She picks at a crack in the wooden floor, "Not here." Her sarcastic attitude is irritating, yet, refreshing.

"I see." I take the top hat off my head, stroking my smooth face, subduing the impulse to laugh.

"What were you doing in our forest?"

Her fingers cease their movement against the ground, and she takes a deep breath, her eyes glare at me and she lifts her injured arm. "Trying not to die, dumb ass."

Dumb ass?!

"You're a little smart mouth who just happens to have all the answers, huh?" I sigh, quirking a brow, taking my top hat off, and running my hand through my hair.

She's not going to be easy to deal with, that's for certain.

"Do you always insult the people who help you?"

"I wouldn't call this help."

"Now, now, don't get snippy. My brothers could have very easily left you in our forest to die, you know."

"I wish they would have." She states, rolling her eyes in their direction.

Dom grins, waving his fingers at her.

"You will find I'm not a man accustomed to being defied."

"Nor am I a woman accustomed to being condescended to." She snaps. "And if you keep doing so don't cry when I rip your tongue from your mouth."

Even Dean cackles at her remark, smoke from his cigar rolling from his mouth as he laughs, "She's a feisty one, all right."

She certainly is.

"Don't make me kill you, trouble. I have no reason to, but you're really making me want to."

"Try me." She growls, and I notice the quiver in her lip and a glimpse of the tears trying desperately to break through the dam she's holding them back with.

She clenches her fists and looks away.

My heart seizes and I want so badly to comfort her, but I know I must refrain. I don't need this distraction when I already have so much going on.

We can't save every stray.

"We've obviously gotten off on the wrong foot. Why don't we try this again," I place my top hat back on my head and stand up, offering my hand to aid her up off the hard floor.

She jerks away from me.

"Fine. Suit yourself." I shrug.

"I will." She glares at me.

"We have guest rooms. Dom will get one prepared for you and we'll see about finding you some fresh clothes." I wrinkle my nose, "You smell like you could do with a good wash too. Dean will show you where the towels are kept and I'll have tea ready for when you are done cleaning up."

"I'm not staying here."

"I wasn't asking."

"I'm not a fucking prisoner." She snaps.

"You're not a guest either," I warn, sifting through the drawer where I keep a small number of medical supplies.

She's seething, her tiny frame shaking with rage, her blue eyes rimmed red, the only sign of the tears she refuses to let fall, "I hate you all." She mutters.

"You can hate us all you want, doesn't make any mind to me, you're stuck here either way." I kneel back down next to her and hold out my hand. "Give me your arm."

"What for?" She asks skeptically.

"I'm going to stitch you up. Now. . .Give. Me. Your. Arm." My words are firm and sounded out with each syllable.

I take one of the small, sterilized needles and thread the stitch through the eye of the needle.

"No." She glowers, her face drawn tight in a scowl, and she folds her arms, backing away from me so fast, that her body hits my desk with a light thud.

Obstinate woman.

I'm going to get it through her thick skull that I'm in charge here and that this is not a goddamn democracy.

I take a step towards her, closing the distance between us. "I'm not going to ask you again," I growl, reaching out to grab her arm.

"I'm not incompetent. I can do it myself." She turns her small nose to the ceiling, clutching her hurt arm to her chest and reaching her other hand out for the needle.

"You should really let one of us help you," I say though I don't know why I even give a fuck.

Let her arm rot and fall off for all I care.

"Well, I'm not going to fall at your feet and beg you to let me take care of you." I spit, hitting my chair, and sending it clattering to the floor and across the room.

Don't lose control.

The demon inside me is lurking dangerously close to the surface. I shouldn't be lettting some dame get under my skin like this.

She's nothing.

Less than nothing.

I shouldn't care if she's hurt. She's just a piece of ass for Dom to play with until he breaks her.

Speak of the devil.

The asshole is standing in the doorway with a grin so wide it stretches from ear to ear.

Dick.

"I should have made popcorn for this shit!" He laughs, letting his shoulder fall on the frame of the door, propping himself up, and crossing his legs.

"Damn it, Dom! You aren't fucking helping." I mumble.

"You're welcome." He laughs.

I flip him off, "Go do something useful, asshole."

"Always telling me what to do." He shakes his head at me before his gaze greedily soaks in the girl.

"You know, I wouldn't mind taking orders from you, little rabbit." He grins.

Her cheeks darken to a rosy hue at his words.

"Out!" I point to the door, though a smirk breaks across my face.

"Fine, fine." He raises his hands in surrender, while slowly approaching the door. "Don't have too much fun without me."

"Why are you being so fucking difficult?" I yell, not understanding why this girl infuriates me the way she does.

"Excuse me?" She looks up, ripping the needle out of her arm, and throwing it to the floor. "I'm pretty damn sure I asked to do it myself and yet you seem to be either fucking stupid or deaf because here you are still trying to be a control freak."

I snort. "That was my fifth fucking needle."

"And it was my fifth time telling you that I don't want your help."

She doesn't want my help, yet she hasn't gotten the first damn stitch in.

"Everything ok?" Dean's head pokes back into my office door.

"She's difficult. I see why you knocked her out now." I answer.

He chuckles. "I didn't knock her out. Dom did. I just carried her in here."

"Whatever," I wave him off.

I grab the girl by the uninjured arm, jerking her up off the floor, and setting her upright on her feet. She hisses at me and her teeth clamp around the soft meaty flesh between my thumb and the first finger on my hand.

She bit me! She fucking bit me!

I snarl, bringing the back of my hand across her face, busting open her bottom lip.

She looks unaffected, ignoring the red smear that forms along her lip, staring at me with cold calculating eyes. She doesn't flinch. She doesn't say a word, toughing out the pain and wagging her finger at me as if I had wounded her feelings.

"That wasn't very fucking nice of you. Do it again and see what happens to that pretty face of yours," she practically purrs at me, sending shivers snaking down my spine.

"And what exactly are you going to do about it, trouble?" I ask through gritted teeth, forcing her to meet my gaze as I wrap her pigtails around my hand, jerking her head back exposing the soft milky flesh of her neck.

The way she's looking at me with those stormy blue eyes shouldn't turn me on, but it does.

She shivers and I'm not sure if it's with anger or desire.

I can feel the heat of her skin through the thin barrier of clothing left on her worn body.

When is the last time she's slept, or eaten?

She tenses in my grasp, "I'll just kill you all while you sleep."

"I sure as hell hope you try." Dom's husky voice says as he strolls into my study, earning himself a slap on the back of the head from Dean.

"Good point," I say, watching the rise and fall of her chest, my cock straining against the fabric of my pants. "You probably would kill us, wouldn't you?"

"With pleasure." She sneers.

I sigh, wracking my brain to think of a way to prevent that from happening.

"Well, then. Once I fix your arm and you get cleaned up and get some food, I'll have some special plans in place for you, trouble."

Dean and Dom watch us intently with hooded eyes.

"What. . .plans?" She asks after a short pause.

"I'm going to tie you to your bed, and you're going to stay there until I figure out what we're going to do with you. You're obviously a rabid animal who needs to learn to behave."

She bucks wildly against me, clawing and fighting against me, but I don't let go, rather, I shove her back and pin her to the wall.

She struggles for breath, squirming underneath my secure grip as I hold her hair with a firm grasp.

"I will fucking kill you! I'll kill you all!" She shrieks, still struggling against my hold.

Blood is still dripping from her busted lip and down the hand that I have wrapped around her tiny throat.

My mouth softly grazes over the soft lobe of her ear, my grip tightening around her neck, cutting off her air supply, "Since you want to act like a bitch, try my patience again and you'll end up chained to the bottom of my desk." I throw her to the floor, her angry yells fading as I walk out of the room, leaving my brothers to deal with the mess they created.

Chapter Fifteen

Dean

She's been asleep for almost fucking two days now. I'm beginning to wonder if she'll ever wake up.

She continued to struggle against us while we were trying to sew her up, and eventually, Dom's patience ran out so, in the end, he decided to knock her unconscious again.

The girl probably has a concussion to go with the rest of the scars, cuts, and bruises that maul her petite frame.

We didn't tie her to the bed since we were unsure of the extent of her injuries so, Dom and I have been taking shifts to keep an eye on her, making sure she doesn't run or cause Hatter to flip shit.

He's been on edge ever since we brought her here, the slightest things setting him off in a fit of rage. It's so unlike him to be so out of control.

In the chair in the corner of the room near the head of the large king-sized bed, I'm hidden in the shadows, watching her, wondering what kind of dreams are playing in her mind as she tosses and turns, occasionally snoring, and twitching as she soundly sleeps.

Jen, the mother of one of the rebels in the nearby village came by and bathed her the best she could so the girl, could keep her dignity instead of having men she didn't even know touching all over her unresponsive body. After cleaning her up, Jen put her in clean clothes and re-dressed her wounds with fresh bandages rather than the muddy rags that she had torn off and used in the woods to stop the bleeding.

In the shadowy corner, my eyes never leave her small form. The darkness of the room is punctuated by the soft glow of the moonbeams that filter through the window. I can hear Hatter shuffling around in the next room, his movements frantic and erratic.

I heard him on the phone with Chester a couple of hours ago. I wonder if it was another lead on who might have stolen our shit.

A soft groan escapes her lips, sending shocks of desire straight to my cock.

I feel this strange attraction to her, one that I can't quite comprehend myself.

Maybe it's the way she looks so delicate and vulnerable, her body battered and bruised, but still so beautiful. Or maybe it's the way she fought against us, refusing to let us take away her freedom.

I wonder what kind of life she led before ending up in our twisted world. It must have been a difficult one for her to be so distrusting.

If the thick scars on her arms are any indicatation, she has been through a lot of pain, probably more than most people can handle. But despite whatever she has been through, she still fights to live—to survive.

I feel this sense of protectiveness towards her as if she's something precious that needs guarding.

The moonlight falling across her face highlights her innocent features. I lean closer, the urge to stroke her face is overwhelming. Her long lashes flutter softly, her eyes darting back and forth beneath her lids and her cheeks flush a bright red as she moans again in her sleep.

The smell of her arousal fills the air, and my nose is overwhelmed by its intensity. It has taken over each and every one of my senses.

The little rabbit is having a naughty dream.

Watching a bead of sweat drop down her pretty face, I palm at my growing erection, imagining what it would feel like to have her beneath me, her body writhing in ecstasy as she comes all over my cock.

A soft sigh escapes her lips as her legs move restlessly beneath the blanket. Her breathing quickens and deepens like she is riding a never-ending crest of pleasure, causing my dick to grow even fucking harder.

My hands ache to feel her silky, soft skin. My mouth salivates at the idea of running my tongue all over her body, tasting her sweetness.

I know she's only dreaming, but the pressure in my balls is almost too much to take. I need to fuck something to relieve the burning need that is tearing through me like a poisonous virus.

My stomach seizes, my hand finding its way down the front of my pants and around my hardened length, pumping slowly.

What the fuck am I doing?

I jerk my hand away from myself and move to the opposite side of the room trying to force the image of her moaning beneath me, her legs locked around my neck as I suck her clit, from my mind.

My abrupt movement causes her to stir. Her eyes fly open, thick lashes blinking rapidly while she takes in her surroundings.

She moves to sit up, her face still flushed, her breathing labored, "You!" She exclaims heatedly when her focus lands on me.

Flinging the comforter off and swinging her legs over the side of the bed, she storms over to me and without a word slaps me in the face--hard.

My head flies to the side from the unexpected impact, a small bit of blood trickling from the corner of my mouth.

My right hand jerks up to my burning cheek, while my left hand balls tightly into a fist and I grit my teeth to keep from lashing out and wrapping my hands around her small delicate neck.

"What the fuck was that for?" I roar, grabbing her wrist when she tries hitting me again. "Why must you insist on being such a brat?"

"Why must you insist on keeping me here?" She reiterates.

My nostrils flare as I drag her small form closer to me, her bright blue eyes meeting mine with contempt and defiance.

"Because we don't trust you. Someone has been killing our men and taking what belongs to us."

"So? Kill them. Either way, I don't see what that has to do with me." She says with ease, an unfamiliar accent poking through her attitude, making my heart skip a beat.

"And how do I know it's not you that we need to kill?"

"Hmmm. I guess that's a good point. You don't. Well, go on then. Kill me." Her challenge has me biting the inside of my cheek, tongue-tied.

My eyes drop to the floor and I release her. I don't want to kill her, but I don't trust her either. She stares up at me with round eyes and a stark look on her face.

"Isn't that what you want, to kill me?" She asks, seemingly confused.

Yes.

No.

Maybe.

Fuck. I don't know.

My shoes echo on the polished wood as I walk over to the bed and sit down, the corner of the mattress sinking with my weight.

I pull my silver cigar case with the Ace of Spades etched into the front of it, out of my pocket, flipping it open and grabbing a Perdomo Champagne out of it, bringing it to my nose before clipping the end.

"Do you mind?" I ask before lighting the tip.

She shakes her head, her hair bouncing playfully around her face, "No. I rather enjoy the scent."

I lift the cigar to my lips, sparking a match and watching as the bright flame licks across the surface, inhaling the taste of smoky oak, with hints of cocoa, and almond. A thick white cloud of smoke hovers above my head like an incoming storm.

"Where are you from...Uh—"

I remember I still have no idea what her name is.

"Alice," Her footsteps are a whisper compared to my own as she breezes across the room and sits down next to me on the bed, "My name is Alice."

"Nice to meet you, Alice. I'm Dean." I smile, holding my hand out for her to shake.

She takes my hand, slowly shaking it, "I can't exactly say the same, can I?" She laughs.

The gesture makes my grin widen, "Touché."

I lean back and stretch my arm out, flicking the ashes from my cigar into a crystal ashtray on the small side table, a thick cloud of smoke billowing from my mouth.

"I'm from a place called London," She answers. "It's entirely different world than this one. There's no magic or nonsense creatures like there is here and it's quite loud. Except for my hospital that is. It's peaceful there."

She's from the Topside.

Good to know.

"I've been there before. One of my favorite cities to visit when we go to the Topside. "So, are you a doctor then?" I assume.

"Not exactly." She says, swinging her short legs back and forth from where they dangle off the bed. "I—" She pauses for a small moment. "I live there."

I take another puff, letting the smoke slip out of my mouth into the air. I run my hand through my hair, leaning forward and planting my elbows on my knees, "What kind of hospital is it?" I question.

"An asylum of sorts."

"So, like a mental hospital?"

Things are starting to make a little more sense about her now.

"Of course not!" She scowls, crinkling her nose. "Well...it is, but it's been shut down for years."

"Are you homeless or something?"

"No!" She shakes her head. "The hospital *is* my home. No one bothers me there and I come and go as I please." She pauses, her finger tapping her chin. "Though, I have been in a mental place before." She recalls. "But that was after my mother died and I wasn't there long. I got out a little while later, and that's when I moved into the old hospital on the outskirts of town, thus, making it my home." She crosses her legs, leaning back on her palms, and shrugs. "It's quite a simple story really."

Simple isn't the definition that comes to my mind when it comes to this girl.

"I see. Why an old hospital?"

"That's easy. So I could kill men like you without having to worry about anyone hearing their screams." She smiles sweetly.

I feel a bit like I've been gut-punched. I definitely wouldn't call this girl normal.

"Men like me?" My brow arches, and I tilt my head to look at her.

"Men who think they can take advantage of other people. Men who think they can treat women like property." Her shoulders square and she looks me straight in the eye, unafraid. "Men who treat women like second-class citizens and who take pleasure in hurting them and taking from them what they see fit."

Her gaze darkens with rage and her hands ball up into fists in her lap.

This girl must have been through some shit to view all men in that kind of light.

I stand up, scratching the scruff on my face that I haven't had a chance to shave yet, "And you see me as one of these...*men?*" I stare down at her.

"Aren't you?" She asks. "Am I not here against my will?"

"Have we hurt you?"

"The other one that looks like you knocked me out." She snorts.

"Only after you tried to kill me!" I retaliate.

She looks lost in thought before she falls back, lying down on the soft bed, and crosses her arms under her head, looking up at the ceiling, "Fair enough." She laughs.

I can't for the life of me figure this girl out. Is she crazy or is she just someone trying to protect herself from a world that has caused her immense pain and trauma?

I slowly sit back down on the bed and we stare at opposite sides of the light grey walls of her room, in silence for a few moments.

"I'm not like these men you speak of," I say, tentatively. "I'm not going to hurt you, and I would never take advantage of your body...Unless you wanted me to." I add with a grin, bringing my cigar up to my lips.

She turns her head to look at me, her eyes searching mine for truth, a light blush blossoming on the apples of her cheeks.

After what seems like a lifetime, she whispers, her voice like soft ribbons of silk when she speaks, "I think I'll have to be the judge of that."

My heart flutters in response.

Whatever her story is, I can sense it's bad. I can even understand why she hates men, and though I would never take from her, I can also understand why she thinks I might.

And for some reason that fucking kills me.

CHAPTER SIXTEEN

Alice

A knock sounds on the door before the golden door handle twists and the one they called Dom pokes his head in.

"So, it's true! The little rabbit has finally come out of hibernation." He says, pushing his way through the door.

I narrow my gaze at him, "To what do I owe the pleasure of your unwanted appearance, creep?" I sneer, as I cross my arms over my chest and lean on one foot so my hip juts out.

"You're cute when you're annoyed."

"You're not." I huff.

He throws himself in the tufted eggplant-colored recliner and kicks his feet up as he leans back getting comfortable.

"Ouch!" He grabs his chest. "That hurts my feelings, little rabbit."

The way the pet name curls off his tongue heats my core. I want to be angry with him, but all I can do is stare, captivated by his smug smile and dangerous eyes.

The colors of his eyes are mesmerizing. It's as if the blue and green are in constant conflict, creating a contrast that looks otherworldly. If heaven were to collide with earth, it would look something like this--a combination of beauty and danger--both pure and sinful all at once.

"I don't care about your feelings."

Lie.

For once, I'm actually finding not caring to be difficult because I do care if I hurt his fucking feelings, and I have no idea why.

Most likely, my body is trying to distract my mind with its traitorous needs. And there is no way in hell I'm about to let that happen.

You better quit your shit, vagina.

"That's not very nice, little rabbit. And to think I came here to ask you if you wanted to join us for dinner."

Has the entire day already passed?

I don't feel like I've been awake that long.

It seems like mere moments ago his twin was leaving my room to do some secret errand the fancy hat guy sent him to do.

I curl my lip, still trying to sort out all these unfamiliar feelings coursing through me. "No, thank you."

My stomach growls, making blood rush to my cheeks in a heated flush.

He notices and laughs.

"Are you sure about that? Dean slaved in the kitchen for the past three hours making sure you had multiple things to choose from just in case there was something you didn't like." He protests.

His reply takes me aback. Why would he do that for me if I'm just their prisoner?

With a deep sigh, I shake my head and look away.

Dom crosses the room quickly, grabbing my chin, and forcing me to look in his eyes. There's something powerful and carnal about his presence that leaves me a little breathless.

"I'm not hungry," I tell him, hoping he doesn't notice the quiver in my voice.

"Why are you lying?" he whispers, his voice a deep, velvety timbre, melting me into a pool of unspoken desires.

I swallow, trying not to focus on the intense gaze that is drawing me in.

He's so close. Too close.

My breath is coming out in short little pants, and my heart is beating erratically inside my chest.

Despite all good reasoning, I can't move away. I'm paralyzed by his gaze.

He tilts his head to the side, studying my face. His eyes slide to my lips and back up again.

My heart skips a beat, but I remain still, trying to show him that he doesn't affect me.

But it's too late.

He knows.

His gaze softens and he releases my chin. His index finger trails ever so softly down my cheek, to the corner of my lips.

He chuckles softly, taking a step back and releasing my chin, "You're not fooling anyone." He says.

I know it's the truth.

I'm starving and absolutely parched. I can't remember the last time I've eaten and the last thing to go in my belly was three bottles of wine.

If I'm going to get myself out of here then I have to keep up my strength, and if they're going to feed me, I might as well take what I can get.

"Fine. If I accompany you for dinner will you leave me alone?"

He smirks, holding out his hand.

I hesitate before taking it, his hand a furnace compared to my icy skin.

He takes my hand and wraps his fingers around mine, pulling me onto the hardness of his chest. Despite the strength in his grip, there is a gentleness to it that catches me off guard.

"No promises, Little rabbit," He whispers into my hair as he inhales my scent, and I can't help but tremble at his touch.

I know that I'm playing with fire.

But I'm willing to risk it if it means getting their trust so I can get to the Queen.

"Now let's go," He says with a tug, leading me towards the door. "Your food is getting cold and I already made you a plate." He grins.

I nod, not trusting myself to speak.

He leads me down a hallway that opens up to a massive spiral staircase, and another hallway full of doors stretches in the opposite direction.

This place is so big it would be easy to get lost in.

"You know you could just let me go," I tell him, my voice a mere whisper.

He chuckles, "Where would be the fun in that?"

He finally stops in front of a large arched doorway and motions for me to enter.

I step in, my mouth gaping in awe at the elegance of the room.

The walls are painted a dark rich green, with black trim, and a golden chandelier hangs from the ceiling, throwing off soft light. A long wooden table sits in the middle of the room, surrounded by high-backed chairs draped in black velvet.

He pulls out a chair for me and places my plate of food in front of me before taking his own seat. I stare at the plate in front of me, feeling the hunger gnawing at my stomach but I don't dig in just yet.

"Where are the other two?" I ask Dom, looking around the room and noticing their absence.

"Dean is finishing up in the kitchen and Hatter had some business to attend to, but he should be coming in at any moment now."

It's hard to believe that Dean is still in the kitchen when there is already so much food spread out on the table.

There's some kind of roasted bird, juicy steaks mound high on a large white porcelain serving plate, a basket full of soft rolls, and various sides and vegetables.

In the very center of the long table, there is a small, tiered tower of bite-sized treats.

My mouth waters as I eye down all the delectable courses set out in front of me.

"There's so much!" I exclaim.

"Dean always cooks a lot of food. Don't worry, it'll get eaten."

"By who?" I ask incredulously, wondering how anyone could possibly consume all of this food in one go.

"Us." He laughs, a lock of blond hair falling over his blue eye. "Dean and I may be men, but we're also wolves. It takes a lot of energy to shift which in turn means that we consume way more than your average human."

"Wow. Okay, then." I laugh.

A few minutes later Hatter strides in, his long black coat swaying around him as he walks. He removes his hat and takes a seat at the head of the table, his eyes locking with mine

He smiles and I feel a warmth spread through my chest.

"Staying out of trouble, trouble?" He asks, removing the black leather gloves from his hands before wiping them on the moist towelette next to his glass of water.

"For the moment," I reply honestly.

Dean enters the room with a large tray of food and sets it down on the last empty space on the table.

"This all looks amazing. Thank you." I tell Dean as he seats himself on the end of the table opposite to Hatter, leaving Dom directly across from me.

"It was nothing, "He shrugs. "Besides, we tend to eat a lot." He says, slicing up a piece of the roasted bird and placing it on my plate.

My mouth waters at the sight as I stare down at the plate of food with anticipation.

"Well, let's dig in then," Dom says, clapping his hands together before digging into his food.

I grab the utensils in front of me and poke at the food on my plate before taking a bite, savoring the smoky flavor of the bird as it spreads across my tongue.

Even though our circumstances are peculiar, this time together feels strangely comfortable.

I glance up to find Hatter watching me, a small smirk tugging at the corner of his lips.

I can't help but blush, quickly diverting my eyes down to the glass of deep red wine Dean poured for me only moments before.

I pick it up, letting the stem go through my fingers, and bring the glass to my lips. As I take a sip of the wine, I feel Hatter's gaze intensify on me. It's as if he's trying to read my very soul.

"So, Alice," he begins, his voice low and as smooth as the wine I'm sipping.

Dean must have told him my name.

"I hear you're from the Topside. How did you come to find Wonderland?"

I gulp down the bite of food in my mouth, "A mirror in a tree. Is there any other way?" I ask.

He shifts in his seat, propping his elbows on the table, and threads his fingers together in front of him. "There are many ways in and out of Wonderland. You just have to know where to look."

"And you would know where to look, would you?" I ask, arching my eyebrow at Hatter.

He gives a resolute nod, "Of course. I would know."

"Where?"

"Nice try, but those are secrets I'm afraid you're not privy to."

Dom stops gnawing on the T-bone steak in his hand long enough to snap his attention to our conversation, "You're not trying to leave us already, are you, little rabbit?" He asks, pushing out his bottom lip.

"I wasn't trying to be here to begin with," I say in a disgusted tone.

Hatter chuckles at my response, a deep, throaty sound that sends shivers down my spine. "And yet, here you are," he says, his eyes flickering over my face.

I feel myself growing warmer under his gaze and quickly turn back to my food, "For now." I assure him.

It was never my intention to stay in Wonderland anyway and had these assholes not captured me, I could have already completed what I came here to do and already have been back in London.

I take another bite, chewing slowly, eyeing the three men, "So what kind of work do you guys do?" I ask, even though I'm pretty sure I already know the answer.

By piecing together snippets of whispered conversations I've heard in the hallway outside my bedroom door, I've come to the conclusion that not only are they brothers, but they also seem to be involved in some sort of risky, illegal type shit.

Hatter leans back, staring at me, "I'm a businessman, Alice, and the whole purpose of the business I run is to help the people of Wonderland retake the kingdom." He answers, taking a sip of wine from the glass before him.

"Like, you're trying to dethrone the Queen?" I ask, shocked that he's actually involved in trying to have her overthrown.

"Precisely." He replies. "Because of the Queen, magic has been forbidden in Wonderland and there are, let's say. . .Dire consequences for the people her seeker catches using it. However, since the seeker can only sense the magic of those who were naturally born with it, that's where me and my brothers come in."

"I'm not following. What is it you guys do to help?" I ask, genuinely intrigued.

Hatter gestures over to the tower of pastries, "I found out that if you concentrate the magic of pixie dust and mix it with certain plants that only grow in Wonderland and then infuse it in treats, much like the ones Dean made here tonight, it will give the person who eats them limited, but untraceable magic."

"And these--*treats*--they help people how?"

"They each do different things," He continues to explain. "Some give you the ability to fly, some allow you to breathe underwater, some give you super strength and agility, invisibility. . .You get the gist. But the one thing that it gives to every consumer is hope, and they need hope. The people of Wonderland have been living in fear and oppression for far too long and it's because of our magic that they are able to stand up and fight for themselves again."

"Yeah," Dean agrees. "The rebellion is something we've been building for years. We've been working hard to give people the power to fight back against the Queen and with the help of the magic that we provide that's exactly what we're giving them."

"Whoa. So, you guys are like illegal magic dealers. That's kind of awesome, but aren't you afraid of getting caught?"

Hatter takes another sip of his wine before responding. "Of course, there's always a risk involved. But the reward of a free kingdom is worth it. Besides, the Queen has been sending her men after us for years and we've made it this far. Only a select few know about what we do, and we make sure to keep our operations hidden. We have a large network of allies which means we never have to involve ourselves in the direct selling of our products. She knows we're selling people magic but she has no clue as to how we make it or where we make it."

I can't believe what I'm hearing. These guys are essentially drug dealers, but instead of dealing with illicit substances, they're trading in forbidden magic. The concept is both exhilarating and terrifying. Yet, I can't deny that there is a certain nobility to it.

I have an interest in what they're fighting for, but that doesn't change the reality that they're holding me captive. But if they're fighting for the people of Wonderland, can they really be that bad?

I could be in chains.

My pussy instantly gets wet upon the thought of being chained up while they torture me with their touch, before taking me hard and rough, fucking all my holes at once until I can't move, can't scream—can't breathe.

This is absolutely fucking ludicrous.

Because I want both; To fuck them *and* kill them.

Jeez, when did I become such a slut?

Dom and Dean throw me heated stares.

"What has you so flustered, little rabbit?" Dom grins, waggling his brows at me.

I choke on a piece of the fluffy roll I'm nibbling on, and squeeze my thighs shut, praying to no one in particular that it will help hide the scent of my arousal.

Hatter must have taken note of my reticence because he shoots Dom a look that makes him instantly go silent, while Dean tries to hide his amusement behind a forkful of potatoes.

"Nothing. It's just warm in here. I lie, my cheeks hot. I finish gulping down the rest of my wine and change the subject. "Are you guys serious about overthrowing your Queen?"

"She's not our Queen but, yes, all the same," Hatter states without hesitation, then, leans back in his seat, twirling a lock of his dark hair that had fallen from its usual swept-back look around his finger.

Maybe I can use this to my advantage and get my hands on some of their magic stuff.

"I'd love to help out," I blurt out, winning myself surprised looks from them all.

"What makes you think we'd want your help?" Hatter questions.

I shrug, "I dunno. But what else do I have to do?"

Granted, yes, helping their cause seems like it would be a great service to Wonderland and its people, but teaming up with this trio of misfits isn't a risk I'm willing to take.

But they don't need to know that.

Call me selfish, but I want the Queen's death to be by my own hands.

I need it.

I've come too far and gotten too close to let my pussy distract me from what's important—avenging my father's death.

Escaping is the only way out of this nightmare, and I'm going to do everything in my power to make sure that it happens.

Chapter Seventeen

Rose

If you had told me that a couple of days ago that my—who I thought to be a dead father—was the beast that the Queen has used to terrorize all of Wonderland, I would have called you a lying sack of shit.

So when it actually turned out to be the truth, naturally, I freaked the fuck out.

I'm still coming to terms with the fact that the father I knew to be gentle and kind, has murdered and eaten hundreds of people, and I helped him do it.

Absinthe and Yelena have still been searching the mountainside for me, surely not wanting to return to the Queen with empty hands.

"What's on the agenda for today?" I ask the dragon-like creature that's my father.

He huffs a smoky breath, seeming to shrug as he lazily soaks in the sun's rays on the bank of the lagoon, hidden behind a waterfall at the bottom of the largest mountain.

I wish more than anything that we could actually talk to each other. I miss the long conversations we used to have as we made star-shaped peanut butter and strawberry jam sandwiches in the castle's kitchen.

I glance at him again and for a moment, I can almost picture the father I used to know. The one who would lift me up and spin me around, the one who would tell me stories of the far-off lands.

I stare off into the surreal blue water of the lagoon, my mind whirring with thoughts. The sound of the rushing water is soothing, and for a moment, I forget about the horrors our kingdom has been suffering and the pain I feel from being forced to assist in the damage caused.

I will never be able to forgive myself for the part I've played in the destruction of a once-thriving land, and neither will my people.

How could I even ask them to?

I may be free from the Queen, but I can never be free from the guilt.

I notice a sudden shift in my father's demeanor. His eyes narrow in on something behind the waterfall, and I turn my head to see what has caught his attention.

My heart drops as I see Absinthe and Yelena standing on the other side of the waterfall. The crashing water hides us, but they will be able to see us if we try to escape.

"What do we do?" I mouth to my father.

He lowers his enormous horns in a warning of caution, shaking his head, indicating that I should stay still for the moment.

My heart is pounding and I'm holding my breath, hoping they just keep going.

Go figure, the day we decide to leave the safe haven of the cave and get some fresh air, we'd run into these fucking assholes.

I don't want to go back to the palace. I don't want to be one of her little pets anymore.

As I watch Absinthe and Yelena approach, I feel a wave of fear wash over me. I can feel my father tense beside me, his muscles coiled, ready to strike at any moment.

The water crashing down all around us is deafening, but I can hear my pulse pounding in my ears. I close my eyes, trying to calm my racing heart, but when I open them again, I see that Absinthe and Yelena have stopped about ten feet away from us.

If they step about six more steps to the left, they'll be able to see us where a large jagged rock splits the water of the fall creating a small insight to the other side, right to our location.

We could take them.

But there's something about the way my father hesitates that makes me believe he can't harm them because of the curse the Queen put on him and I can't take them down. Not by myself.

Fuck!

I don't know what to do. I can't just make a run for it and leave my father here. What if they kill him?

Tears prick the corners of my eyes, my father notices and his gaze softens, a silent understanding passing through us.

He nods to the small cave just big enough for me to crawl through, but small enough that Absinthe and Yelena wouldn't be able to fit through since they are both much larger than me.

However, that also means that he won't be going with me.

No!

I won't leave him. Not when I just found out he's alive. This isn't fair.

He nods again, this time more desperately because now Absinthe is two steps away from being able to see us both together and if they know I'm not dead or injured, they'll know he saved me.

He's doing what he has to do to make sure we both make it out alive.

I take one last look at my father, his eyes soft and pleading, before I nod back, indicating that I understand what he's trying to do. It's tearing me apart inside to leave him behind, but I know that's what needs to happen if we're going to survive this.

With silent tears streaming down my face, I turn and as quietly as I can crawl into the entrance of the cave.

My heart is pounding, and I can hear my breathing echoing against the walls around me. The darkness is suffocating, but I try to control my fear.

I hear footsteps growing louder and I press my back against the cave wall, trying to make myself as small as possible. The footsteps stop outside the entrance of the cave, and I hold my breath, waiting for them to leave.

But they don't.

Instead, I hear Absinthe's voice echoing through the caverns.

"Shit!" He yells, my heart dropping when the sound of his axe swinging into the rock reverberates through the small hole, ringing through my ears. "WHERE IS SHE?!" He roars.

"I bet the bird knows." Yelena's voice filters in.

I hear the whoosh of her flames and the screech of the Jabberwocky.

Bitch!

She's the first person I'm going to kill when I figure out how to get this fucking necklace off. I'd gladly rip her heart out and serve it to the Queen.

"The Queen is expecting you. She's not going to be happy you let the girl get away." She says.

I hear the thunderous clapping of his leathery wings as he takes to the sky to report to the Queen.

After he is gone, I hear Absinthe again, "His head is going to look good hanging in the main hall of the clubhouse." He laughs.

The sound of their footsteps begins to fade, and I crawl further into the cave until I feel something brush against my hand. I quickly pull back and try to stifle the scream in my throat as I realize it's just a cobweb, not some creature lurking in the shadows.

I crawl deeper and deeper into the cave, my only source of light coming from the faint glimmers of sunlight filtering through the cracks in the rocks. My knees ache and my hands are scraped raw by the sharp edges of the rocks, but I keep going, pushing myself further even when my hand slips off a wet rock and it slices through the soft flesh of my palm.

"*Ahhh*!" I hiss as sharp pain lances up my arm. "Fucking great!"

Just my luck.

I press my injured hand against my chest and continue forward for what feels like hours until I finally reach the end of the cave and collapse, my breath coming in short gasps. I can still feel the sting of pain on my hand, but now it's joined by a throbbing ache in my knees and feet. But at least I'm safe for now.

I close my eyes, taking deep breaths to steady the thumping in my chest. I feel like I'm about to pass out.

My fingertips dig into the ground as I drag myself out of the small opening of the cave and into the open air.

The sun is just starting to set, casting the surrounding forest in a warm golden glow. I take a moment to breathe in the fresh air, the scent of pine needles and damp earth flooding my senses.

Now what?

The top of the mountain where my father's list is located is still a far reach, but I can probably make it there by morning if I start now.

I stand up, using the rocky wall of the small cave I just came out of to support my aching body. I take a step forward and immediately stumble, catching myself on a nearby tree, my injured hand jolting with pain. I curse under my breath and look down at my palm, only to notice that the wound has started bleeding again.

Why am I so damn clumsy?

My father used to say that I got all of my grace from my mother which, unfortunately, was none at all.

He told me of a ball they once hosted before my mother fell pregnant with me and how she was the most beautiful woman there. He told me how her jewels sparkled, bringing out the brilliance of her eyes, and how her gown turned the heads of everyone there when she began to descend down the double staircase of their palace only to make it halfway down before she tripped on the tail of her dress when her heel got caught in it and she fell the rest of the way down.

She didn't get hurt but she was so embarrassed that she began to cry. My father said he took her hand, gently pulling her from the ground and she turned to the whispering crowd and said,

"In life, there will be many stumbles and many falls. However, it is not the fall that defines us, but the strength we muster to rise again."

My father told me that was the moment he fell in love with her all over again and he knew he had chosen the right woman to spend his life with.

It was my favorite story as a child, especially after we lost her, and it has stuck with me all these years. And now, more than ever, it feels like a mantra I need to live by.

Taking a slow steady breath, I look around, the sun is almost gone from the sky now, and it is already getting dark. The forest around me is as still as a grave and a light chill is creeping in, sinking deep into my bones, eliciting a shiver that runs down the length of my spine.

I wrap my arms around myself, trying to fight off the chill as I take a step forward. It's now or never, I remind myself, and I push forward into the darkness of the woods.

The trees close in around me as I continue on my journey, their branches reaching out like bony fingers ready to grab hold and drag me into the shadows.

I hope my father is ok.

I don't know when I'm going to see him again, but if I can just make it to his cave then I can wait it out until he returns. He's bound to come back eventually, right?

I mean...He has to.

AMBER BUNCH

Chapter Eighteen

Dom

I wonder if she would scream if she woke up to find me next to her, watching her sleep.

Her body is lax and pressed against me, with her ass snuggled right into my groin.

She's quite the cuddler.

Funny, since she's such a little firecracker when she's awake. I would have never guessed that about her.

It's been so long since I've felt this at peace.

Lying here next to her, I don't hear the screams or mournful howls of my dying pack that fills my head on a daily basis.

She's like an angel who traded in her halo for horns. There's something wild and untamable about her, a walking hurricane that can bring both destruction and beauty.

She's the embodiment of contradictions—the storm and the sun, her soul a swirling mix of light and dark, calm and chaos all wrapped up into one perfectly imperfect girl.

I find myself completely and utterly captivated by her presence; there is something about her that drew me in and now I'm entirely fucking hooked.

It's not just her beauty, although that is certainly a part of it. It's the way she challenges us, the way she pushes Hatter to the brink of insanity with her sharp wit and fiery attitude, the way she has softened Dean, and the way she makes me feel less alone.

I realize that I want her in a way I've never wanted anyone before.

It's dangerous, this desire that burns within me, but I can't help it. I want to possess every inch of her, to claim her as mine.

She stirs slightly, pulling her knees closer to her body, her light snores making the corners of my lips tug upward.

Her smell is intoxicating, filling my nostrils with a sweet, seductive scent and I inhale deeply, wanting to hold onto it forever.

I trace the outline of her jaw, my heart thudding so loud I'm afraid the sound will wake her.

I lean in closer and place a gentle kiss on her temple, my lips lingering for a moment before I pull away.

Her body tenses.

She's awake.

Her hand finds its way behind her, landing on my face, she pats it for a second before she flips around to face me, "What the fuck are you doing you fucking creep?!" She yelps, scrambling to get out of the bed.

She's in one of the black t-shirts that I gave her to use until the stuff I asked Jeremiah to have Nova order for her arrives at Henry's shop. I figured since Nova is a girl, she'd know what to get our little rabbit so she can have more than our clothes that completely swallow her delectable figure.

Our clothes never looked as sexy on us as they do on her, though.

"You were nicer when you were sleeping." I pout.

"What the hell is wrong with you?" She tugs at the hem of her shirt, trying to cover her bare thighs.

I lean back on my elbows reveling in the way she flounders under my gaze, "A lot actually." I laugh.

"Clearly." She backs herself in a corner, her legs trembling, her eyes widened in fear, and she points to the door. "Get out. Get the fuck out, right now!"

"Or what, little rabbit?" I hop off the bed, covering the distance between her and me in a matter of seconds. "You gonna scream for help? I mean, you could. . .But who's gonna save you?"

My dick is so fucking hard.

She gasps, her nostrils flaring as her chest heaves from the heavy breaths escaping her throat, her eyes meet mine, the panic in them making me even harder, though, I didn't think that was possible.

"No one. That's who." I whisper, boxing her off by leaning my hands on the wall above her head.

I can hear the quickened pace of her heart and smell the sweetness of her pussy as she grows slick. She's scared but she's also turned on and I think that's what pisses her off the most.

She wants to hate us, but it's a fight she'll eventually lose.

"Get away from me." Her voice comes out in a breathy huff, one that makes my cock twitch in my pants.

She eyes the door, and I can see the wheels spinning in her head. She wants to try to run from me, but there is no escape.

I lower my head, my lips so fucking close to hers, "Do you know what happens when a rabbit attempts to flee from a wolf?" I ask.

"No, and I don't care to know." She folds into herself, shaking her head violently.

I grab the back of her neck, sliding my tongue across the curve of her throat, "He hunts her. He finds her, and he makes her scream as he eats her." I whisper in her ear, before nipping her earlobe.

Her pupils dilate, not out of terror but because she's aroused.

"You're a fucking psychopath."

I lean in further, my lips ghosting against hers, "A lunatic...A loon...A madman." I bite her bottom lip, pulling it into my mouth before releasing it and resting my forehead against hers. "Sounds like we're two peas in a pod, little rabbit."

She closes her eyes tightly, her fists clenching at her sides as she tries to fight the desire she's feeling.

"I...No...Uhh..." She's stuttering, and I take the advantage to put her out of her misery.

I capture her lips with mine, my tongue delving deep into her mouth, tasting her. She tastes sweet and innocent, but she secretly has a dark side that is as dark as my own. A side that is full of rage and bitterness, thirsting for dominance, a side that craves the kind of sick love we can offer her.

I think that's why I'm so drawn to her.

I press my body against hers, loving the way her curves mold to mine. My cock is thick and rock hard, and it's ready to be buried in her wet cunt.

I'm lost in the moment, in her kiss, in her tongue tangling with mine.

I pull away, my breathing ragged as I look down at her. She's dazed, but I'm more so.

My lips trail down her jawline to her throat. "I'm going to have you, little rabbit," I whisper in her ear. "I will break you, make you scream my name, make you cry as you beg me for mercy while you cum on my cock. I will be the reason your foundation crumbles and you fall apart at the seams...and I'm going to enjoy every delicious fucking second of it."

AMBER BUNCH

Chapter Nineteen

Alice

Soft lighting cascades across the living room of Hatter's manor, casting shadows upon the silky drapes and ornate furnishings of the living area.

It's a haven for the damned, a place where secrets are whispered like ghosts through the hallways and unspoken desires are given free rein.

My gaze falls upon a small, unique-shaped bottle perched delicately upon the mantle. "Drink me" is etched into its glassy surface, the words taunting me with their enigmatic allure.

My arm moves almost involuntarily as I go to pick up the little blue bottle from its spot on the mantel. As soon as I have it in my grasp, I can feel the weight of its contents shifting around inside.

"What is this?" I ask Hatter, holding the bottle up to the light so I can get a better look.

The liquid inside shimmers like liquid starlight, its bright golden hue capturing the essence of the twisted beauty of the magic I believe to be inside.

Hatter strides toward me, his steps confident and strong, with a dangerous determination that closes the distance between us.

His eyes are narrowed and locked onto mine, a fire burning behind them that sends a shiver down my spine. "That," He said, snatching the bottle from my unsuspecting fingers, "Is none of your fucking business."

"It's some of that illegal drug magic, isn't it?" I ask, my eyes sparking with wonder and excitement.

He shoves the potion into his pocket, his face inches from mine, "Stop meddling in things you have no understanding of," he hisses, his breath tickling my skin.

Okay.

Someone needs a juice box and a nap.

There's this intensity in his demeanor, a guardedness that makes me question just what kind of magic is being contained within that seemingly innocuous bottle.

For him to be so protective over it, it has to be something good.

"Just tell me!" I whine.

Hatter's eyes bore deeply into mine, "Curiosity can be a dangerous thing, Trouble." He whispers, his voice low and warning. "Especially in Wonderland."

"You're no fun." I sulk, before he tears himself away from me.

"Come now. Can't you at least give me a hint as to what it does?" I ask, trying to sound as innocent as possible, though I know it's futile.

I pout, my bottom lip jutting out slightly. Hatter's countenance remains unchanged, his eyes steely and unwavering.

"Drop it, Alice. It's not for you to know," he says sternly, his voice firm and final.

I can sense the undercurrent of tension in his words, and it only piques my curiosity further.

With a huff, I give up my line of questioning, knowing it will get me nowhere.

Instead, I plop down on the couch next to Dom, whose presence has been almost forgotten amidst my failed interrogation.

I grab the TV remote from his hand and begin flipping through the channels, propping my feet up on Dom's lap.

"I was going to complain, but if you're going to touch me, I think I can be persuaded to do otherwise." Dom jokes, though, I know he's not entirely kidding when he says it.

"Hey, how are we even able to watch TV in Wonderland without the internet?" I ask. "Is there some sort of twisted version of Wi-Fi here?"

Hatter smirks, clearly amused by my question. "No, Alice. There is no Wi-Fi in Wonderland. However, I created a device that mimics the Topside's internet. It's far from perfect, but it serves its purpose."

"Wow, that's pretty clever," I reply, genuinely impressed.

I would have never taken Hatter for the inventive type, but then again, there is so much about him that still remains a mystery.

"Thank you," he says, inclining his head slightly. The momentary warmth in his expression quickly vanishes, replaced once more by his usual guardedness.

"Does everyone have access to this...This mimicry of the Topside's internet?" I question.

Dom leans over me, reaching to grab a bowl of green colored chips, popping a handful in his mouth before answering, "Only those who work for us do. But once we overthrow the Queen and take back Wonderland, we plan to make it accessible to all."

I nod, then my fingers go back to dancing across the remote, mindlessly flipping through the channels as my thoughts wander.

Anxiety churns inside me, a quiet but firm reminder lurking in the depths of my consciousness.

I came back to Wonderland with a purpose, but it seems that every step I take, only leads me further into the temptations of wanting to stay here.

As I'm lost in my thoughts, Dom nudges my leg with his knee, "Is everything okay, Little rabbit?" His voice breaks through the haze of my thoughts, the concern in his tone, inescapable.

"Oh, yes. Fine," I lie, plastering on a smile that doesn't quite reach my eyes. "Just lost in thought."

"Be careful not to get too lost," he laughs softly, his gaze lingering on mine for a moment longer before he turns back to the TV screen.

As we sit here, our silence is punctuated by the flickering images on the screen.

I settled on a comedy show about two waitresses that live and work together in New York City a place in the States I've always dreamt of visiting.

"Where's Dean?" I wonder aloud, taking note of his absence.

I haven't seen him since earlier this morning.

Hatter and Dom both answer at the same time giving me conflicting explanations.

Hatter sighs, stopping his consistent pacing in front of the fireplace, "For future reference, we're not inclined to tell you our every whereabout. You are a prisoner, perhaps you should start acting like it."

"Harsh." Dom mumbles beside me.

Before I can respond and give him a piece of my mind, Hatter's phone rings, its shrill tone slicing through the tense atmosphere like a knife.

He quickly answers the device, his face hardening as he listens to the voice on the other end of the line.

"Good, and you're sure they're going to know something?" He questions.

He nods, the corner of his mouth curving in a devilish smirk, *"Yea, I know. Thanks, Henry."* He says, turning to where Dom is still laid back, munching on chips as he rubs his thumb on my calf.

"Is there a problem?" He ventures, acutely aware of the sudden shift in energy that seems to saturate the room.

"Seems we've got a lead on a couple of bartenders who might know the whereabouts of the assassin we believe is involved in the murders of our men and theft of our pixie dust shipments," Hatter says, a dangerous edge to his voice.

Dom sits up straighter, his eyes gleaming with excitement.

"Sounds like it's time for a little adventure," He grins, his hand sliding up my leg.

I push his hand away, scowling at him, and he lets out a throaty laugh as he sidesteps one of the elegant couch pillows, I throw at him.

Hatter rolls his eyes, "This is not a game, Dom. We have serious business to take care of."

"But it doesn't mean we can't have a little fun along the way," Dom argues back, still grinning.

Hatter makes a noise of annoyance, before turning to me, "You're staying here with me."

"Great." I retort. "Sounds fun."

"Dom, go grab Dean. I want you two to go talk to these guys and find out where this guy lives. I want to know if he has family, where he eats, what time he takes a shit—you know what to do."

Dom nods in agreement, already heading for the door.

"You know we'll take care of it," He says, pausing in the doorway to meet my eyes. "See you soon, little rabbit. Keep my spot warm." And he winks.

"Don't make me puke," I say, though the tingly sensation I'm feeling in my stomach is certainly not nausea.

"Dom," Hatter warns.

"I'm going ain't I?" Dom groans as he slips out the door, grumbling as he marches down the hall on his way to grab Dean.

Hatter turns to me, "Is there anything you want to watch?" I ask, offering him the remote.

"TV isn't really my forte but thank you for the offer."

"Is there anything else you do outside of whatever you do in your office?"

He laughs, "Books. I enjoy reading books."

"Wow."

"What?" He questions.

"I'm just surprised to find out that we actually have something in common."

"You like to read?"

"I love it, way more than watching television if I'm being honest. Do you have any books I could choose from?" I ask, my eyes growing wide with anticipation.

Books were always my escape, a doorway to another world, another life, where I could forget about the harsh reality of my own problems and live vicariously through the characters on the page.

And now, being in Wonderland and surrounded by dangerous men who are holding me captive, books seem like the perfect distraction.

Hatter nods, "Of course."

He leads me through the maze-like hallways of his mansion, eventually arriving at a massive doorway, the doors creak as he parts them and gestures to me to enter.

I step inside the room, and my eyes widen in amazement. The room is filled with shelves from the floor to the ceiling, each holding hundreds of books of every genre imaginable. The room is lit by a warm, cozy light, and the air smells of the aroma of bound leather.

As I walk through one of the aisles, my fingertips trace over the spines of books; I can feel Hatter's presence behind me. I turn around to see him standing at the entrance with his arms crossed over his chest. He looks so fucking sexy standing there, his hair unkempt, his sleeves barely containing the biceps spilling out of them.

It almost makes me want to like him.

Almost.

His piercing gaze follows my every movement as I hesitantly go to pick up a book before my gaze snaps back to his as if to silently ask permission.

A small smirk tugs at the corners of his lips as he sits down in one of the many recliners, waves his hand, and says, "Go ahead, trouble Take your pick."

CHAPTER TWENTY

Dean

My hands grip the steering wheel tighter, the muscle in my leg twitching as I press the clutch and kick it into sixth gear.

Hatter is sending us to check on another lead that he received from Henry, earlier today.

Judging by the fact that there was no evidence left behind at either scene and that we only know of one man who's as good as us at leaving no traces behind, we think we finally have our guy.

Alex Frost.

He's an ice assassin who can produce weapons made of ice from his body, which he then uses to kill his targets, making it almost impossible to link him to the murders.

He's skilled. Very skilled.

I doubt he's working alone but we can at least find out who hired him if we can get these guys to give up his location.

Dom is in the seat next to me, looking like he's seen a ghost. His knuckles turn white as he tightly grips the handle above his head, his eyes widening in terror as the back end of the car kicks out and I hit the gas, drifting around a sharp bend.

I can feel the adrenaline surging through my body as I take the car faster and faster down the winding road. The wind whips my hair around my face, and I can hear Dom's ragged breathing next to me.

"Could you slow the fuck down?" Dom asks, his jaw resembling stone with how hard he has his teeth clenched.

I glance over at him, his skin glistening with sweat as his eyes roll back in his head. Blood drips down his chin from his protruding fangs and little patches of fur fade in and out, sprouting up on the back of his hands before disappearing back into his skin as he strains to fight off the transition.

If he shifts inside here, he'll destroy the entire cabin and we'll wreck. I don't want to ruin this car; I just picked it up a few weeks ago and this is the first time I've taken it out since bringing it here.

I laugh, feeling the rush of excitement coursing through me. There's nothing like the feeling of driving at top speed on an empty road at night. It's exhilarating—freeing, and it makes me feel invincible.

"Sorry, brother. I got a little carried away." I tell him, running my hand through the dark mop on my head to remove the stray strands that are flying into my eyes.

I need a fucking shower.

I wonder if Alice would like to join.

I can picture the soft peaks of her breasts with little water droplets running down her hardened nipples and down to dip between her legs as I have her spread open with her back pressed against the wall while I flick my tongue across her clit, grinding into her sweet pussy until she wraps her legs around me and begs for me to slide my cock deep inside of her.

My dick twitches in my jeans at the thought as I pull a little harder on the steering wheel, sending the car into a sharp turn that sends Dom slamming into the door of the car.

"God damn it, Dean!"

We're here anyways.

I slam on the brakes, bringing the car to a screeching halt and Dom jabs me in the jaw before he rips open the passenger door and storms off.

"I fucking hate it when you do that." He growls.

I follow after him, shaking my head and laughing as he disappears inside the entrance to the pub that Nova hid out at before finding sanctuary in Neverland.

His hands are shoved into his pockets and his shoulders are hunched.

He's pouting again.

"Dom!" I call out, from behind him. "Dom, I'm sorry!"

"No, you're not!" He snaps. "Now shut the fuck up so I can do my damn job and get the fuck out of here."

"So grumpy."

"I wonder fucking why, Dean."

The pub is mostly empty, with the exception of a few sirens seducing a couple of guys at the corner of the bar and a few men sitting at a distant table too distracted by their card game to notice anything going on around them.

As we walk across the room, I notice two burly men entrenched behind the black stone bar. They share a long look between the two of them before their eyes settle on us. Their expressions harden and their brows knit together as we approach the bar and sit down in the two bar stools in the far back corner.

They already know who we are.

"We don't want no trouble here, man." The shorter of the two states. "You're welcome to grab a drink if you want but-"

"We're not here for the drinks, though, I will oblige and have a bourbon," I reply, reaching into my jacket for a lighter as I bring a cigar up to my lips preparing to ignite the end. "We're here for information. No trouble."

"Well," Dom begins. "As long as the two of you cooperate, we won't have any issues. You'll have to forgive my brother for being so transparent. He doesn't know any better." I roll my eyes as Dom slings his arm around my shoulder when he says the last part.

The taller bartender has a thick accent, and his ears are a shade redder than his face. His beard is starting to grey, and he has a couple of faded scars beneath his eye.

"Okay," he sighs, rubbing at his head before sliding a glass across the table. "What do you need to know?"

"We're looking for someone."

"Got a name?" The short one asks.

He's a tad on the pudgy side and has a squeaky voice. He's watching us warily, jumping at every little noise as if we're venomous snakes eager to strike their prey.

"His name is Alex Frost. He's tall, kinda skinny. White hair." I raise an eyebrow before proceeding to light up my cigar. The bartender cocks his head and furrows his brow, looking back and forth between us.

"No. I've never heard of him." He replies. I can hear his heart racing and he's sweating more than is normal. I lean forward, resting my elbow on the table and my head in my hand as I fix the poor sap with a glare.

"Are you sure?" I ask, smoke curling around my face as I take another puff of my cigar blowing it directly in his face. "We've heard he likes to visit here from time to time."

Dom throws back the rest of the amber liquid in his glass, grinning from ear to ear as he slams it down, shattering it on the pudgy man's hand that's busy wiping away at the countertop.

"Oops." He chuckles, licking at the side of his mouth. "Looks like you're gonna need stitches, man. See, the thing is, we don't believe you. You seem like a smart man, so tell me something—Is he worth dying over?"

The short man doesn't say anything, he just clutches his hand in pain as the blood starts to seep through his fingers.

The tall one comes forward and speaks, "I never met the guy, but I heard he's a mean son of a bitch. I'm sure he's capable of handling himself and I damn sure ain't about to lose my life for the likes of him."

"He'll kill us." The short whispers.

"Sam, they'll kill us." He points to me and my brother. "Do you not know who they are?"

A wrinkle forms between Sam's eyes as he tries to place who we are. His mouth drops into a small *O* as the realization kicks in, "I—I'm so sorry fellows. I didn't. . .I'm not. . .Can I get you anything else?" His tongue tumbles over his words.

"I wouldn't say no to another drink," Dom says and Sam quickly fills his glass again with his good hand.

"So, where can we find him?" I ask.

"I've heard that he has a little one-room cottage somewhere near the mountains where the Queen's Jabberwocky lives when he's not out on a job." The tall bartender chimes trying to take some of the heat off his buddy.

"See, Sam." I smile, patting his shoulder. "That wasn't so difficult, was it?"

The pudgy man clenches his fists and grits his teeth as he shakes his head, his lips pressed tightly together in fear.

"Well then, I think we're done here," I say, standing up from my seat and butting my cigar in the tarnished ashtray behind the lip of the bar.

"Thank you for your time. You have such a lovely. . .Establishment.

Dom grins devilishly, finishes his drink, and blows the frightened men a kiss. "Talk to you soon, boys."

Sam looks like he's about to throw up.

We walk out of the pub and get in the car.

"You think Hatter has murdered Alice yet?"

Dom cackles, leaning his arm out the window, "I'm more worried about our little rabbit killing him."

I notice how he calls her ours, and how I don't hate it.

I know we're all attracted to her madness. She has somehow crept beneath the surface of our skin, igniting every nerve ending with a blazing fire.

She's our poison. Our plague.

And she's just as broken as we are.

She's awoken Hatter, in a different way though, and I'm not sure if it's a good or bad thing yet.

She's either going to be his undoing. . .or she's going to become the one who finally takes on his beast, and wins.

A PURSUIT OF MADNESS

CHAPTER TWENTY-ONE

Alice

The rage he hides behind that perfect businessman act reminds me a bit of my own.

I wonder what or who made him that way.

Everything about him is cautious, he's a man who's always in control, always calculating his next move.

As we sit in silence, I can't help but notice the way his eyes linger on my lips, and the way he bites his own lip as if he's fighting the urge to taste mine.

The tension makes me squirm in my seat, the book in my hand doing little to keep my mind distracted from the peculiar man sitting in the chair across from me tapping his fingers on the arm of the chair as the glow of the warm fire in the massive stone fireplace in front of us, dances in his eyes.

Suddenly, he stands up and begins pacing back and forth in front of the fireplace. His hands are clenched into fists, and I can almost feel the anger radiating off him like heat waves.

He whirls around to face me, his eyes wild, "Forgive me. I'm not much for company at the moment."

I set my book down on the small black table beside my chair, curling my legs up in the seat, "You haven't been much for company since the moment I met you in my opinion. You're grumpy and rather boring."

He scoffs, his eyes flashing with a dangerous glint, "Is that so? Perhaps I should show you just how interesting I can be."

My heart races as he stalks towards me with a predatory grace. I feel a shiver run down my spine at his words, the sudden darkening of his gaze making my heart race. He steps closer to me, towering over my smaller frame and I almost feel a slight sense of vulnerability.

"I highly doubt that." I laugh, tossing my hair over my shoulder. "I can't possibly imagine anything about you to be interesting."

Without warning, he takes a step forward, his hand finding its way to the back of my neck. His grip is firm, and I can feel his nails digging into my skin. My stomach twists into knots and I can't tell if it's from fear or excitement.

He leans down, his words lingering in the air between us like electricity, "Oh but, Trouble," He whispers softly into my ear, "You have no idea what I'm capable of."

I can feel my heart pounding in my chest as he leans closer to me. I can feel his breath on my skin and my body begins to respond to him in ways that I can't control.

I know that I should push him away, to stop him from coming any closer, but a part of me wants him to continue.

I inhale sharply as his breath tickles the skin of my neck. His grip tightens, and I feel my pulse throb against his fingers.

I'm sure he can feel it too. It's as if he's testing me, seeing how far he can push me before I break.

My thighs have grown slick and my pussy clenches at the thought of his hands on me. At the thought of a man as dark and self-destructive as him bending me over, ripping away my soaked panties, and fucking me until I'm too sore to walk.

And the fear he instills in me only makes me want it more.

My mouth falls open and my tongue darts out, wetting my bottom lip in anticipation. I feel my heart pounding in my chest as we stand here, frozen in some kind of standoff.

"Yes. You're pathetic and dull." I breathe, my voice huskier than I meant for it to come out.

He jerks me up out of my seat, backing me up against the stone mantel, hot flames lick at my heels.

My pulse races, betraying the calmness of my exterior, despite the collected expression on my face, my heart skipping a beat when he presses himself into me and I feel the hardness of his cock.

"Are you scared?" He asks his breath ragged against my ear. I look up into his eyes, his face dark and brooding as it hovers over mine.

I swallow hard and my voice comes out in a whisper, "No."

His hand moves from my neck, trailing a slow-burning path down the sensitive skin of my neck and down to the center of my chest. My body trembles at his touch and goosebumps form along the path of his fingertips as they trace a path against my bare skin.

"You should be."

I bite my lip, and his gaze drops to my mouth. I watch, frozen as his head lowers to mine, his lips mere centimeters from my own. I glance back up at him and my heart leaps to my throat as I feel his warm breath on my lips.

"Do you want me to be scared?" I whisper.

"Perhaps." He smirks, and I feel his lips brush mine.

The fact of the matter is—I'm absolutely terrified.

Terrified to let these men in. Terrified to trust them, but also—I'm also terrified of the reality that I may not be able to help myself if I stay here much longer.

What if I fall for them and it ends with my heart beating out of my chest, shattered on the floor?

What if it ruins me?

Would it be worth it?

Absolutely not!

I suck in a shaky breath steeling my nerves, and then, I bring my knee up as hard as I can sending it straight into his dick.

He lets out a strangled cry of pain, dropping his arms to hold his probably now bruised cock.

I take this opening and rush towards the hall that leads to the front door. I hear him snarling behind me, his voice has become a raw, primal animalistic sound as he pursues me.

I make it to the stretch that leads straight to the exit. I'm only a few yards away from making it out of that door.

My legs pump as hard as they can but right before I can make it there, I'm tackled by a hard body.

He turns me over onto my back, his knee pressing into my chest, forcing the air from my lungs.

I shriek as his fingers tighten around my hair, the sharp pain making my eyes water.

"You fucking bitch!"

I claw at the hand pressed against my trachea, but he has the advantage of leverage and size, and I can do nothing but let out pained gasps.

My body trembles with terror as my vision blurs and darkness closes in, but there is also a twisted sense of pleasure radiating throughout my veins. I'm engulfed by a wave of ecstasy, my skin tingling as I succumb to the forbidden desire coursing through me like a raging inferno.

The fact that I am so aroused by this makes me realize how disturbed I really must be, but I have already accepted my own fucked up nature a long time ago.

It's a weakness I've come to terms with and I don't expect anyone to understand it. I deal with my trauma in a way that would make most people vomit, I'm sure.

I can feel my pussy clenching with need, the pulsing between my thighs returning with a vengeance.

I want to stop him, to escape, but I can't, my body won't let me. His fingers release their grip from around my neck as he pants raggedly, his body still pinning mine to the floor.

"Do that again and next time I'll crush your fucking windpipe."

"Is that a promise?" I wheeze, my neck still burning from his grip.

I know I shouldn't egg him on, but I can't help it.

Maybe I want him to hurt me. Of course, I do.

The thought sickens me, but the rush of pain is addictive, an endless cycle of abuse that rids me of my feelings for a short while.

It's a funny thing. . .What trauma can do to a person, and I guess mine has given me two really fucked up sides—the submissive one and the depraved one and he seems to bring out both.

"That all depends on you, Trouble. If you keep this shit up I'll have to start doling out punishments for your disobedience." He rumbles.

I clench my eyes shut, the arousal burning through me, my pussy soaking my panties even more.

"Punish me, then, big boy." I taunt breathlessly.

Did I really just say that? Fuck.

He snarls, rolling off of me, grabbing his hat that fell off during our tousle, and cramming it back on his head in a heated fury.

His usual perfectly slicked-back black hair falls carelessly around his face, some sticking to the shaved sides of his head from sweat.

If looks could kill, his steely glare would be lethal. But for all his anger, he takes a moment to take a few deep breaths, calming himself, likely so he doesn't do anything impetuous.

"Be careful what you wish for." He pants out before straightening his jacket and yanking me to my feet.

My mind is hazy, lost in the euphoria and confusion of all that just happened.

I want to push him further, make him lose all of the control he desperately holds onto, but before I can the front door swings open, and the twins walk in.

Great.

"Did we just interrupt something and if so, can we join?" Dom asks teasingly, pulling his shirt off no sooner than the door closes behind them.

I wish he would learn to keep his damn clothes on.

His tight, tanned chest is on display as he moves, his shorts riding low on his hips, and my eyes are naturally drawn to the bulge of his cock.

He's huge, and he looks like he is in a pretty good mood now that he walked in on me and Hatter all flustered.

I gulp, swallowing my drool before it can deceive me, though I know they can sense my arousal, so I'm sure it already has.

"No, I was just leaving." I snap, trying to ignore the ache between my legs.

Hatter simply shakes his head before vanishing into his office, no doubt seeking a familiar refuge after our encounter.

I watch him walk away before huffing at the twins and stomping off to the room they gave me, slamming the door behind me once inside.

I can hear Dom laughing at my tantrum as I shove my face into the silk pillowcase and scream as loud as I can.

I hate them.

I hate them so fucking much.

How did I let myself get into this damn mess, and how the hell am I going to get myself out?

I have to get the fuck out of here. I feel like an animal trapped in a cage.

I'm suffocating, no matter which direction I turn, one of them is there and I can't take it anymore.

Biding my time until I can kill them and escape, is the only plan I have, and I damn sure can't mess it up.

So, for now, I will play nice, and participate in the little games they want to play.

I'll let them think they've won—that I've given up on fighting them, and when they drop their guard because they feel comfortable around me, I'll slit their fucking throats.

Their hold on me won't last forever.

I can see the cracks in their façade, and I'm determined to find a way to break them as they have vowed to break me.

I will not be their toy and I will not be their prisoner. They have no idea what I'm capable of. . .but they *will* find out soon enough.

Chapter Twenty-Two

Dean

Her hand is over her mouth stifling a yawn as she shuffles into the kitchen, hair swept messily over to the side, and she's scratching under her ass cheek through the baggy sweatpants she has on, yet I still find her sexy as fuck.

"Would you like some tea, gorgeous?" She jumps when she hears the sound of my voice.

"Oh! Um...Yes, thank you," She squeals. "I didn't know anyone else would be up this early. I was having trouble sleeping."

The sky is an inky black, and no light has broken the darkness. A few stars still shine brightly, glimmering like glitter, but they are beginning to fade as the first hint of dawn creeps across the horizon.

I watch her clumsily shuffle over to the counter, her ass swaying irresistibly with each step. I can't help but imagine pressing her against the counter, ripping off the shirt that she has tied beneath her breast showing off her slim waist, and roaming my hands all over her body as she moans my name.

"I couldn't sleep either," I say. "So, I thought I might as well make myself useful and make some breakfast."

It's cute how she tries to hide her tiredness and disheveled appearance by combing her fingers through her ruffled tresses and rubbing the sleep from her eyes.

She boosts herself up onto one of the chairs at the breakfast bar and runs her hand along the smooth black stone, "This place is so lovely. Everything is so elegant, I'm almost too afraid to touch anything." She admits, taking the steaming mug I offer her.

I laugh, "I promise you can touch whatever you want."

Pink tints her round cheeks.

"Hatter's mother and father designed it years ago. We've made minor adjustments and added extra security systems, but other than that, we've tried not to change it much. Why chase perfection when there's so much untold beauty in broken things? We've come to appreciate the magnificence of imperfections because honestly, we're all a little fucked up in our own way."

"That is true." She smiles, sipping her tea thoughtfully before speaking again, "If I may ask, what happened to Hatter's parents?"

My brows drop as I lean my back against the counter next to her, "His mother died when he was just a baby. She fell ill and neither doctors nor magical healers could cure her. They never found out what caused it or what exactly the illness was. His father raised him alone until he was framed for the King's murder and executed."

Her face contorts, a frown forming on her lips and tears misting her azure eyes, "I—I'm sorry. I didn't know." She hesitates. "Wait, so there used to be a King of Wonderland?"

"Yes, and under his rule, all of Wonderland thrived. The King remarried a few years after the death of his wife so his daughter would have a woman figure to help raise her and prepare her to one day take over the rule of the kingdom. And man didn't that slap him in the face."

"What happened to the King's daughter? Was she murdered too?"

"No. Now she works *for* the Queen." I spit. "She's the reason my pack was slaughtered. She has the power to sense magic, and if she senses it, the Queen sends her executioners and sometimes some of her guards if there are a lot of people to round up. Then, depending on whether they decide to put up a fight or surrender, they'll be transported to the prison or they are killed right then, along with most of the town. Most people surrender in hopes that it will save their loved ones, but entire towns have been wiped out and burned to ash by the Jabberwocky and the Queen's executioners simply for standing up for their rights as a living, breathing, being."

The terrified look on Alice's face sends a sharp pang through my chest. I didn't mean to upset her, but unfortunately much like ourselves, Wonderland has a dark past.

She reaches her hand out and places it gently on my shoulder, "You lost your entire pack?" She asks, a twinge of shock in her voice.

I nod, choking back the knot forming in the back of my throat.

I don't normally dwell on it the way that Dom does. I keep the memories suppressed, locked away in a cage deep inside the back of my mind. I don't want to remember. I don't want to feel that pain.

"The only reason Dom and I didn't die that day was we ran out to the meadow, disobeying our mother's warning. We were pups and our bones ached to run. I convinced Dom to come with me. We knew we weren't supposed to shift, we knew it was dangerous, and yet, we did it anyway." I swallow, shaking my head to hold back the onslaught of tears that threaten to fall from my eyes. "We heard the screams, the fighting, but by the time we got back to the forest, our entire pack was gone. All of them—dead."

"That's awful." She whispers, her gaze fixated on me.

My breath catches in my throat and my pulse races in my neck as she stands up, placing herself in front of me, laying one hand on either side of my face, her eyes darting back and forth between mine.

"No one deserves that—no one." She says, but it's her next words that reach into my soul and drive their way through my chest like the tip of a broadsword. "It's not your fault, Dean. You can't blame yourself."

It's as if she can read me like one of her books.

I bow my head, my vision blurring as the first tear falls and hits the floor. The knot in the back of my throat swells and a sound I don't even recognize breaks free from my lips. I can't hold back the emotions anymore.

An avalanche of guilt and regret fills me, boiling up from deep within like molten rock spilling from a volcanic fissure.

How could I not blame myself?

How could I not hate myself?

I lost my entire pack.

I failed them.

And now they're all dead because of me.

My nose stings from the pressure of the tears. I can't stop them.

There's too much loss. Too much anger. Too much pain.

Her fingers that are gripping my face let go, sliding down and around my neck, pulling me into her embrace where I crumble into her soft, warm body.

The wispy fray of her hair tickles my face as she reaches up on her toes and places a kiss on my cheek.

"There's nothing you could have done." She whispers in my ear. "It isn't your fault."

I've been told this countless times by my brothers and it hasn't changed how I feel about it. So, why do I want to believe it when it's whispered by her lips?

She pulls back, wiping the wetness from my cheek, her stare formidable as she gazes into my eyes.

My lips come crashing down on hers. It's messy and rough but it's exactly what I need.

She doesn't stop me, rather she kisses me back even harder, her tongue clashing against mine in a heated battle.

Her body presses into mine, and my hands snake along the column of her spine until they're smoothing down her shapely ass and pulling her closer to me.

She pulls back, panting and breathing heavily.

Her cheeks are flushed, and her eyes are clouded as she stares at me. The heat of her core against my swollen cock is enough to replace all rational thinking and I find myself picking her up, and sitting her on the counter, positioning myself between her legs.

I can see her wetness seeping through the crotch of her pants. I can feel her desire emanating from every inch of her body, and it only makes me more aroused.

I groan, and my greedy hands grip the back of her neck pulling her into me until our lips meet again.

My cock is throbbing between my legs, craving to be deep inside her.

My lips move slowly down her neck, and she leans her head to the side, giving me better access.

I barely register the fabric move as my hands move down to her waist and yank down her pants, sliding one finger along her slick center and savoring the moan that leaves her lips.

"Do you want me to stop?" I ask.

"I—I don't know." Her voice is husky, but she doesn't move to stop me.

Taking that as permission to keep going, I place one thumb on her clit and push two fingers deep inside of her, sliding them in and back out again.

She whimpers, her head falling back, her eyes fluttering shut.

My heart pounds as I move my fingers inside of her.

She's fucking soaked.

"Dean," My name leaves her lips, the soft and innocent sound surprising me as it reaches my ears.

Her muscles tighten around me, and I have to muster every ounce of willpower I possess not to lose control right then and there.

My fingers curl against her walls, eliciting a louder moan from her and she bucks up against my hand, her mouth falling open with her cries of rapture.

Using my other hand I unbutton my pants, tugging them down and letting them fall around my ankles while I continue to pump my fingers inside her sopping cunt.

I'm almost convinced that she needs this just as much as I do.

I feel her start to tremble, and I know that she's close.

She leans back on her elbows to balance herself and the large mounds of her breasts jiggle with each thrust of my hand.

My thumb traces circles on her swollen nub and I watch with anticipation as her lips part with every one of her moans.

I thrust my fingers into her a few more times before her muscles tense and her legs press against my hand, and that's when I know she's reached her climax.

Shivers wrack her body as wave after wave of intense pleasure crashes over her, and the most gorgeous shade of red colors her features as she throws her head back, crying out as she comes.

"Ohhh, Fuuuuck." She rides the words out.

I pull my fingers from her, licking them clean before I drop my boxers, and grab my shaft, smacking the head of my dick off her pussy with a wet, *thwack.*

She jerks and I smack her again, her eyes rolling back in her head with each sharp slap.

Slowly, I push into her tight pussy, restraining my own desire to slam into her like a desperate man.

My cock pulses as I move in and out of her, feeling the grasp of her vagina as it tightens around me with each push of my hips.

I look up at her just as I slide all the way into her, and not being able to hold back anymore, I pull back, slamming all the way back until I'm bouncing off the soft bulb of her cervix.

Her eyes fly open and connect with mine, a look of astonishment shining in them, "Oh fuck, Dean!" Her knees fall open even wider, "Yes!"

My hands cup her ass as I pound into her, meeting her hips with every thrust.

"Harder!" She screams, and I'm happy to oblige.

I smirk down at her, as I move faster, plunging deeper into her pussy.

The room is filled with sex, the scent of her lust, and the sound of our skin slapping off of each other.

I pound into her over and over, feeling the tension start to build inside me.

My balls slap off of her ass as I continue my assault. She starts to convulse beneath me and I can feel her pussy begin to clench and pulsate around my shaft.

"Keep going, don't stop!" Her legs wrap around me and I rub her clit, pushing her into another orgasm.

"Oh shit, I'm coming!" She declares, grinding up into me.

I'm right on the cusp of my own climax.

"Fuck, Alice." I growl, "You're so tight. Are you going to be a good girl and come for me again?"

"Yes!" She screams.

The feeling of her throbbing around me propels me over the edge, and I grit my teeth, my cock twitching as my orgasm surges through my shaft, and I flood her pussy with my hot cum.

I slow down my movements and close my eyes, savoring the feeling of her as she clamps and quivers around me.

She's so fucking gorgeous.

Her eyes are blazing with delectation, her lips parted in ecstasy, and her cheeks are flushed. Her hair is wild around her face and her body is slick with sweat.

She is an absolute vision and her beauty radiates through the room with every tremor of her orgasm.

Every part of her is flawless.

I hear a shuffling from behind us. From the heat of the moment, I didn't even hear Dom come in.

"Aww, man!" He moans. "Why didn't I get invited?"

Chapter Twenty-Three

Hatter

I spent the night in my office, trading in my suit for a pair of old sweatpants and a long-sleeved shirt to run over the numbers of the shipment we received in this morning.

Everything is as it's supposed to be.

This time.

I've avoided Alice at all costs since yesterday, not wanting the distraction of her oh-so-many personalities.

She's a challenging one that's for sure, and without a doubt, she infuriates me to no fucking end.

I still have to finish the payroll and cut checks.

Though, I suppose that will just have to wait until after we get back.

My tea tastes especially bitter today which is unusual as Henry never gives me anything other than the best when it comes to his tea leaves.

The cup is still full and untouched aside from the sip I took and promptly spat back out. Dean's tea brewing skills are much better than mine, so that could be why it didn't appeal to me.

Either way, I need to pick up some fresh tea since we'll be passing through the town his shop is located in today anyway. Plus, I don't want to have to listen to his old ass bitch me out over the phone again.

As much as I hate the idea, Alice will be coming with us. We can't leave her here by herself, she's already proven that she can't be trusted not to run.

But I also don't want to put her in danger. Not that I don't believe she can't take care of herself, but because a part of me wants to protect her and keep her safe because it's clear no one ever has before.

I turn back to the payroll list, flipping to the next page, and making a note to send Rupert's check to his widow and their children. It will be his last paycheck, but I will make sure that his family is taken care of and that they need for nothing.

I hear the faint knock.

"Go away," I grumble to the door, not wanting to be bothered.

The rapid tapping begins again but slightly louder this time.

Annoyed, I open up the filing drawer of my desk and place the paperwork inside, locking it before walking over to the door, opening it just enough to see Alice standing on the other side of it with a tattered, worn book in her hand.

"No." I go to shut the door then her tiny bare foot pokes through.

She needs shoes.

I need to ask Dom if Nova ever got her clothes and toiletries sent to Henry's shop. Hopefully, they'll be there waiting to be picked up today when we stop in.

I don't know if the little troublemaker is going to like what Nova picked out for her but at least it's better than her having to wear our clothes.

"I'd like to speak with you," She says firmly, not taking no for an answer.

I let out a small sigh and then reluctantly open the door wider for her to come in. She steps into the room, holding the book tightly against her chest as she looks up at me with her big, innocent cerulean eyes.

The last thing I want is to have a conversation with her, but I know that I can't avoid her forever.

Not when I'm holding her prisoner here until I can make sure she's not the one killing my men.

As much as she is a burden to me, I can't deny the fact that she also intrigues me. She is unlike anyone I have ever met before, and I find myself drawn to her in ways that I cannot explain.

She bounces on her toes as she waits for me to acknowledge her, biting her lips as her eyes dart around the room.

It's that vindicated demeanor of hers that is going to be the fucking death of me.

I take a deep breath, trying to mask my irritation as I walk over to my desk, gesturing for Alice to follow me. She skips behind me, still holding her book.

I sit down in my leather chair and motion for her to take a seat in front of me, and she perches in one of the two chairs in front of me that are ordinarily meant for my brothers or business partners.

"What do you want, Alice?" I ask, failing to keep the annoyance out of my voice.

Her eyes widen slightly at my tone, but she quickly regains her composure.

She fidgets with the edges of her book, her gaze shifting nervously between me and the floor. "I just wanted to apologize for what happened the other night," She says quietly. "But I want you to let me go."

"I can't do that."

"Can't or won't? You know deep down it wasn't me who took your magic drugs. So, why are you truly keeping me here? What do you want with me?"

What do I want with her?

It's a question I've been asking myself since the moment I laid eyes on her.

Why did I really keep her? And why does it make me sick to the stomach to even think about letting her go?

I lean back in my chair, studying her as she awaits my response. My mind races with conflicting thoughts and emotions.

I can't deny the truth in her words; I do know that she's not the one responsible for the missing drugs, but there is something about her that makes it hard for me to let her leave.

She's intoxicating, a toxin that's crept its way under my skin. An addiction—a high that I never want to come down from.

"Both," I answer honestly, straightening the papers into a neat pile on my desk.

Alice's eyes narrow at my response, and I can tell she's not satisfied with it.

I can't give her a straight answer because I don't even know why I'm keeping her here.

She just has a certain allure, an irresistible magnetism that makes me want to possess her in every way possible—to own her.

I try to stifle the dark desires that stir within me, but it's becoming increasingly difficult.

Her pretty face crumbles as tears build up and spill down her cheeks. My heart shatters into a million pieces watching her fall apart in front of me.

I've grown so accustomed to her witty comebacks and her mile-high attitude, to see her so—broken, is punishing.

"I won't let you keep me here," she says, her voice low and steady. "You can't control me forever."

But I know I can—if I choose to do so.

And there would be nothing she could do to stop me.

It's a dangerous thought. One that makes my dick hard, my breathing erratic, and my blood run hot.

"I'm not trying to control you," I say with a shrug, trying to play it off coolly. "I just need more time to figure out the truth."

"You're a fucking liar." She says her jaw twitching from her tightly clenched teeth.

She stands up from her chair, her eyes locked onto mine with determination, rage, and defiance.

Despite her petite frame, Alice is a force to be reckoned with, and I adore that about her. Though, I would never admit that to anyone else.

I watch as her angry tears fall, each drop like a shard of glass through my heart. The pain in her eyes mirrors the agony within my own soul, and it almost feels as though this cruel world has conspired to break the both of us.

She walks in slow, measured steps until she is inches away from my face, her hand planted firmly on my desk.

"You're pathetic. What a foolish notion you have that you can control everything and everyone around you. Control is merely an illusion, a fabrication of your own mind to avoid delving into the heart of the problem—the thing that you are really trying to control—yourself." Her eyes are like daggers, piercing through me, chipping away at the ice around my soul until my darkest secrets are exposed.

I can see the danger in her glare, the threat of her strength and resolve, her hidden vulnerability and need for freedom.

But why is she so desperate to get away, to want to face the dangers of a strange land she only just arrived in?

She may not be guilty of robbing me, but she definitely has some kind of an agenda, and I know there's certainly something she is withholding from us.

I have this weird feeling that perhaps she's been here before—in Wonderland.

Yet, I've been to every town, every place in Wonderland, and not once have I ever laid eyes on her.

She would be hard to forget.

"I'm right, aren't I?" She asks, her voice breaking, as residual tears slip down her cheek.

She is right.

I need to stay in control, but she doesn't understand why. She doesn't understand the depths of depravity I'm able to reach if I surrender to my darkness.

"You don't understand, trouble."

"Then make me understand." She challenges.

I take a deep breath, trying to steady myself. It's frustrating that she thinks she has all the answers when in reality, she knows nothing.

She has no idea what I've been through, what I've had to sacrifice, what I'm fighting so hard to achieve.

"I can't just make you understand, Alice." I snap, my voice louder than I intended it to be. "You just look at the world as if everything is so black and white-as if everything is so simple. Nothing is simple and nothing is black and white! It's cold, grey, dark and terrifying. That's the world we live in! How can you possibly understand unless you've experienced the kind of loss, destruction, and pain that I have? Only to just turn around and become one of the monsters you're trying to save the world from? You don't!"

She blinks, surprised by my words, the concern in her eyes quickly turns to rage, "Screw. You." Her fist pounds the top of my desk, sending my neat stack of files scattering to the floor before she turns to storm out.

Fuck.

What made me utter those words? It's apparent she has endured a great deal of pain in her lifetime and here I am, acting as if it is insignificant, showing no empathy to her traumas but expecting her to empathize mine.

I hesitate, then grab her by her shoulder, turning her back around so she's facing me, her eyes swollen from her tears.

"Alice?" Her name's a question on my tongue as I take her face in both of my palms, guiding her head to look into my eyes. "I-I shouldn't have said that."

"Save your fucking breath." She says, twisting away from me.

I reach for her hand.

"Don't," She sneers, retreating away from me and towards the door. "I don't want your pity."

"You think too highly of yourself if you think I pity you, trouble," I reply, knowing there is no truth to my words.

She glares at me, and for a moment I swear I see a hint of hurt behind the stone mask she's hiding behind. Her hand lingers on the doorknob before she finally yanks open the door and storms out of the room, leaving me standing there jaded and alone.

I let out a frustrated sigh, running my hands across my face.

My words have only worsened the situation, but it's for the best. If I have to be the fuel that keeps the fire inside of her ignited, to keep her from letting her guard down so she won't fall victim to her own emotions, then I'll gladly be the villain she sees me as.

Because as long as she hates me, she won't keep trying to save me.

Chapter Twenty-Four

Dom

My little rabbit is upset.

I watch from the shadows as she flees from Hatter's office, her blonde locks bouncing behind her as she runs down the hall.

She continues down the hall until it dead ends, I wait until she has rounded the corner before I decide to follow.

I can almost taste the saltiness of her tears just from the stench of the despair that's emanating from her in thick waves.

I catch up to her just as she reaches the end of the hallway, her body is heaving with sobs. I place a hand on her back, and she flinches away from me, her eyes red and puffy.

"Get away from me!" she snarls.

"What's wrong, little rabbit?" Her expression softens when she hears the fervency in my voice.

"Nothing," She sniffles, keeping her eyes on the floor.

"Doesn't look like nothing to me."

I feel a twinge of satisfaction as she looks up at me through her tears, her eyes wide with dismay. I take a step closer, pressing my body into hers, brushing the back of my knuckles down the apple of her cheek to chase a stray tear away.

I can feel the way her body trembles under my touch, and a hungry part of me wants to take advantage of her current state. But I know I must be patient; I need to bide my time until the moment is right because I want her to remember the exact moment when I destroy her.

She doesn't know what she needs from me just yet—but I do.

She needs me to break her, to tear her down and rip her apart so she can heal and build herself back up again, even stronger than before.

My little rabbit is so delicate and yet, so strong. I can see the fight in her eyes even as she tries to hide it from me. I know it won't be easy to break her, but I'm ready for the fight. I need it.

"What did my asshole brother do now?" I coo as I stroke her cheek with the pad of my thumb, watching her eyes flutter shut.

"He—It's not him." She shakes her head, her foot tapping against the marble floor of the foyer leading to the library wing.

Whatever it is, it has her in shambles. She tugs at the end of her hair, ripping away small tendrils of hair with each sharp pull. Her eyes are wild and her breathing is rapid.

She tries to pull away from me, but I tighten my grip on her, pulling her closer into my embrace. I can feel her heart racing against my chest, and it ignites something dark and possessive in me.

Poor, little rabbit. . .So desperate to leave her cage.

My face is mere inches away from hers, "Then tell me. . .What is it that has you so upset?" The demand is more of a plea.

"It's just—everything." She whispers, defeat resounding in her tone.

She looks up at me, her eyes bloodshot and her lower lip quivering, so I wrap my arm around her shoulder and give her a small push, "Come with me." I say guiding her to the massive arched entrance of the library.

The scent of old books fills my nostrils as soon as the doors open. The mixture of the dust and the muskiness is overwhelming to my overly sensitive nostrils, but I take a seat on one of the large red velvet armchairs near the fireplace that looks like it hasn't been lit in years and pull her onto my lap.

She tenses, frozen in place, and I can feel the heat rising from her skin, "Talk to me, little rabbit. Let me help you."

With how antsy she was out in the hall, something is clearly gnawing at her, eating her alive from the inside out.

"I don't need your help!" She bites out.

"Alright. Fine." I dump her off my lap, letting her fall on the seat of the chair. "If you need anything I'll be in the kitchen."

As soon as my hand touches the door she calls out, "Wait."

I turn around to face her, raising an eyebrow in question.

She hesitates for a moment, seemingly unsure of what to say, before finally speaking up. "I don't want to talk about it just yet but would-would you mind staying here with me while I read?" The words leave her mouth so softly I can almost feel the insecurity in them.

I nod my head and make my way back towards her. "Of course, I'll stay with you," I say as I take a seat next to her on the armchair, nuzzling my face in the softness of her hair before I pull her back into my lap.

Her body is tense as if she's trying to shrink away from me but she soon relaxes, her shoulders drooping as she flips through the pages of her book, though her fingers are still slightly shaking.

I watch her intently as she reads, her eyes scanning the words on the page. Her face remains expressionless, but the way her brows furrow and her lips press together in concentration tells me that she's fully engrossed in the story in front of her.

The library is illuminated by the dim, golden glow of antique low-hanging lamps with faux candles that dance in sync with one another. The flickering light casts shadows on her face, accentuating her cheeks and lips in the soft light.

Her locks flow in an even motion around her face, swaying rhythmically as she reads from side to side. The tips of her hair curl softly at the ends with each gentle bob of her head.

The lush tendrils sweep over her shoulders and frame the sides of her face, lightly touching her flushed cheeks. Her lips are slightly parted as she reads some parts out loud in a whisper, letting the silence of the room carry them away.

She's an exquisite vision of perfection, captivating in every possible way. She exudes an aura of effortless beauty that is unparalleled by anything this land has ever witnessed.

I could stare at her for an eternity and still not be satisfied.

I want to see her soften in my arms and relax against my chest; her body cradled by mine as I shield her from the world. I want to taste her lips and make her moan as I explore her body.

I want to feel her nails dig into my back as I take her on my lap, filling her so full of my cock until she shatters, breaking apart every wall she has ever built. I want her screams piercing my ears and my name rolling off her tongue.

I want her.

All of her.

The good, the bad, and the crazy.

She's becoming my sick obsession, and I don't think I'll be able to just walk away from her when the time comes.

One thing I do know, though.

If she's able to sink her claws into Hatter, the way she's already got them sunk in me and Dean—we're all fucking screwed.

Chapter Twenty-Five

Alice

The warmth of his body is like a comforting embrace, radiating against my body like the sun at the peak of a summer day.

He patiently waits, brushing his fingers through my hair as I read, his breath tickling the nape of my neck. His closeness is alluring, and I find myself getting lost in the solace of his touch.

I close my book and turn to face him, placing a hand on his chest. His heart beats steadily beneath his shirt, and I feel a sense of comfort knowing that he's here with me.

"Thank you for staying with me," I whisper, admiring his mismatched eyes.

"I can't think of anywhere else I'd rather be than right here with you, little rabbit." His words make my stomach flutter and heat sink to my core.

He seems to have this knack for making me feel special as if I'm the only woman in the universe that matters to him.

Which I highly doubt.

With looks like his, I can imagine he has plenty of women to choose from.

"I'm sure you have plenty of other things better to do than wasting your time with me." I blush.

"Not a single one." He grins.

"Nonsense."

He palms my cheek, "Let me prove it to you." His lips move closer to mine, and I can feel his warm breath on my face.

"Dom." I breathe, my hands moving to push him away.

"Fuck, little rabbit. I wonder how my name will sound on your lips when you're coming all over my cock." He growls. "I know you want me. I can feel it. I can tell in the way your body responds to my touch."

He's right. I do want him. I want him so fucking bad.

The need to feel him inside of me is maddening, but I know I shouldn't. I've already fucked up and let my guard down once already.

I can't give in to them. I have too much to lose.

I'm so close—so fucking close.

Revenge is at the tip of my fingers; I just can't fully grasp it yet.

Not until I can rid myself of the Black Spade Brothers.

"Please, Dom!" I gasp, trying to pull myself away from his grip.

He groans, tugging me back against his chest, and nuzzles his face in my neck.

He plants kisses up the side of my neck, then along my jaw. I melt in his arms, my resolve weakening as he grazes my skin with his teeth, biting the soft flesh between my neck and my shoulder.

He nips my neck with his canines, and I struggle to stifle a loud moan.

I feel an inner warmth radiating from my core and throughout the rest of my body. An inferno builds up in the depths of me, threatening to devour me entirely.

"Dom. Please." I beg, desperate for him to stop because I know I won't be able to resist him much longer.

I open my mouth to protest, but he silences me with his lips, his tongue seeking entry. I moan as he explores my mouth, his tongue delicately tracing my bottom lip and twirling around my own.

He moans into my mouth, his kiss turning hungry and demanding.

My skin is burning, and there's only one person who can quench the raging fire that has taken over my body—him.

I crave his touch on my flesh, taking in every contour of my skin with his mouth, savoring me as if committing it to memory.

The thought alone has me so fucking wet.

The ache in my pussy grows heavier, throbbing and begging for his cock.

Grinding myself against him, he groans into my mouth, the vibrations from his chest bouncing off of my breasts and straight to my sensitive nipples.

I want to rip my shirt off and feel my skin against his, but the thought of breaking the kiss is too terrifying.

I need his lips on mine.

I *need* him.

It's frightening that I'm so wrapped up in a man that I barely know anything about.

I've fucked up big time, giving in to temptation, but at this point, it's too late to stop now.

I've crossed the line, and there's no going back.

My nails dig into his back, and I bite his bottom lip.

My heart races as I anticipate feeling his skin against mine, my breath quickening as I imagine the taste of his body lingering on my tongue.

He pulls back, ripping my shirt off, and he sucks in a breath of surprise, his eyes drooping from lust, "No underwear?" He questions hungrily.

I shake my head. I don't want to talk.

"Good girl." He praises me.

I smile, my body on fire.

I grab at the hem of his shirt and pull it over his head, exposing his toned, chiseled chest.

He pulls me down in the chair, spreading my thighs open, my pussy hot and throbbing, begging to be touched.

Then, he lowers his head, circling his tongue around my clit, dipping lower, and running the thickness of it through my wet folds.

"You taste so good." He groans, before plunging his tongue inside of me, pressing and flicking it around the soft flesh of my inner walls.

I can barely hear myself think, my body is on sensory overload.

The way he's looking at me, the feeling of his warm tongue caressing my pussy, the way he's parting my lips, plunging his fingers inside of me as he sucks my clit into his mouth, I can't describe it, but I've never felt anything like it in my life.

He spread me apart, exposing my clit more fully to his tongue, licking and nibbling on the throbbing mound.

He moves his tongue up and back down, slowly, and gently caressing my clit as I push his head into me, writhing around in the chair, my body buzzing with arousal.

He inserts a third finger inside of me, working them in and out in a steady motion. "Oh!" I moan, rearing up against him, but he places a hand on my stomach, holding me still as he continues to work my hot sticky cunt.

"Is this what you want?" He taunts, slamming his fingers in a bit rougher, causing me to cry out.

"Yes!" I can feel my muscles clenching him, and my back arches, my eyes rolling into the back of my head.

I'm moaning, writhing, and panting. I tense up right before the muscles in my body seize, and I cum hard, my pussy spasming around his fingers.

I want him inside of me.

Now.

He stands, drops his shorts, wraps a hand around his cock, and strokes himself as he watches me tweak my nipples between my fingers.

I can see my juices dripping down the center of my pussy and into the crack of my ass, pooling around the tight puckering hole.

Lifting me up like I'm the weight of a paperclip, he positions himself beneath me in the seat of the chair, leaning back slightly so he can freely move his hips. He then sits me down on his lap with my back to his chest, as he holds my thighs high in the air, opening me up to take him.

He's so fucking hard.

The head of his dick is tinted a purplish red from the amount of blood circulating through it.

He spreads my pussy apart, pressing the head inside me. I cry out as he sinks deeper inside of me, stretching me wide, filling me until I'm practically in pain.

But damn it feels so fucking good.

I ride up and down along the length of his shaft, my pussy dripping every time he pulls back.

His hands cup my ass as he slams into me. "Yes! Fuck me!" I scream." Fuck me harder!"

I'm rocking my hips, bucking, grinding, and twisting, as he works my clit with his hand, stroking the sensitive area while he yanks me up and down, impaling me with his dick.

"I warned you, little rabbit." He hisses. "I will break you. I will ravage you. And at the end of it all, your pussy will belong to us--you will belong to us."

"Oh my God!"

My body is rippling with euphoria from his heavy thrusts.

I can feel it growing inside of me, gradually intensifying until it finally results in an eruption of pleasure so intense, so brutal, that my scream is loud enough to wake the dead.

I'm convulsing, my pussy gushing around his thick shaft.

"Yes! Come for me," He grinds out through his clenched teeth. "I want to see that pretty pussy dripping."

He continues to pound into me, rubbing my clit like he's trying to make it explode.

I scream out his name as the climax pulls my body taut, then releases me, making me feel like jelly.

My body melts into his as I gasp with pleasure and emit a low, satisfied moan.

He trembles in response, his dick growing ever larger, swelling until it's almost unbearable—in the best way possible though.

His fingers bite into my hips, holding me steady as he spurts his load into me.

He's groaning, panting against my neck. He then takes my mouth in a fiery kiss, and I taste the sweetness of my pussy on his lips while he stills, his cock twitching, jerking, and throbbing as he spills himself into me, filling me up until his seed is spilling back out of me.

I'm shivering, slick with perspiration, and sticky with the mixture of our cum, but he doesn't let me go. Instead, he holds me close, wrapping his arms around me with his cock still buried inside me.

I crane my neck around to look at him, and I can feel his cum running down my thighs as he slips out.

I know I shouldn't have let this happen. I shouldn't have given in so easily, but damn it. . .They make it so fucking hard to not want them.

Dom rubs his thumb along the side of my face, "You're perfect, little rabbit. Every little thing about you drives me insane. I could die right here, right now, and die the happiest wolfman to ever dwell in this entire universe."

"Ha. Ha." I dryly laugh.

"I'm serious." He insists. "You're everything I've ever wanted. . .And everything I've never had."

I feel a knot in my stomach and my chest grows tight at his words.

A sudden wave of emotion washes over me, and my breath catches in my throat, my heart thumping hard against my rib cage.

I don't want him to say these things, and I damn sure don't want to feel the things I feel when he does.

The one thing I know for sure though, is if I don't put a stop to it soon, I'm scared I never will.

Chapter Twenty-Six

Dean

We should be leaving in the next hour to head to Henry's, so what the hell is taking all of them so damn long?

I strain my ears, listening closely to where everyone is in the house.

Hatter is tapping a pen on his desk, probably brooding over paperwork as usual and it sounds like Dom and Alice are somewhere in the library and it sounds like they just *shared* a moment.

My cock stiffens as I reminisce about the moment she and I shared earlier this morning.

But ultimately, I'm just glad she's becoming comfortable with us.

The kitchen smells of freshly roasted coffee and spiced vanilla, an aroma that normally wouldn't be present in our home since we prefer to drink tea, but has become a scent I've grown to love since Alice's arrival.

Though I don't know how she drinks the shit.

I went down to the warehouse and found a can of coffee that belongs to one of the security guys after I noticed she never finished her tea. When I confronted her about it, she admitted that she didn't like it but she didn't want to be rude.

I finish plating the table and bring over a couple of baskets of biscuits and set them down then make my way to the kitchen and back over to the stove to stir the pan of eggs, not wanting them to burn.

It's a gorgeous morning, and the sun's bright rays are filtering in through the cracks of the heavy curtains.

Grabbing the fabric, I thrust them open exposing the large sliding glass doors that lead out to a large black oak deck overlooking the pristine white sanded beach.

Our entire operation lies beneath the beauty of the crashing waves of the shore and putrefied skeleton trees that haunt the beach.

I can't believe the amount of time that's passed since my brothers, and I departed from Neverland and came back here to start our business dealing illegal magic and starting the rebellion.

I grab a cigar and step out onto the deck, the salty sea breeze whipping through my hair and cooling my heated skin. It's a stark contrast to the warm, cozy kitchen, but I need the fresh air to clear my head.

As I exhale a plume of smoke, I can hear the light footsteps that unmistakably belong to Alice. I turn around just in time to see her enter the dining room; Dom hot on her heels.

Alice's eyes widen ever so much as they land on me, and she offers a smile that doesn't quite reach her eyes. "Good morning," she greets before sitting down at the table and cramming her face into the book she carried in with her.

She's remarkable.

Her hair is a tangled mess of waves that frame her delicate features, and she's wearing a faded, too-big t-shirt that swallows her petite frame, her legs bare.

I try to focus on my cigar, but my eyes keep flicking towards her, almost involuntarily.

Her eyes are swollen and red as if she's been crying.

"Alice," I say, my voice low and smooth. "Is everything alright?"

She looks up from her book long enough to nod.

I can't help but feel a tinge of concern for her, but I know better than to pry. Alice isn't the type of person to open up easily, and I respect that. Instead, I turn my attention back to the ocean, taking in the beauty of the waves.

Dom joins me on the deck.

"You're late," I complain punching him in the shoulder.

He chuckles deeply, his eyes scanning the beach below. "Or right on time." He gestures back to the food still piping hot on the table.

"Sometimes I wonder how I got stuck with you as my twin." I sigh.

"Easy my dad fucked your mom."

"Could you be any more immature? That doesn't even make sense."

I meet my brother's gaze and nod over at where Alice is sitting, "She ok?"

"*She's* perfectly fine, thank you. And she's also quite capable of speaking for herself." Alice says without even looking up from the book laid out in front of her.

"I didn't mean—"

She cuts me off with a wave of her hand, "It's fine."

Dom and I exchange a look and then I finish my cigar, butting it in the tray before going back to the kitchen.

I wash my hands, grab a cup out of the cupboard, and fill it three-quarters of the way full with coffee. Then, I grab the ceramic vat of homemade spiced vanilla cream I made this morning, to bring out with me, and place it on the table in front of Alice.

She takes the lid off the cream, sniffing it, "This smells delicious."

"It's something new I made this morning. I hope you like it. I can't promise it's going to taste very good." I laugh, rubbing the back of my neck.

"Thank you so much, Dean." I'm sorry I snapped. You didn't deserve that. You've been nothing but kind to me." Her cheeks bloom a bright mahogany.

Dom follows me out of the kitchen, his hands full of bowls containing scrambled eggs, bacon, and gravy.

Alice looks up at the sound of Dom's footsteps and watches as he sets the bowls of food down in front of her. She pushes her book to the side and takes the cup of coffee, pouring a generous amount of spiced vanilla cream into it.

The aroma of the coffee mixed with the sweet scent of vanilla fills the air.

She takes her first sip of coffee, her eyes flutter close, and she lets out a small sigh of contentment.

"It's absolutely amazing." She breathes. "Thank you."

"I'm glad you like it," I reply.

Hatter walks in with a scowl on his face.

He's been grumpy ever since whatever happened between him and Alice the other night.

He doesn't say anything to any of us, just pours himself a cup of tea and sits down at the head of the table.

The tension is palpable, it's clear that he's still upset with her and vice versa. He looks over at Alice, his mouth opening like he's going to say something, only to snap shut again.

"So, you ready to see more of Wonderland today, Little rabbit?" Dom asks through a mouthful of bacon.

"You're letting me leave?" She practically screams, her eyes lighting up.

"No. You're coming with us because we have business to attend to and you can't be trusted to not kill our guards and run off." Hatter interjects.

"That's absurd."

"Is it though?" Dom asks, leaning back in his chair.

I almost choke on the biscuit I just shoved in my mouth, sending crumbs flying all over the table.

Alice glares daggers at Hatter before turning to Dom. "What kind of business?" she asks, intrigued.

Dom smirks at her, "The kind that's none of your concern. All you need to know is that you're coming with us." He says.

"You can't just fucking kidnap me, keep me captive, tell me that you make illegal drug magic, and then bring me along just to keep me in the dark about whatever this business stuff is. It's not fair." She groans.

"I don't have to be fair," Hatter says.

"I don't remember asking you for your input." She retorts.

I expect more of a fight from him but he just sighs and shakes his head, his eyes flashing red for a split second, "Just hurry up and finish eating. We need to get going. We have a long day ahead of us."

He's starting to slip, his grip on reality is faltering; the demons inside him are winning in their struggle against his mind and

I don't know if he'll be able to claw his way back out of the darkness this time.

"Tell you what, little rabbit. . .When I bring the *business* back home, I'll let you come down to my torture room and have a front-row seat to witness how we get information out of those who cross us. Should make for a bloody good show." Dom says, waggling his eyebrows. "I'll even let you join if you want."

"What has this person done?" She asks.

"Besides fuck with us? He's been an assassin for the Queen, regularly in fact. He's killed women, children, and entire families--all for a contract."

Her eyes flash with fury as she contemplates his offer and then she flashes him a smile, "Sounds like fun."

"Good," Dom smirks. "Now finish your breakfast so the fun can begin."

Henry's teashop has an inviting atmosphere. Vines grow up the walls in some areas and it's a bright white in the sections that haven't been covered by the greenery.

The sound of a bell dings as Hatter opens the door, announcing our arrival, and the scent of fresh earthy, tea, flowers, fruits, and herbs fills my nose.

Henry waves at us from behind the counter with a half-ass smile pulling at the wrinkles on his face, "Good to see you boys. . .Finally." He grumbles, his mustache twitching as he eyes Alice. "Who's your lovely company?"

"This is Alice," Hatter says.

"A pleasure to meet you, Alice," Henry says, leaning over the counter to get a better look at her.

"Nice to meet you too." She nods, as she runs her fingers over the small items on the counter.

"Actually!" He points a scraggly finger in the air. "I just got some things in a couple of days ago that I believe are yours." He hobbles out from behind the counter and disappears into the stockroom, a little later coming out with a large trolly full of bags and boxes, all for Alice.

We didn't know what she'd like so we just had Nova get her a bit of everything. Clothes, makeup, snacks, candles, body wash, you name it, we made sure she had it.

Alice's eyes widen as she takes in the overflowing trolley of gifts. "Oh my—" she trails off, at a loss for words.

Her cheeks are a bright red, I can hear her heart rate speeding up as her eyes skim over all the commodities.

Hatter and I exchange a quick glance, both amused by Alice's reaction.

I can't help but find her innocence endearing. It's a rarity in this world of madness and bloodshed.

"Would you like to go change, Trouble?" Hatter asks her

"Can I?" She replies sarcastically. "Wouldn't want your prisoner to run away now, would you?" She scoffs.

"Dean and Dom will go with you."

Alice raises an eyebrow, glaring at Hatter as she crosses her arms, poking out her hip, "Excuse me?"

"As you said. . .I wouldn't want my prisoner to escape." Hatter grins.

"I fucking hate you." She mumbles with a roll of her eyes.

"I know," Hatter replies smoothly his lips twitching.

"You would think you were married to her rather than her being your prisoner." Henry teases.

Dom and I help her grab a few bags of clothes, lead her to the back of the store where the bathrooms are, and hand them off to her as she goes inside, the lock clicking behind her.

The minutes pass by and she has still to emerge from the bathroom.

I knock on the door, "Everything ok?" I call out.

No reply.

"Dom, go see if Henry has a key. I don't want to break the door unless I have to." I whisper low enough that only he can hear.

He nods and goes back up front, Hatter following him back, absolutely livid.

"There's only a tiny window in there but it's not big enough for someone to fit through," Henry states, sifting through a brown leather satchel, mumbling to himself. "Ah, here it is!" He pulls out a key, twisting it in the lock and the door pops open.

"Thank you, Henry. We got it from here." Dom warns.

The old man throws his hands up, shuffles back to the front of the store, and precedes to polish teacups.

"Alice?" I call out, pushing the door open halfway and poking my head in.

The clothes she had on are lying on the floor and she is nowhere to be seen.

Fuck.

The bathroom is empty.

She apparently climbed out of the window that none could fit through.

How ironic.

Hatter's fist slams into the mirror shattering it, "Find her." He growls, dark clouds swimming in his eyes.

Dom and I nod and head out the door, shifting so we can better follow her scent.

"And Dom." He calls after us, "Don't be gentle."

Chapter Twenty-Seven

Alice

Fucking idiots.

That's what they get for trusting someone they barely know.

The wail of a wolf calling out somewhere behind me makes my blood run cold. The sound seems to fill the air, echoing off the trees and sending chills down my spine.

They've already realized I'm gone.

I had hoped I would have had a little more of a head start before they noticed I was missing.

I should find someplace less exposed, so I'm not as easy to locate.

About a mile or so ahead of me is a range of mountains. If I can make it there, I should be able to hide myself.

I'd taken the opportunity to change out of the dingy old shirt and into something more fitting so I didn't have to worry about fighting it while running. I tugged on a pair of jeans and a plain black tank top, black athletic shoes, and threw my hair up before I took off.

I take a deep breath, steeling my resolve as I begin to make my way towards the mountains.

My heart is beating so hard I can hear it in my ears. I quicken my pace, hearing the howls of the wolves as they get closer.

I can feel their presence, and I know they're on my tail, but I can't let them catch me. I have to make it to the mountains.

The ground beneath my feet is slick and wet, the mud sticking to my shoes as I run. I jump over fallen logs and stray branches making sure to stay away from the main road.

I don't know what I'm going to do when I reach them, but I know I have to keep going. There's no turning back now.

There's no way I can outrun them but maybe I can outsmart them. I pull the small spray bottle of perfume out of my front pocket and spray it downwind hoping to confuse them. I can feel the panic rising in my chest. I'm running as fast as I can, but I know it won't be enough.

The mountains are a towering mass of rock rising in the sky, their jagged peaks casting a long shadow over the land. Trees line the slopes, their leaves rustling in the wind. The air is crisp and clear, and the clouds circle around the peaks, like wisps of smoke.

I'm almost there.

My legs throb and my lungs burn from the exertion and the icy bite of the wind but I made it to the trees. A stream trickles down the mountain, culminating in a pool at the bottom that is illuminated by a waterfall crashing against its surface.

My throat is dry and my chest is tight. I throw myself behind a tree and gasp for air. My hands shaking, I press one to my chest to try to calm my raging heartbeat.

I have to take a break.

The water looks cool and inviting. It's serenely clear and probably one of the prettiest things I've seen in a very long time.

Tiny rainbows of fish decorate the water, darting back and forth under the surface causing little ripples.

Plants with finger-like tendrils and small blossoming flowers pepper the ground around the basin of water along with rings of speckled mushrooms.

Small flying creatures buzz around. They're small and delicate, with shimmery wings that sparkle in the light.

They seem almost fairy-like with their colorful forms as if they were made out of precious gems.

Like tiny comets, they move quickly, zigzagging their way around the plants and blossoms. They bring a lightness to the air as they flutter around, carefree and beautiful.

The splash of the waterfall mists my face as I draw nearer. I'm parched and it's the only source of water around from what I can see so I chance going over to the edge and kneel down dipping my hands in the icy water.

I cup it and take a small sip letting it slosh around in my mouth before swallowing. It's cold but delicious and feels so good against the back of my burning throat.

I close my eyes, allowing this one moment of peace and solitude, and the thundering of my heart slows down as I sit back against the rock of the basin's edge.

The light breeze brings goosebumps to my skin, and I shiver, although it isn't particularly cold out.

I've already stopped for too long.

Pushing myself up off the ground I ready myself to continue running only making it about two hundred feet to the left of me where the trees are thicker before my attention is grabbed by the sound of breaking twigs.

My stomach twists and I feel sick, nausea taking hold of me. Looking around I don't see anything, but I swear I can feel the sensation of being watched.

They're hunting me, stalking me, preying on me.

At any point, they could attack, yet they choose slow deliberate torture just to fuck with me.

I know I have to keep moving, but my legs feel like they've turned to cement.

The sound of twigs snapping again echoes through the silent forest, but this time it sounds much closer and coming from directly behind me.

I turn quickly almost slipping from my disjointed swivel to meet the clashing eyes of a wolf.

It's Dom.

His lip is curled back in a snarl, exposing his sharp teeth. His nostrils flare and his eyes darken as he flaunts his canines at me, and I can hear Dean circling back around me so they are cutting me off from two separate directions.

I could try to run left or right, but it would be no use, they're both faster and stronger than I am.

My chest and stomach lurch with nausea as I feel bile gather at the back of my tongue.

Not knowing what to do, I run in a blind panic. I double back sprinting for the dense woodland to the left of me.

The rush of adrenaline pushes me to run as fast as I can before finally, I can no longer see them.

"That's right. Run, little rabbit." I hear Doms's voice call out, and his husky laugh follows. "Because when we catch you, we're going to devour every stunning little inch of you. And once we're finished, you'll be left weeping for our cocks."

I feel my pulse racing in anticipation as his words ignite a wildfire within me. I can feel the heat of it coursing through me, igniting every nerve ending, exhilarated by his threat.

I hate my body for reacting this way.

Why can't my vagina just listen to my head instead of my libido?

I. Don't. Fucking. Want. This.

Chapter Twenty-Eight

Alice

I can feel both their stares on me, watching my every movement as I scramble across the haphazard tangle of roots and sharp branches of trees.

"Eat shit!" I scream in no direction in particular.

"There's nowhere to run." Dean mocks. "Anywhere you go, we will find you."

"Who do you think you are? Following me, stalking me, playing your sick little games." Defiant, I shuffle on, my breath hitching in my throat.

"Believe me, little rabbit. . .There's only one game I want to play, and that's how fast I can make you come." Dom growls from directly behind me.

A heavy weight has settled in the pit of my stomach, and my insides are quivering like a million fluttering wings. It feels like a thousand bricks are strapped to my feet, each one made of lead as I try to run.

I'm disgusted that I'm turned on by this. It's wrong, and I know it's wrong but it excites me like nothing ever has before.

I always knew I was fucked up, but this-this is ridiculous.

I'm so used to only getting excited when I'm deepest in my work back home. When I'm cutting into the flesh of the damned, surgically removing the malignant tumors that call themselves saints, they're like a cancer that eats away at anything, and everything good until there's nothing left behind but corruption and evil.

This sensation is unfamiliar, yet I am invigorated by the thrill of it, however, I'm not sure how to process it just yet.

"You smell so sweet," Dom whispers close to my ear, placing one of his large palms against the middle of my back and reaching around with the other wrapping it around my throat.

Gently, he squeezes with just enough pressure to make me whimper. I can feel the hardness of his dick pressing into my ass.

His teeth skim across the exposed flesh of my shoulder, nipping at me with lengthened canines.

"Careful, Dom." Dean comes out of nowhere, his tanned naked body fully on display for my viewing pleasure. "Try not to break her...Just yet."

His gaze is both passionate and wrathful as his eyes hold mine. Sweat drips down his chest trailing the perfect V of his stomach, his muscles rippling as he slowly approaches me.

His hair is a wild and disheveled tangle of dark strands, highlighting his gorgeous face and I find myself wanting to run my fingers through it while his face is pressed between my legs.

The firm hands of Dom squeeze harder around my throat, his long fingers running across the smooth skin finding their way into my hair, "We're going to have to punish you, little rabbit." He tsks, pulling my head back and running his tongue up the length of my throat.

My skin is flushed, my body is on fire, and my panties are completely soaked.

"You shouldn't have run away but I'm so fucking glad you did because I enjoyed the chase."

"Fuck you."

Dean's hands cup my face, running his thumbs over my bottom lip. "Are you sure that's what you want?" He grins. "I can only hold Dom back for so long."

"Stop," I say though it comes out sounding more like a breathy moan. "I don't want this please st—," I try again but he cuts me off.

"Don't lie," he whispers, his warm breath touching my sensitive flesh. My body is on overload.

I try to shake my head, but it only makes Dom's hold on me tighter. They both continue to toy with me, their touches, sending volts of electricity to my dripping cunt.

The way he looks at me, the way he takes in my body, licking his lips like I'm his last meal, it makes me feel so small and powerless.

"Oh, how I'm going to shatter you, little rabbit," Dom whispers, his breath tickling my neck. "We're going to use you in ways that you can't even imagine. Your body will be so overwhelmed with pleasure that you'll beg for more."

I find myself trying to resist them even though my body aches for more of their touch.

"I won't." My words are defiant, but I can't help but feel like I'm telling a lie.

"Yes, you will." Dom kisses my neck, slowly trailing his kisses down to my collarbone, his tongue lapping at the small dip of my neck, "And you're going to love every fucking second of it. Aren't you?"

I would be telling a lie if I said being pressed in between the heated flesh of Dean and Dom wasn't the hottest thing I've ever experienced, and probably the most terrifying too.

It shows me that there's a very delicate balance that exists between my fear and desire.

Why won't they just go away?

"No, what I'll enjoy is cutting off your dicks and shoving them up your ass!" My voice is soft yell, but it's my last effort to protect the little bit of pride I have left.

"You're so fucking cute when you're angry, baby," Dean chuckles, holding his hand out in front of him and twisting it in front of my face as his fingernails turn into sharp claws.

He flicks one out, easily slicing through the front of my thin tanktop.

My body quivers at his touch and I feel my nipples harden to a painful degree. A wave of desire washes over me, causing my pussy to clench with the need to be filled.

Dean's eyes glisten at my reaction, and he looks over at Dom before his lips curl in a sadistic smile.

"Don't you dare fucking touch me!" I snarl, and the direction I intended for my words is muddled when Dom places his thick cock against my ass.

"Do you want to be angry, little rabbit? Do you want to hate us for having the power to make your body feel like this?" The sound of my jeans being torn rips through the air, and a scream lodges in my throat.

I can feel the cool rush of air between my legs where he tore my pants away, exposing my thighs, and leaving me with only a thin piece of lace to cover my pussy.

I manage to turn my head slightly, spitting in Dean's face, "I'll kill you! I'll kill you both!" I screech.

Dom reaches around me, pulling my thong to the side, and dips his fingers inside me, "Dirty, little rabbit. You're so fucking wet for us." He growls, pushing farther inside me.

My whole body shakes when I feel Dean rake his claws along my stomach, just barely putting pressure on my skin. I feel his fingers trailing up my stomach until he reaches the middle of my bra.

With a swift motion, he cuts through it and my breasts tumble out, and he scoops them in his hands before sucking one of my nipples in his mouth, his tongue massaging circles around the hardened bud.

"Oh god," I whimper, unable to look away.

Dean's face is flushed, his cheeks a deep shade of pink, and I can see every vein in his neck and arms standing out as he strokes himself, a little drop of pre-cum dripping from the tip.

From behind me, Dom slides his dick between my ass cheeks, still squeezing my neck as he continues to pump his fingers in and out of me with slow short motions.

The sensations are overwhelming, causing me to cry out, and my head falls back onto Doms's shoulder, my eyes rolling back in bliss.

I can feel my mind giving in, losing the battle against my body.

The pleasure is more than I can stand, "Please don't—" My body convulses.

"Please don't what?" Dean questions, pinching my nipple lightly, drawing a desperate cry from me.

Dom finishes tearing away my panties and slips his arms under my thighs, lifting me up, and spreading me open for Dean.

My breaths are quick shallow pants, I can feel myself spiraling closer to the edge of ecstasy, and I'm powerless to stop it.

I don't want to stop it.

Dean buries his face in my pussy, his teeth softly scraping and biting at my clit before he swirls his tongue around it and draws it in his mouth, sucking and releasing it over and over again.

I can feel my orgasm building, but I don't want to give them the satisfaction of seeing me succumb, so I begin struggling against their restrictive holds.

"No!" I pant, bucking my hips forward, trying to escape.

"Don't fight it, little rabbit. You're going to cum for us whether you want to or not."

Dean's tongue flicks over my swollen clit again and I'm riding the precedence, my body is on fire, and their touch is so close to sending me over.

I know they're both drawing this out, torturing me, driving me to the edge at their own pace.

Dean continues his assault, not giving me a second to breathe before he plunges his tongue into my wetness and draws me into his mouth.

I give a helpless moan as Dom stretches me open wider for him.

"Please! No more!" I sob, writhing in Dom's arms, but it's too late.

My body shudders and I let out a loud cry. Waves of intense bliss ripple through me as I experience the most powerful fucking orgasm of my life.

"Good girl. Cum for us." Dom's mouth is at my ear, his voice is deep and husky.

"Fuck." Dean moans against me before he's coming in spurts all over his hand.

Dom releases me, spinning me around and forcing me to my knees in front of him.

"Open your mouth," Dom commands as he taps his raging cock against my lips.

"Ah! Fuck yes." Dean pumps his hand a few more times, catching the last few drops of his release on his finger before sliding it into my mouth.

I'm still experiencing bliss as the salty, coppery taste of Dean's cum fills my mouth.

I moan quietly and Dom grins down at me, his eyes burning with lust or depravity.

I can't tell.

With gentle pressure, he runs his hand along my jaw, tilting my chin up, then grabs my hair and pulls my head back so I'm looking at him before he squeezes my face, forcing my mouth open.

Holding my head in place, he guides his cock into my mouth, and I close my lips around him, swirling my tongue over his head and sucking him deep.

He groans loudly, his grip tightening in my hair. "Such a good little rabbit." His hips jerk roughly as I take the full length of him into my mouth, his cock pressing against the back of my throat.

Dean is still dazed from his release and is propped up against a tree watching us.

Dom's pace quickens, his thrusts becoming harder causing tears to flood my eyes.

"I love the way you gag for me." He groans as he pulls me back by my hair.

Shame burns my face.

I shouldn't be enjoying this. I shouldn't want this.

Suddenly, I remember that the lagoon isn't that far away, and if I can make it back there, there's a small opening in the rock that I may be able to fit through.

When he slams into me again, I bite down as hard as I can, pouring all of my frustration into the bite.

Dom roars—loud and thrashing and falls to the ground clutching his bleeding dick. I scramble to my feet and take off not thinking about the consequences.

Footsteps pound the ground behind me but I don't stop and I don't look back.

I make it to the waterfall, and run to the small hole in the mountainside, dropping to my knees and crawling quickly inside.

I think I'm almost home free when I feel a hand close around my ankle.

I scream, kicking my legs trying to break free. My foot connects with something, and he curses, releasing me and I pull myself inside the tight space.

I don't pause until I'm sure that they won't be able to catch up with me and I let out a whoop of victory laying back on the jagged stone wall to catch my breath.

Good luck being able to track me a mile inside solid rock.

Jerks.

Chapter Twenty-Nine

Rose

He's back!

I wonder what horrors the Queen had him partake in this time.

I hear the thudding of pebbles bouncing against the ground, their noise ringing around the entrance to the cave and traveling through its tunnels.

The large cave is illuminated with the soft glow of torches along the walls.

Hanging tapestries and rugs cover the floor, items I assume to belong to the owners of the bones that litter the Jabberwocky's labyrinth. Stone pillars are nestled between the entrance and the back of the cave, providing a few dividers of privacy.

The center of the cave boasts a large firepit, warming the cold stone area and giving a soft ambiance of light.

In the very back corner, I've made a bed of blankets and animal hides, and a long body pillow made by stuffing a torn piece of fabric with the feathers of the birds I've been hunting for food and tying the frayed ends together.

And it's still better living conditions than what the Queen offered me growing up.

I get up from where I'm seated by the fire and walk towards the front entrance of the cave but stop in my tracks at the sound of footsteps.

One way too light to be my father's massive, clawed feet.

Did they find me?

It's been at least a week since he saved me at the falls and went back to the Queen's castle.

I hold my breath as the footsteps draw closer, and I try to steady my shaking hands. As much as I want to convince myself that I'm safe here, away from the Queen's grasp, the fear of being discovered never quite leaves me.

The footsteps get closer, and I hold my breath, trying to prepare for the worst.

Trying to steady my shaking hands, I back away slowly, scanning the room and quickly realizing I don't have any proper weapons to defend myself so I grab my slingshot I've been using for hunting and pull back a rock, waiting for the intruder to approach.

A figure pokes around the corner, entering the vast room, "Hello?" A female's voice calls out.

It's certainly not Yelana.

So, who is this strange girl?

I don't budge, and I try not to breathe, as her footsteps get closer, hoping she doesn't notice me.

The girl approaches, but I can't make out her face in the dim lighting.

She moves with a cautious grace, and as she steps closer to the fire, her features are illuminated.

She's stunning, with long golden hair and big blue eyes, and she's not wearing any clothes. Mud streaks her body and blood is dried on her bottom lip.

I watch as she slowly walks around the cave, touching the tapestries, and observing her surroundings. She doesn't seem to be a threat, so I lower my slingshot, making sure she doesn't see me.

"Who are you?" I ask, stepping out of the shadows, trying to assess her intentions.

She jumps at the sound of my voice, whirling around to face me, her eyes going wide as she raises the heavy-looking leather book in her hands like a weapon.

I can see the fear and the confusion written all over her face, and I realize that she's just as lost as I am.

"I could ask you the same thing," she retorts, her voice steady but with a hint of anxiety.

I take in her appearance again, trying to put my finger on why she seems so familiar. "Have we met before?" I ask, taking a step closer to her.

"I—I don't think so." She replies, lowering the book and taking a step away from me.

I step back too, trying to give her some space.

She seems like she's been through a lot, and I don't want to scare her any further. "I'm sorry if I scared you, I didn't mean to." I lower my voice, trying to sound as reassuring as possible.

She looks at me skeptically, but the fear in her eyes slowly dissipates.

"It's alright," she says, finally relaxing a little bit. "I'm just. . .Not used to this kind of situation."

I can't help but notice the way her body shivers in the cold dampness of the cave, "You poor thing. You must be freezing!" I say, running over and grabbing her a blanket, wrapping it around her shoulders.

"Where are we?" She asks, looking around the cave once more.

"It's my home for now."

I watch as she pulls the blanket closer around her, her eyes scanning my face. I can see the questions forming in her mind, but before she can say anything, I take her hand and lead her over to the makeshift fire pit in the center of the cave.

"Let me get some firewood and I'll get a bigger fire going," I say, walking to the exit of the cave.

As I step out of the cave, I take a deep breath, feeling the crisp night air fill my lungs. I can't help but feel a sense of relief that I'm not alone anymore. It's been so long since I've had another person to talk to, and she seems nice enough.

As I gather the firewood, I can't shake off the feeling that I know this girl from somewhere, but I can't quite place where.

Once I have enough wood, I head back into the cave and start to arrange it in a small pile near the fire pit, placing a couple of them in the hot embers.

The fire continues to grow in size, giving off a pleasant warmth that fills the cave. Once I am pleased with the temperature and give a satisfied nod and sit down on a large rock, holding my hands over the fire.

The girl watches me intently, her eyes following my every movement.

"I never got your name," I say, breaking the silence.

She hesitates for a moment before responding, "Alice."

Alice. The name sends a jolt through my body, but I can't figure out why. I decide to brush it off and continue the conversation.

"That's a beautiful name," I say. "My name is Rose." I hold my hand out to shake hers.

Alice hesitates for a moment before taking my hand, but when her palm meets mine there's an electric feeling that rushes through my veins as I feel the warmth, and smoothness of her skin against mine.

I quickly pull my hand back, hoping she doesn't notice the pounding of my heart.

"Rose," Alice repeats, testing the name on her tongue. "So, how did you end up living in this cave?"

I take a deep breath, unsure of how much to share. But there's something about her that makes me want to open up. I take a deep breath and lean back against the rock, feeling the heat of the fire against my skin, and my heart tightens as a wave of pain washes over me, memories flooding back to me like a tidal wave. I push them away, focusing on Alice instead.

"It's a long story," I say, avoiding eye contact.

"Fair."

"What about you? And are you ok? Did something happen to you? Like—" I pause, not sure how to ask without possibly offending her, so I just blurt it out with no remorse. "Is there a reason you're naked?"

Her cheeks flush, turning a deep red and I instantly regret my words.

"You don't have to answer that!" I yelp. "I am so sorry, I shouldn't have asked. It's none of my business. I-I was just worried that maybe you got hurt."

She nods, clearly relieved. "It's a long story." She offers.

I laugh, "Fair."

"Well, Alice." I get up, wiping my hands on my pants. "I hope you're hungry. I was just about to make some food. It's not much but-" I shrug.

"I appreciate your kindness, but I don't want to intrude any more than I already have."

"Are you kidding me?! I'm a cavewoman. I would love the extra company."

Her laugh is a melodic sound, like a gentle breeze brushing against a stream on a warm summer day. The light, airy notes linger in the air, and I find myself smiling in response.

"Maybe just for dinner then." She says.

As I start preparing the food, Alice watches me intently, her eyes following my every move. The silence is thick between us, but it's a comfortable one.

Alice stands up, her long hair flowing down her back like a waterfall. As she walks toward me, I can't help but notice her curves and the way they move, hypnotizing me like a siren's call. I shake my head, trying to clear my thoughts.

Now is not the moment to be sidetracked.

"Would you like some help? My friend back home loved to cook and I rather enjoyed helping her when she was rummaging around in the kitchen."

My breath hitches, and I can feel the heat rising in my cheeks at her closeness. I nod quickly, handing her a knife and some vegetables to chop.

"That would be great." I manage to say, trying to keep my voice from betraying me.

I'm so damn nervous and I don't know why.

As we work together, our hands brush against each other, and I can feel the electricity between us. Alice's eyes meet mine, and for a moment, I forget about everything else.

"Sorry." She murmurs softly, breaking the spell.

"It's fine. It was my fault anyway. I wasn't paying attention." I assure her.

The silence returns, even thicker than before, as we continue to chop and prepare the food.

My heart is a loud drum in my ears, I can feel the sweat starting to trickle down my back, and I realize that my nervousness around Alice is not going to subside anytime soon.

Her presence is tantalizing, and to top that off, I feel oddly drawn to her in a way that defies any explanation.

After we eat, I use a blanket, cutting it, and tying it strategically into a not-so-great-looking dress that she can use to cover herself.

I wish I had more than just the clothes on my back to give her, but I have nothing more to offer her than a full belly and a place to sleep.

Alice looks down at the makeshift dress when I hand it to her, a small smile playing at the corners of her lips. "It's perfect," she says softly, her eyes meeting mine.

"Far from it." I giggle. "I'm sorry I don't have more."

"You've already done so much! Please, don't apologize."

She drops the blanket that wrapped around her and it falls to a heap on the floor. Her full round tits are revealed, and my eyes widen with surprise. I can feel my mouth go dry as I try to regain my composure.

Alice doesn't seem to notice, picking up the dress and slipping it over her head.

I fleetingly look away, feeling guilty for my inappropriate thoughts.

Alice must have noticed my discomfort because she clears her throat, breaking the tense silence. "Thank you, again, for everything. I truly appreciate it."

"Of course. Come on, let me show you where you can sleep." I say, gesturing towards the makeshift bed. "I'll sleep somewhere else for the night."

"You don't have to do that!" She exclaims. "I refuse to take your bed from you. Really, I'm fine."

"I insist. Besides, I don't sleep well these days so it wouldn't even be getting used."

Alice nods, seemingly accepting of my offer. She follows me over to the pile of blankets and pillows, and I watch as she settles in, making herself as comfortable as possible given the circumstances.

"Look." She says, sliding over to the wall. "There's plenty of room for us both."

I swallow hard, my mind racing with thoughts I know I shouldn't have. But as Alice pats the space next to her, inviting me to join, I find myself unable to resist.

Without a word, I crawl into the makeshift bed, curling up next to Alice's warm body. I can feel her breath on my neck.

"See? Plenty of room."

"Mmmhmm." I squeak, my body stiff as a board.

I try to push away the thoughts that invade my mind, but they only get more vivid with each passing second.

Her body is so close to mine, her warmth seeping into my skin and stirring something deep within me. It's been so long since I've felt this way—since I've been intimate with someone and that has only happened once or twice before.

I hear her yawn deeply behind me and she snuggles into the bed, "Goodnight, Rose." She whispers, sleep already in her voice.

Staring off into the darkness, I try to steady my breathing, a smile tugging at my lips, "Goodnight, Alice."

Chapter Thirty

Hatter

I should have gone myself.

Why did I trust them to bring her back, and what's more, why do I care that she's gone?

The twins have been keeping me informed through our bond on what's been going on and they refuse to come back until they find her.

Is she hurt?

Hungry?

Dead?

I find myself worrying about her well-being way too much.

No matter what I do, my mind keeps going back to her.

My thoughts have circled around and twisted themselves into knots until I've become completely consumed by them, and the only thing left in my fucking head is her.

Though, I do believe that Dom has been the most impacted by her absence.

He hasn't shifted back since they lost her.

His mournful howls fill the night sky as he calls to her. It's his way of letting her know that he's not going to give up on finding her, and that we *will* get her back.

Minutes have turned into hours and dread has settled in my bones.

I pace back and forth, my eyes darting towards the door every time I hear a sound. The room is silent except for the ticking of the grandfather clock in the corner. Time seems to have slowed down and every second feels like a lifetime.

My pacing quickens, I can't sit still, not while she's out there somewhere...Alone.

I can't shake off the feeling that something terrible has happened to her.

I'm losing control.

I can feel it, the madness that is always at the edge of my mind threatening to take over.

I've never felt like this before—so vulnerable and exposed. It's like I'm empty without her, and the only way to fill the void is to find her.

A suffocating and oppressive shroud has fallen over the house—over me.

I make my way to the door and fling it open, the night air hitting me like a physical blow.

It's dark, the only light coming from the moon that hangs high in the sky.

The world is bathed in shadows, and it's the perfect playground for those who are lost and unfamiliar with the treacherous landscape.

I know that Alice is a fighter, but this world is unforgiving, and there are so many things that could go wrong.

She doesn't realize that the monsters she's used to in her world are nothing compared to the monsters she will face here in Wonderland.

Like the one that slaughtered Alex Frost.

He was dead when I arrived at his home.

I knew as soon as I came up to his house, something wasn't right.

The door was hanging from its hinges, and the handle had been mangled and twisted, snapped off the frame. The wood of the door was deeply cut by some force, creating large, jagged gouges in the surface.

I tried to piece together what had happened, but the only thing that made sense was that whoever had caused his death, was most likely the same person who's been murdering our guys and intercepting our shipments.

Alex was smart and he was by no means a weakling, yet, it seemed like he never even had a chance to fight back. The scene was pretty brutal. Alex was lying on the floor on his back, his eyes staring up blankly at the ceiling. His throat had been ripped out, a large gaping hole left in his neck, and there were deep cuts across his chest.

Judging from the chaos and destruction that had been left behind, it seemed more animalistic. With each murder, the killings have become more and more ravening, almost like they've been done by something that's not entirely human.

What if Alice suffers the same fate?

I can feel a rage like nothing else as my anger swells inside me, boiling and churning until I can hardly contain it. It starts from my chest and spreads throughout my body, a burning sensation that covers me like a blanket.

My blood boils in my veins and my muscles constrict, clenching in response to the fury that threatens to overwhelm me. I hate being stuck here.

With everything going on we can't all risk being out in the open at the same time, and I promised the twins that I would stay at the manor in case she came back, but this not knowing is an absolute fucking nightmare.

As the night wears on, my impatience only grows and festers. My mind is a swirling pandemonium of thoughts and emotions, and I can't make sense of any of them.

The stillness of the house is maddening as I sit in the parlor, staring at the clock.

Every second hand of the clock makes its presence known in my head, and I feel like a timer is counting down to some impending ruination.

My eyes dart around the room, searching for anything that can distract me from the thoughts that are circling around my head. I get up and walk towards the window, gazing out into the yard that surrounds the mansion.

The moon is shining brightly and casting a pale glow that gets quickly eaten by the darkness.

But that's just the way of this world, isn't it? Beauty and darkness coexisting, always vying for dominance.

I take a deep breath, trying to calm my nerves, but it feels like an impossible task.

Suddenly, jarring me out of my trance, Dean's voice fills my head, *"We caught her scent."*

Thank fuck.

"Do you know where she is?" I reply, relief flooding my veins.

"Somewhere at the top of the mountains, I think. It was faint, but I'm pretty sure we're heading in the right direction."

I let out a sigh of consolation, my muscles relaxing as I feel the weight of the worry, subtly shifting on my shoulders. At least now, we have an idea of where Alice might be.

"Ok, stay close by. I have a few of our guards watching over the property, keeping an eye out for her as well. How's Dom?" He cut

the connection from our bond a couple of hours ago, probably the moment he began to lose hope.

"He'll be fine. She was just another conquest, a faceless vessel of pleasure that had the audacity to challenge him and dent his ego. He'll get over it soon enough." Dean lies, trying to sound both un-swayed and pacifying but we both know she is so much more than that.

For all of us.

"Watch your backs," I say. *"Whoever this son of bitch is that's killing off our men is still on the loose and he's been keeping tabs on us somehow."*

How else would he have known about Alex and gotten to him before us?

"We'll deal with him when you get back here with, Alice. When we know she's safe."

"Indeed. It's time we end this shit. Be careful, Dean."

"Always. See you soon, brother."

My mind goes silent, leaving me alone with my ravenous thoughts once more.

While I am relieved that we have found out where Alice is, I feel like the worst is still yet to come.

We still have to figure out who's been taking our shipments, and what they're using the dust for.

What I can't seem to figure out is how this person is always one step ahead of us.

I feel like we're pawns in a game of chess.

They think they have all the power, but they'll soon find out that I'm the fucking king of this board and I have a few tricks up my own sleeve.

Check mate mother fucker.

CHAPTER THIRTY-ONE

Alice

"Good morning." I look up to meet her magnificent emerald eyes.

Her smile is warm like the sun breaking through the darkest clouds of my existence.

"Good morning." I smile back. "I hope you slept well."

Her cheeks glow a bright red, like the hair flying in wisps around her face.

She's beautiful.

Her peachy skin is flawless, unblemished with a few freckles sprinkled across her nose, and her lips are plump and inviting.

"I did, thank you for asking." She takes a seat next to me and reaches for a stone pot used for steeping coffee. "Want some?" She asks, leveling out scoops of coarsely ground coffee beans and placing them in the round cone cylinder at the top.

"Yes. Thank you."

"So do you know where you're heading once you leave here?" She questions.

I nod, pulling my bottom lip between my teeth, chewing on the sensitive flesh, "The Queen's castle."

Her face drops for a moment, but she quickly smiles and grabs two cups to pour the coffee in. "Do you work for the Queen?" She asks and I can hear the tension in her voice.

"Oh, fuck no!" I exclaim. "I intend to kill the bitch."

Her jade eyes widen in shock and disbelief, but something else flickers there too. Something akin to admiration. I can tell she's intrigued by my answer, even if it's not what she was expecting to hear.

She hands me a cup of steaming coffee and takes a sip of her own before asking, "And why do you want to kill the Queen?"

I put my nose to the edge of my cup, savoring the aroma of the coffee, it's not Dean's but beggars can't be choosers.

I take a deep breath, bracing myself for the memories that I knew this question would bring up, "Outside of her just being a shitty person that murders the innocent people of her kingdom—she took everything from me." I admit. "She took the only person that ever loved me. My father. He was the most important thing in my life. And she took him away from me." My words trail off as I stare down at my coffee, watching the steam rise up in spirals.

I can feel her gaze on me, but I don't look up.

I can't look at her. I can't look at anyone. I only see the past.

Vivid images flash through my mind of the last time I saw him, how his dead lifeless eyes glimpsed into my own right before he took his last breath.

She speaks gently, her voice full of empathy. "I'm so sorry, Alice. That must have been difficult," She murmurs.

I give a small nod, pausing to take a sip of the coffee as I try to organize my thoughts and will away the tears in my eyes.

"The Queen has taken so much from our people—our land. Wonderland used to be a much brighter place many years ago before she married the King." Rose says, her eyes filling with tears too. "That's what she does—tears families apart and destroys anyone and anything that gets in the way of her desperate hunt for power. She's the reason why our kingdom is so impoverished, why people are homeless, and why children are starving. Yet, she sits in her castle and feasts every night on the people's work while her subjects try to survive in the ruins of the once glorious Wonderland. She's a wretched creature who thinks only of herself—a greedy monster that deserves to perish."

I can feel the anger and pain radiating from her words, and I know that I'm not the only one seeking revenge against the Queen.

Maybe in Rose, I have found an ally.

I meet her moist eyes, "Did she take someone from you too?"

"Yes." She whispers. "She took my father too." She puts her mug of steaming caffeinated liquid to her lips, taking a sip.

My heart aches with sympathy for her and I give a sage nod in recognition of the connection we share.

We sit in a comfortable silence for a moment, our thoughts consumed by the Queen and the pain she has caused so many.

"What about your mom?" I dare to ask.

She shakes her head.

"Oh." I look away, regretting that I asked. "I'm so sorry, Rose."

Rose's eyes soften, "It's okay. It was a long time ago." She reaches out and puts a hand on mine, giving it a comforting squeeze. "We all have our battles to fight. And I plan on fighting mine until the end."

I smile at her determination, feeling grateful to have met her. "Me too," I say firmly. "And I won't rest until the Queen is held accountable for her actions."

Rose nods in agreement, her eyes locking with mine in a silent understanding.

"I don't even know what my father saw in her." I fume.

"You—your father was with the Queen?" Her question is a whisper as all the color drains from her face.

"Yes. When I was just a little girl." I tell her. "She seemed quite lovely at first with her kind words and caring ways—she made it easy for my father to fall, but that of course, was before he found out that she was a ruthless, vindictive cunt and she murdered him."

"What about your mother? Why was your father not with her?"

Ice forms in my veins, "She was just as vile as the Queen, if not worse." I clench my jaw, rage making my vision turn red. "She was an evil tyrant in my world. She victimized innocent children, abusing them and offering them along with their innocence as a sacrifice to sick individuals--all for wealth and power."

"Oh, Alice! You poor thing. What did she do to you?" Rose asks, her body stiffening next to me.

Fear and revulsion are written all over her face.

I grit my teeth as I recollect her cruel manipulation, "I was nothing more than another dollar in her pocket." I admit. "She used me as a pawn in her twisted games," I admit, my voice trembling with anger. "She was wretched, she tossed me to her snarling hounds like a piece of meat." My veins boil with rage and shame. "She convinced me that my own father wouldn't love me because I was unclean, tainted, and unworthy of his affection—that no one could ever care for me.

Rose grabs my hand, "That's not true, Alice. You deserve all the love in the world."

I try to hold back the tears that threaten to spill down my face but fail miserably.

A sob escapes my lips, and Rose pulls me into an embrace. She cradles me in her arms, murmuring softly in my ear in an effort to calm me down.

I sob into her shoulder, "I don't think that woman was capable of love. As far as I'm concerned, she was soulless with no heart whatsoever. Needless to say, it's become hard to trust—or to love anyone now." I confess, my voice trembling.

"I can understand that." She whispers.

Remaining in her arms, I allow her warmth to comfort my aching heart, "I hope she was punished."

"She was. I killed her." I sniffle.

Rose's eyes widen at my confession, but she doesn't pull away from me.

Rather, she cups my face in her gentle hands, wiping away the tears with her thumbs, "Good. You did what you had to do," She says softly. "And you shouldn't carry the weight of her sins on your shoulders. You're not responsible for her evil deeds."

Memories of the night she died flash in my mind. The decision to kill her had been made as soon as I got home from the hospital after I had been punished for my father's infidelities and lies.

I couldn't allow her to hurt me or another child ever again.

She needed to be destroyed—to be punished for all the things she had put us through and allowed others to put us through.

The scene of her demise had been horrifying—for everyone but me that is.

I can hear my mother's screams, smell the burning of her flesh, and the metallic twang of her blood still coated on the blade of the knife I used to give her just a small crucial taste of the pain she had caused me.

She was angry at first when she woke up to me in her room, but that quickly changed when she realized she couldn't move and she saw the hunting knife in my hand that my father had given to me on my birthday earlier that year.

"This will only hurt for a little bit, mother." I laughed as I plunged my knife deep between her legs.

Her scream was met with my laughter.

I remember how she vomited on the bedsheets, her wails and pleas for me to stop, but I continued to assault her like I had been assaulted so many God-forsaken times.

Afterward, I covered her mangled body with kerosene, flicked a match, and threw it on my way out.

My mother along with two senators, a couple of millionaires who wanted to know what it was like to fuck a little girl, and none other than Sully himself, died in the fire.

I was the only one to survive that night.

The cops arrested me, and I was put in an institution for a little while they tried to charge me with five counts of murder and wanted to give me an insanity plea, but ultimately all charges were dropped, and I was let go because there was absolutely no proof. They had nothing to go on other than their suspicions.

But deep down the judge knew better, and I know he did because he had been coming to my mother's "parties" for years.

Of course, there was no way he would risk challenging it for fear of getting caught himself, so he let the case go and sent me on my merry way.

It's been years since that night, and I like to think I have moved on quite nicely on my own.

"How did your father not know?" Rose asks.

"He worked until late at night. My mother made me swear I wouldn't tell a soul and the other children weren't kept at my home; they were hidden at a different location. I finally broke down and told him, and that was around the same time we stumbled on the portal to Wonderland. He wanted to keep me safe, so we left my mom, and we stayed in an old, abandoned building in the middle of the woods up until we moved to Wonderland, where he died. I had nowhere else to go after the Queen killed him, so I went back home, hoping my mother would change her ways, but that was a joke."

"I suspect the Queen didn't show her true colors at first, and that's why you and your father didn't know about what the Queen was doing to the kingdom?"

"Correct. My father was a broken man when he met the Queen, an empty shell of who he had once been before the treacheries of my mother made him weak. He wanted to be loved, wanted, needed—he needed to feel like he was worth something. And at first, he found that with the Queen." I pause. "Little did he know she would betray him. It all changed so quickly. One day, I was playing in the halls of the palace with another little girl, and I heard them arguing. I couldn't make out what they were saying so I cracked the door to her tea room and heard her telling my father to leave me with my bitch of a mother." I shiver as I hug myself, though it doesn't do anything to lessen the ache in my chest. "She was making him choose between me and her. . . And when he told her he would always choose me. . .She killed him. She beheaded him right in front of me. She was going to kill me too."

"Oh, Alice!" Rose exclaims. "What happened? How did you get away?"

I take a deep breath and a sip of my coffee before I continue, "She sent her guards to hunt me down, but the servant girl not much older than me that I had been playing with, saved me. She helped me escape to the gardens through hidden passageways the servants used to get around the castle so they weren't seen by the monarchies. If it weren't for her, my fate would have been sealed and I would have never been able to evade my death. I barely made it to the portal before some lunatic in a mask and some pyromaniac lady murdered me—the Queen's executioners. Once I was back in London, the glass disappeared. I went back to the tree I first found it at, every day for years, and nothing ever changed until recently. Hints how I'm here now."

Rose's jaw drops in shock, and her cup slips from her grasp and crashes to the ground.

With a gasp, she rises to her feet, eyes wide as she chokes out, "Alice." Her voice quivers as she speaks her next words. "I think I'm the one who rescued you."

Chapter Thirty-Two

Alice

"What? How?" I ask in disbelief.

Rose looks down at the floor and takes a shaky breath. Her pale cheeks flush red as she mumbles, "I—I was the servant girl who helped you. I became nothing more than a tool for her to continue her corrupt reign. She took away my true power with this." She holds out a stone on the end of a thin silver chain, hanging around her neck. "I was scared. I felt helpless against her."

I feel my stomach churn, unable to process the reality of what she just confessed.

Waves of disbelief crash through me, pulling me under as I struggle to comprehend how the worlds brought us back together.

"You saved me?" I whisper back to her, standing up to meet her tearful gaze, my hand brushing against her cheek.

"You said she took your father from you...Who was he?"

She pauses for a moment, her eyes darting away from mine, "My father is the former King of Wonderland." She says softly.

Holy shit.

What are the fucking odds?

"You're the Queen's seeker. The princess that turned against her own people—so I've been told."

"Yes." Her lips curl in disgust as she looks away from me, her voice firm as she replies, "I was a token of her propaganda—a device she could use to control the people. I'm ashamed of my part in the fall of Wonderland. I may not have killed them directly, but I am the cause of so many deaths. I'm a monster—a murderer." She sobs.

"Rose. Don't." I murmur, "You were afraid. You were a little girl who lost both of her parents and didn't have a choice. You have nothing to be ashamed of. Regret is a natural response to the choices we make--there's never a perfect decision in a fucked-up situation."

Her blood-shot eyes meet mine, "I'm a coward. I ran away. I couldn't do it anymore. I couldn't be the reason another person was imprisoned or sentenced to death."

"That doesn't make you a coward, Rose. That makes you a strong fighter who chooses to stand up for herself and do the right thing."

"Thank you." She sniffs, "I just hope one day, my people will be able to forgive me."

"You don't need absolution from them. What you must do, Princess is to no longer accept their mistreatment—take your rightful place as the Queen of Wonderland and set it right again. Reclaim the kingdom and continue the legacy of what your parents intended for the realm."

"I can't do that, not now. Not after what I have done." She shakes her head, "I'm useless. I can't even control my magic anymore, and I don't know how to run a kingdom; I don't know how to rule it. The kingdom needs my father."

"I thought she killed your father or had him killed?" I question my mind still reeling as I try to process all the information. "Wasn't a man convicted and beheaded for his murder?"

"Yes, but she didn't kill him, though. She cursed him."

"Cursed?"

"She bound him to the body of a beast—the Jabberwocky."

Holy shit!

She continues to blow my mind.

"Your father is the Jabberwocky?" I gasp.

She nods, "This is his cave. He helped me escape, but she has control over him somehow. She uses him to destroy entire villages when her executioners aren't enough to fight against the rebellion. It's awful."

This whole time she's had the King right under everyone's noses.

A gasp escapes my lips as the truth of her reign dawns on me. No wonder she has been able to stay in power for so long.

"This is why she needs to be stopped."

My heart aches for Rose and her family. I can only imagine their suffering, and then it dawns on me, "Oh, Rose. . .I'm so sorry. I can't imagine the pain you must have felt watching my father with her after what she did to you and your father. I'm so sorry if my being there back then attributed to your agony." I apologize gingerly brushing away her crimson hair from her beautiful face.

She holds my gaze, her ruby lips pulling up into a gentle smile. The tension in my chest begins to ebb away, and my heart flutters in a way I hadn't expected it to.

Her hands move up to grab mine, "I appreciate that, Alice, but I never blamed you. We were just kids. We had no control over what she did, and I felt absolutely no reason to hate you, or your father. Actually, I enjoyed having you there. I got a chance to be free of the Queen's chains for a while. It was a nice reprieve to have you around."

The depth of her words soothes my soul.

"It was nice having you too. I always felt at ease around you, and you were the very first friend I ever had." I admit, my heart fluttering in my chest again.

I am acutely aware of the warmth of her hands in mine, of how close our faces are, and of how gorgeous she looks with the light of the warm fire dancing on her face.

Her eyes light up suddenly, "Do you remember the time we were in the gardens the summer the rocking horse flies migrated to the castle?" She asks.

They are small, vividly colored creatures with graceful wings that glisten in the sunlight with a rainbow spectrum. They zip through the air with speed and agility, performing intricate maneuvers as they go, making them quite difficult to catch.

"How could I forget?" I reply, smiling as the memory washes over me. "We had spent hours chasing them around, trying to catch them in our jars."

Rose nods, her smile widening. "And then we released them all at once, watching as they flew away in a colorful blur. It was magical!" She exclaims.

"It was." I concur, chuckling at the memory. her smile is contagious making me grin. "Your laughter has always been so infectious." I muse.

Her cheeks turn a rosy shade as she responds to my words. "Being with you made me so incredibly happy. It was like nothing else existed when we were together—I didn't feel bogged down by the drudgery of my daily life or weighed down by the demands and expectations of the Queen. You made my life more bearable in what short amount of time you were there. It was because of you that I remembered what happiness felt like, even if it was an ever-fleeting emotion." Her smile fades. "She has taken away everyone's happiness. She poisons everything she touches—a venomous witch that brings only destruction."

"You won't have to worry about the Queen much longer, Princess."

"I wish that were true." She sighs.

My hand sweeps up her jaw, and she turns her face into my touch, "I promise. Here soon, she won't be able to hurt anyone else."

"How can you be so sure?" She asks, her eyes searching mine for an answer.

"Because, like I told you before—I'm going to kill her."

She looks at me in awe while I hold her close, still hugging her as she weeps silent tears onto my hands. I can feel the warmth of her body pressed up against mine, and everything inside me screams to kiss her, to hold her tight, and to never let her go.

Our lips are almost caressing each other's, I swallow hard, moving closer when she doesn't stop me and our mouths seal together in a passionate embrace, my hands still caressing her face.

I explore her mouth with my tongue, gently stroking her own, and I feel her gasp against my lips.

My body responds to our passionate kiss, my nipples stiffening and my pussy wetting with arousal. I break off the kiss, taking a deep breath before running my hands underneath her shirt to capture the tender buds of her nipples, caressing them in circles.

She lets out a breathy moan and I push her shirt up over her head, exposing her to me.

I take a moment to drink in the sight of her in the flickering glow of the fire.

She looks ethereal, her flawless skin resembling porcelain, and her small, pink nipples perched perfectly atop her petite breasts.

I lower my head to her breast and capture her nipple in my mouth, sucking hard and hearing her moan in approval.

Then I slowly pull away, her nipple leaving my mouth with a wet *pop*, as I bring my hands to them, caressing her hardened buds with my thumb and forefinger.

I circle my thumbs in a slow delicate motion and pinch; her mouth parts with a moan, her head falling back, exposing her long, delicate neck.

"Do you want this?" I whisper in her ear.

"Yes." She answers breathlessly.

And I kiss her again, this time harder than before, and her hands claw at my back, pulling me flush to her body as her hands wander down to my ass, her fingernails lightly tracing my feverish, tingling flesh.

The sound of rocks being kicked reverberates in the hollow stone cave from the tunnel behind us making my stomach instantly sour, and my blood run cold.

I turn to face the direction of the intrusion and I see a dark figure standing in the darkness.

We're no longer alone.

Chapter Thirty-Three

Alice

"Isn't that sweet," A man's voice I don't recognize seeps from the shadowy tunnel.

We both spin around to see a massive, masked man carrying an axe almost the size of him stalking towards us.

It's the same man she saved me from all those years ago.

"Alice, run!" Rose shouts.

I don't have time to register what's happening before Rose's hand grips my wrist and drags me down one of the other tunnels. I can hear them running after us as we race through the darkness, pebbles, and bones crunching beneath our feet.

"Fuck! What are we going to do? What are we going to do?" She panics.

"We have to find a place to hide or a way out of here." I gasp as another tunnel comes into view.

"Over here!" Rose grabs my hand and tugs me into the new passage.

It's so dark I can't see my hand in front of my face. I squeeze my eyes shut and focus on Rose's footsteps as she leads me through the tunnel.

"Turn here!" My eyes pop open as she flings me around a corner and stops, grabbing a chain from where it hangs from the ceiling of the cave.

A net full of stones is stretched across the area, a cunning trap that had been set by Rose, I presume.

"If you keep following this tunnel, it will lead you out to the other side of the mountain."

She's trying to save me again.

"No! We can make it out together, please!" My words, a plea.

"Alice, no! I can't go with you! He won't kill me, the Queen needs my power to stay in control, but they *will* kill you."

"I'm going to find you," I promise her. "I will find you and I will end this bitch once and for all." Tears burn my eyes, as I hug her close to me.

"You have to run now," she whispers into my ear. "Run!" She pushes me back, yanking the chain and rocks begin crashing down, filling the space between us.

"Rose!" I scream though I know she can't hear me anymore.

I won't give up on her.

I will find her again.

I turn and run as fast as my feet can carry me, crashing against the solid rock walls in the darkness.

I trip a few times, but I don't slow down.

As I come up on the exit a blast of heat hits me in the face, stealing the air from my lungs, and I stumble back, shielding my eyes from the blinding light.

What the fuck was that? I ask myself, blinking to regain my vision.

A tall lean woman balancing a ball of fire in her palm sneers at me before trying to blast me again.

I jump backward, my back slamming into the hard wall of the cave, the scorching flames singing my lashes as it whizzes past my face.

I grab the largest rock I can manage to find in the dark, and keep my back against the wall, sticking closely to the shadows.

"Come out, come out, wherever you are." She sings.

She makes a dash for where I'm hiding, her fiery ball of death flying above her hand as she swings it from left to right.

I smash the rock as hard as I can into her face, catching her off guard, and dropping her to the ground before I leap on top of her, landing my knee in her chest. I bring the rock above my head preparing to smash it down on her head and she grabs my right side, burning through the dress Rose made me, searing my skin.

A scream rips from my throat as I nearly drop the rock I'm holding in my hands.

"Well, well, well, you're a feisty one. I like that." She spits blood from her mouth, the rock I believe I broke her front tooth with. "I'm going to savor ending your life."

"I'm not fucking dead yet." I snarl.

She bucks up, sending me flying above her head and I clash to the ground, my skull connecting with the hard floor.

I lay there a moment, stunned by the impact, and she raises her right leg, planning to stomp on my face. I grab her by the foot, twisting it and yanking her forward bringing her down on top of me. My hand stretches, reaching for the stone. It's just out of my grasp.

She laughs, flames dancing in her eyes, "Bye, bye." She says, her voice eerily calm and sinister.

I reach for the stone again, my fingers so close, it's nearly in my grasp. I can feel the warmth of it, there's only an inch between my fingers and the smooth surface. Finally, my hand finds purchase and I bring it up as hard as I can, and it connects with her temple.

She falls over and I mount her waist, clenching my thighs around her, bringing the small boulder down on her nose with a loud crunch. Then, again, over and over until she's no longer moving, gurgling sounds spill from her mouth as she tries to breathe.

I wait there, straddling her chest, the rock in my hand, watching the blood flow from her face like a river, and finally, she stops moving, her eyes glazing over, becoming unfocused as she stares into space. Her body goes limp beneath mine and I roll off her, every muscle in my body aching.

I hear more footsteps, and I stand up, wiping at the blood that splattered across my eyes in my assault.

"I am too fucking tired for this shit!" I yell, but pull the rock up, getting ready to attack if I need to.

"Little rabbit?"

Dom!

I've never been so damn relieved to hear a familiar voice as I am right now.

"I'm here!" I almost scream, dropping the rock and running in the direction of his voice.

As I run towards Dom, my heart beats so fast it feels like it might burst out of my chest. When I see him, I can hardly believe it.

"How—why are you here?"

"I told you. You aren't going to get away from us that easily." He smiles, pulling me into his chest.

"Holy mother fucking shit. What the hell happened here?" Dean asks, his eyes wide at the sight of carnage behind me.

"She attacked me. I—I think she's dead," I say, still shaking from the adrenaline.

Dean presses a kiss to my forehead and then goes to examine the woman's body.

"No shit." He says, impressed. "It's Yelena."

He takes his foot and flips her head to the side, kneeling down and pressing his fingers to her neck, "She's still alive, but barely."

"Grab her." Dom grunts.

"Already on it," Dean replies, throwing her over his shoulder like she weighs nothing.

"Ahhh!" I groan, losing my balance and Dom picks me up, cradling me in his arms.

My side is burning and throbbing, and I can feel the warmth of blood and melted flesh sticking to my shirt.

"Fuck. You're hurt!"

"It's just a flesh wound." I lie, wincing as pain shoots through my body.

Dom carries me out of the clearing, holding me tightly against his chest. I rest my head on his shoulder, feeling safe and protected with him and Dean with me.

I should have just told them the truth, told them about my history in Wonderland and with the Queen. Maybe it's not too late. They want her dead just as much as I do and I trust them. They could have let me go, but they didn't, and I know it's not just because they think I'm the person who stole from them.

No.

They care about me.

And *Rose* cares about me. And as much as I hate to admit it. . . I fucking care about them too.

But they don't even know Rose.

What would they say if I asked them to help me save her?

As we walk, the adrenaline that had gotten me this far begins to wear off, and my body is starting to ache all over. My wound feels like it's on fire and my energy is fading.

I let out a weak chuckle, "I'm starting to think I fucked up a little."

"Maybe a little." Dom jokes.

I go silent for a few minutes.

"You still with us?" Dean asks, walking swiftly ahead of Dom, his eyes constantly scanning through the trees.

If the Queen's executioners were out here that could mean some of her guards are too.

My mouth is dry, making it hard to speak so I nod unconvincingly.

"Hang in there just a few more minutes, little rabbit. We're almost home."

CHAPTER THIRTY-FOUR

Hatter

I'm already waiting for them when they arrive, running to wrap a blanket around Alice as soon as they come into view.

Dom finally flipped his connection to the bond back on and told me Alice had been injured badly by Yelana.

I catch a glimpse of the black charred skin on her side as I cover her, "Fuck, trouble. What did you get yourself into now?"

I take her from Dom, running the entire way back to the house, up the stairs, down the hall, and into my office.

The large soft, black velvet lounger is plenty big enough for her small frame. I gently place her down on her uninjured side and get to work on cleaning the wound.

The burn is too severe for me to fix on my own, I'm going to need magic.

"Dean!" I yell, pulling up the sleeves of my white button-up shirt. "Dean!" He's already by my side before I call him the second time.

"What can I do?"

"She needs healing magic. It's the small vials with the blue liquid down in my lab at the warehouse. They're on the third shelf on the storage rack on the very back wall."

"Third shelf, back wall. Got it." He confirms and takes off at an unnatural speed.

Her breathing is becoming shallower with each fleeting moment.

"Hang in there, trouble. You're going to be ok."

"And you're a liar." She lightly laughs, coughing and wincing from the pain.

I can't help but smile slightly at her quip, despite the situation. Alice always knows how to bring levity to the darkest moments.

"I may be many things, but a liar is not one of them. Dean will be back any moment and you will be better as soon as the magic kicks in." I assure her as I kneel down, taking her hand in mine, my lips tugging up at the corners as I brush a strand of hair from her face, her pale blue eyes connecting with mine, "Besides." I speak softly, placing my lips on her hand as I squeeze it. "You're mine, trouble. And I never stop fighting for what belongs to me."

My smile quickly fades as her breathing becomes more labored, her eyes flutter closed, and her entire body seizes.

She's going into shock.

I place another blanket on her and elevate her legs.

Hurry the fuck up, Dean.

I don't know how much longer her body can take this.

Hot tears rush down my face, "Hang in there, trouble. I'm right here." My heart tugs in my chest. "Don't give up on me now."

Her face is so pale, and her lips have a slightly blue-ish tint to them as she tries to suck in a breath.

No. No. No.

This can't be fucking happening. Not when I just got her back.

"DEAN!" The anguish vibrates through me.

The thought of losing her sends my mind in a whirl, the beast within me tugging at its chains, wanting desperately to trade places with her, to take away her pain.

"GOD DAMN IT, DEAN! FUCKING HURRY!"

Not even a minute later, Dean is rushing through the door with the entire tray of vials.

His face drops when he sees Alice's small, lifeless body and he almost drops the tray from how badly his large hands are shaking as he rushes to hand one to me.

Reaching behind her neck I lift her head, remove the cork with my teeth at the same time, place the tiny glass to her parted lips, and pour some of the liquid inside her mouth, being cautious not to pour too much so she doesn't choke.

"Is she—" Dean goes to ask but I cut him off.

"She's going to be fine." I snap, not sure whether to believe it myself.

I place the vial back in her mouth, emptying its contents.

Dom stands by the door, watching over us with the most helpless look on his face I've ever seen.

He knows there is nothing he can do so he just watches as a few stray tears drip from his clenched jaw.

Seconds feel like hours as we wait. When the magic begins to work, alleviation washes over me, and I release a deep breath that I hadn't realized I was holding.

Her respirations grow smoother, her chest rising and falling with more ease, and her complexion begins to return to normal, the tension in her small frame, dissipating.

I stand up and walk over to Dom, resting a hand on his shoulder. "She's going to be okay now," I tell him softly, trying to offer some comfort.

He looks up at me with a glimmer of gratitude in his eyes before grabbing a vial of healing magic and turning to walk back out of the door.

Now that he knows Alice will be okay, he'll be taking Yelana down to his torture room to start on her interrogation.

"I'll go make some tea, and have some food made for when she wakes up." Dean offers, leaving us alone.

I sit beside her on the lounge, intertwining my fingers with hers. Her hand twitches softly within my grasp, a sign that she is slowly emerging from unconsciousness.

About an hour later her eyes blink open and she sighs deeply, stretching her arms above her head.

"You're safe," I say calmly when a look of panic settles on her face as she attempts to gain hold of her surroundings. "How do you feel?"

"I don't know," Alice says groggily, blinking several times to clear the sleep from her eyes. "My head is swimming and my body feels heavy."

"That's the effect of the healing potion. It will wear off in a few hours. Are you in any pain?"

She shakes her head no, scooting herself up the back of the lounger so she can sit higher up comfortably.

I watch Alice closely, noting how vulnerable she looks in this moment. She is still processing the events that transpired in the last few hours.

"You're ok now," I assure her.

Alice nods her head, her eyes scanning the room as if searching for something. Her gaze lands on me, and a flicker of recognition crosses her face.

"Thank you," she whispers, her voice barely above a whisper.

I offer her a soft smile before standing up, giving her some space to adjust.

"No need to thank me. I'm just glad you're ok now."
She looks down at our intertwined hands, "Hatter?"
"Yea, trouble?"
"We need to talk."

CHAPTER THIRTY-FIVE

Alice

I told them about everything.

My past, my history here, how the Queen killed my father—about Rose.

Everything.

"She's the Queen's seeker, Alice!" Hatter bellows over the table. "She turned against Wonderland when she began helping the Queen."

"She's the reason our family is gone. She led them right to us, and they killed our entire pack. Our entire pack!" Dom chokes out, his jaw clenched tightly and trembling with rage.

The last thing I want to do is hurt the twins or Hatter. I'm lost and this is tearing my heart into pieces.

I know the losses they encountered at the hands of the Queen—and Rose. But I also know that she didn't have a choice.

"She's a victim of the Queen's power," I argue. "She was just as young as you were when the Queen had your pack executed. It's not her fault."

Dom shakes his head, "She's one of them. I don't care that she was forced to do the Queen's bidding. She's one of them."

"Hatter, please."

"Absolutely not. It's too much of a risk." He says, crossing his arms, glaring at me from across the table.

"How can you defend her?" Dean grumbles across from me as he snips the end of his cigar.

"You don't understand! I *have* to save her." I tell them, my voice almost a whisper as I try to swallow the lump building in my throat. "I owe her my life."

"No." Hatter repeats.

"I'LL JUST DO IT BY MY FUCKING SELF THEN!" I scream, my anger finally seeping through.

Hatter and I stare at each other, our breathing ragged. The air between us thickens with tension, and we both know that we're at a crossroads.

"I have to do this."

He takes a step back, his face twisted into a scowl, "Don't you see what's at stake here? You could get yourself killed! And for what? A girl you barely know?"

"I knew her before I knew any of you! And I know her enough to care about her," I retort, my voice growing in octaves. "The same damn way I care about the three of you, okay?!"

"Fuck, little rabbit." Dom cringes. "You make it almost fucking impossible to say no to."

"You're putting yourself at risk by doing this. You're risking everything we've worked for." Hatter says, his tone dropping to a low, menacing rumble.

"Maybe not," Dean says, taking a drag from his cigar.

Hatter sighs defeatedly, "Regardless, we need to figure some shit out first."

"What better time than the present for a rebel uprising?" Dean smiles, walking up behind me and squeezing my shoulders, kneading at the knots twisting my muscles.

Hatter rubs his temples, "I don't like this."

I turn my attention to Dom, and he rubs his palms over his face, exasperated by my pleas, "Fuck it. If this is something you need to do, Little rabbit, I'm in."

"Thank you," I say, my voice wavering.

"We're all in, at this point," Dean says.

I take a deep breath, trying to calm myself.

It's not their fault; they don't understand why I need to do this, and I can't explain it to them--not in a way that they'll understand. Hell. . .I'm not sure I even understand it myself.

I just know I don't want to give up on her, and I don't want to have to live without her.

The three of them exchange a look as if they are silently agreeing that there's no other way.

"You two are never any fucking help," Hatter says, leaning back in his chair. "Fine. We have enough people now. We can save Rose *and* take the kingdom back."

I jump up, squealing, and run around the table to give each of them a hug.

I'm grateful for their unwavering support, even if this might be a borderline reckless idea.

"Thank you," I whisper to Hatter when I make it over to him placing a kiss on his cheek.

"Don't thank me yet, trouble. We still have to find out where she's being kept first, and then we have to succeed."

I know he's right, and I know the danger that lies ahead, but I also know that I'm doing the right thing.

Rose needs me, and I won't stop until she's with us and she's safe.

"Just one more thing," I say it as a question more than a statement.

"Anything," Dean replies, grabbing my chin and gently kissing my lips as the trio surrounds me, the heat of their bodies smoldering against mine.

"Leave the Queen to me," I demand when our lips part.

Dom tucks a loose strand of my hair behind my ear, "Whatever you want, little rabbit. We'll give you whatever you desire, all you ever have to do is ask."

Chapter Thirty-Six

Alice

I should have known this was coming.

He stands above me, his arms folded on his chest, glaring down at me with desire burning in his eyes before he forces me down to the floor so I'm on my hands and knees.

Hatter is unlike the twins; his desires are unrestrained and feral.

The broken part of me revels in it.

Goosebumps erupt all over my body, and I find my body trembling with anticipation.

He pulls the heavy leather belt from his waistband in one even swoop, popping it on the desk when it releases from the last belt loop.

I can feel my heart racing as I watch him approach me, the leather belt dangling from his hand.

I know what's coming, and I want it just as badly as he does, yet I can't help but feel a rush of fear mixed in with my excitement.

"You understand now that running from us was a bad idea, correct?" He questions, stalking around me as he speaks.

"I—I understand." I choke out, my throat tight.

"Good," I growl through clenched teeth. "Because I still owe you a punishment, and there won't be any running away this time. There is no escape."

My pussy is already wet, clenching with eagerness.

"You've been a bad girl," he says, his voice low and commanding. "You know what happens to bad girls, don't you trouble?"

"Mhmm," I squeak.

"You will fucking speak when I ask you a question." His belt comes down hard across my ass.

My nipples are hardened peaks, and the wooden floors are rough on my knees as I rock forward from another forceful smack of his belt.

"Yes! I understand!" I shout, taking another lick from his belt.

Sharp, electric jolts send sensations of delight coursing through my body straight to my dripping cunt, chasing away every inhibition I possess.

I moan, arching my back, as my head dips to the floor.

The thin satin material of the red split hemmed camisole dress I have on is smooth and cool against the abused flesh of my ass, soothing the burn just a little.

He reaches out with one hand and grabs me by my arm, his grip strong and vice-like. He pulls me until I stumble back and I'm in a position where I'm sitting on my heels in front of him.

A studded collar has been placed around my throat with a chain connecting it to the desk in his study.

His pistol is cocked back in his right hand as he uses his left hand, the one with a tattoo of a large spade that has a face that's half demon and half man in the center of it, to pry open my mouth.

Part of me wants to scream in fear as panic creeps through me, but then there's the other part of me that wants to scream as he's thrusting into me from behind, filling and stretching me at the same time he strikes me with his belt.

How can I be this fucking turned on and terrified all at once?

"Do you like being chained up? Does it make your pussy wet knowing you belong to me? To know that you're our little slut to do with as we please?"

"You're a sick son of a bitch." I spit, though my voice sounds anything but angry.

He shakes his head, tsking me, squeezing my cheeks a bit tighter "Such vial words for such a pretty little mouth." He says, before sliding the tip of his gun into my mouth. "I'm going to enjoy making it shut up."

I'm so horny and I want him to take me already.

"Wider." He demands, and I close my eyes, quivering in expectation as I comply with his command.

Obviously, I know he's not going to shoot me. He's only doing this to degrade me. To show his dominance by forcing me to capitulate to his wants and desires.

"Good slut. Now make it pretty for me." He orders, his voice a low growl as he presses the gun further in and I'm forced to open my mouth as wide as it'll go, as he presses it against the back of my throat. He releases it after a moment and a drop of saliva slides down my chin.

Tears of both arousal and fear of the unknown are already staining my face as I swirl my tongue around the weapon in my mouth, tickling the inside edges, and tasting the bitter tang of the metal.

He lets go of my face, leaving the gun in my mouth, and lifts the hem of my night dress. My arousal is already dripping down both my thighs as his fingers stroke over my slit, smearing my juices up to my sensitive bud, then rubbing it in slow agonizing circles.

He moans at the sight of my gushing pussy. "You're so fucking perfect." He rasps, his voice strained.

He takes the gun from my mouth, stands me up, and pushes me down on top of his desk, spreading my legs open.

"What a pretty pink little pussy." He says, his voice growing hoarser by the moment, his cock bulging against his pants. "I hope it can handle what I'm about to do to it."

His fingertips make a trail up my thighs and to my entrance. I whimper in response, and he laughs ruggedly.

"So eager." He says.

He traces the barrel of the gun over my sensitive clit, which sends pleasurable chills through my body. I feel helpless and invigorated at the same time, craving more with each sinful stroke.

I break out in a fresh sweat as he pushes it against my hole, sliding in just a bit then slowly pulling back out again, before gently grinding it against my clit once more.

My body moves towards his touch, yearning for the pleasure to never end.

"Please," I beg, shame rushing through my body as I speak the word I hate the most.

I'm disgusted by it.

I was taught to never beg.

But here I am.

I don't want to say it but I want more—I *need* more.

"Please what?" He taunts, smirking unapologetically as he continues to tease me.

"Please fuck me." I whimper, my shame solidifying my desire for him all the more.

His eyes darken at my words, "Are you going to behave yourself, trouble?"

"Yes!" I moan as he slips the tip of the barrel inside me.

My face twists with primal lust at the intrusion, and my pussy grinds against his hand, crashing into him involuntarily.

"Hatter!" I scream, growing impatient. "I want you!" I demand.

"You're not in control anymore, Alice. Not here. Not when you're with me." He runs his tongue over my inner thigh, goosebumps rising in unison across my body as he presses the gun deeper inside me.

I moan louder as pleasure and pain meld together in a swirl of maddening eroticism, and my head spins with a dizzying need for release.

He pumps it harder, faster, his breath growing labored as his thrusts take on a new urgency and I gasp uncontrollably.

My legs quiver as he rubs his thumb over my clit, "You're mine now." He breathes, his mouth hot against my skin. "Ours."

He slams into me harder, and I cry out, "Say it, trouble. Tell me you belong to us." He growls.

"Yes!" I pant. "I'm yours."

I'm floating in the stars, so close now. I should be ashamed that I'm giving him this much control over me, but he needs this.

He needs control.

And I need to know that I can give it to him.

His eyes are dark, nearly black with desire, and his jaw is tense with the fervor to take me.

But he won't. Not yet.

I close my eyes and revel in the sensation of him taking possession of my body.

I'm lost, so lost.

The warmth of his fingers pressing against my clit, the coldness of the metal hitting all the right places, massaging my inner walls as he moves it at an agonizing pace, all of it combines into a tornado of ecstasy, swirling my mind into a euphoric blur.

It should be wrong, but it feels so right.

My breath catches in my throat, and I gasp, "Harder."

"Be a good girl, and I will." He growls.

"Please," I whisper.

My pussy is throbbing, and my body is on fire. I can't take much more of this. He grinds against me harder, and I feel myself getting closer with every stroke.

"Let go, Alice. Let go for me."

I'm panting as I submit to his command.

My orgasm rips through my body as he brings me to the finish line, my pussy pulsing and pounding in time with my erratic heartbeat.

He pulls the gun out of me and it makes a sloppy wet squelching noise as he does.

He then places it on the desk, and takes off his jacket and shirt, revealing hard abs covered in scars, and then lastly drops his pants.

He's so fully engorged, that the head of his cock is pushing through the top of his boxers, pre-cum dripping from the tip.

He looms over me like a fucking God, every inch of his muscular body tense with need. He towers above me, his hands brushing softly against my skin as he showers me with passionate kisses. It's like a divine experience, feeling him worship my body with every carnal touch.

He pushes my dress up and over my head, massaging my breasts before dropping his boxers. Taking his cock in his hand, he strokes it roughly before placing himself between my thighs and rubbing it up and down the dripping slit of my pussy.

He grabs my legs, spreading them as wide as they'll go, and pulls my ass to the edge of the desk as he brings his face up to mine.

He whispers, "When I'm done with you, I want you to be unable to walk. I want you to still feel me inside you even after we part. Now beg me for it, Alice. Beg me for my cock." He grunts, pressing the head of his cock against my throbbing clit and I immediately comply.

"Please!"

I'm spinning so quickly.

I don't know up from down anymore.

He's teasing me, spanking my clit with the head of his cock, and a loud whimper rushes from my throat, my eyes fluttering in their sockets.

"Good girl." He says, running his tongue over my lower lip and biting down. "You are so fucking good."

I'm practically squealing at his praise.

I'm dying to feel him inside me, stretching me wide. My pussy is so wet and so ready for him. He's taunting me and I'm dying to come.

He strokes my slit a few more times, and then, finally, mercifully, lines up at my entrance and pushes the tip in slowly as he takes my mouth in a brutal kiss, stealing the moan from my lips.

He thrusts his tongue into my mouth, mimicking his hips rocking against mine as he pushes himself deeper into me.

Waves of pleasure rush over me as he pulls almost out and then slams back in again.

My head falls back but he isn't having it and he grabs the chain attached to the collar on my throat, wrapping it around his fist and forcing me to watch as my pussy stretches over his massive dick and my cum spills down his shaft from the orgasm that's rocking through my body.

My hands claw at his back as he forces his cock deeper, each thrust making me gasp for air.

Gasps and moans of pleasure spill from my mouth, his rhythm becoming more and more erratic, and I feel another orgasm rushing to the surface.

He reaches down and starts massaging my pussy as his thrusts get faster, "Fuck yes. Cum on my cock." He moans, sweat beading above his brow as his own climax builds.

"Oh Fuck!" He roars at the top of his lungs when I start to clench around him. "So. Fucking. Tight." He groans.

I come undone, screaming his name as my pussy milks his cock, his own orgasm taking him over.

He quickly jerks back spurting his cum out all over my stomach and my drenched cunt.

"Holy fuck." He mutters, loosening his grip on my chain.

We're both sweaty and spent, still dazed by the euphoric high of pleasure.

He kneels down, kissing my stomach in small kisses and I watch as my juices drip from his cock.

"That was fucking incredible." He says, standing up and leaning over me.

"Mmhm," I reply, unable to form words at the moment.

He takes the collar off of me and lifts me to my feet, "Let's get you cleaned up. Are you hungry?"

We'd already eaten dinner before he brought me in here to dole out my punishment but after a session like that, I could definitely eat again.

"Starving," I reply.

"After we get you fed, Dom has asked for your assistance downstairs. He said Yelana is close to breaking and he wants you to be there when she finally cracks."

Dom, you're so fucking wonderful.

We could be on our way to rescue Rose in the next couple of days if she gives us the location. We have to have a plan in place first.

We can't fail.

I refuse to fucking fail.

A wicked smile forms on my lips, "Perfect."

CHAPTER THIRTY-SEVEN

Alice

Yelana is hanging from chains. Her wrists and legs are spread apart, mangled from being suspended in the air. She's unconscious, her head lolled over to the side, blood dripping from almost every part of her body.

Dom is standing across from her, a knife in his hand, a devilish grin on his face.

The crazed look he has would scare most people but I find it absolutely fucking sexy when his gaze fixes on me as I walk in the room and he holds out the knife to me.

"Coming to join me?" He asks, a devilish grin breaking the solemnness of his face.

He is familiar with the type of job I used to do in London, and he takes pleasure in it; takes pleasure in knowing that I'm no different than him when it comes to punishing evil.

I glance to where Yelana is dangling. She's hanging motionless in the air, not even a twitch of a finger and her chest is moving in slow shaky motions.

"Absolutely." My hand trembles as I take the knife from him, but not from fear--from anticipation and excitement.

Dom grabs a small vial of liquid and dabs some of it on his finger before he shoves it in Yelana's mouth.

Though her wounds begin to mend, the recovery process is slow and limited. It makes her aware of her condition but does little to provide much relief from her discomfort. She tries to lift her head, but her body can't hold up to the strain.

Blood drips out of her mouth, down her neck and her wrists, the wounds slowly closing, but still fresh and raw. Her eyes are bloodshot, and her lungs are rattling from the effort of breathing.

"She's all yours, little rabbit.

I walk over to her, placing the blade against her face, putting just enough pressure to make her cringe.

"You're going to tell me where Rose is being kept." My voice is soft and sweet, as I slide the metal across her cheek, a small amount of blood pooling at the sharp edge of the blade.

I will do this so that she feels the full weight of my actions, not only physically but emotionally. I want her to be afraid of me and I want to revel in every second of it, I want her to suffer.

I'm not the only one that's enjoying this.

Dom stands behind me, stroking my back with his free hand, his other palming at his erection.

"I'm not telling you shit." She wheezes.

I smile as I push the knife in deeper making a small, thin cut.

"Oh, you will," I say confidently. "It's only a matter of time before you do." I continue to taunt her.

"Fuck you!" She spits at me, blood coming out with the words.

I drag the knife down, making a parallel cut on the other side, fully knowing it won't kill her. It's more about inflicting pain, and she knows that.

She's breathing hard, cursing at me between her pants.

"Rose told me about you. You were mean to her." I say, running the knife to the center of her breasts. "She said you were mean to everyone." I continue, making shallow cuts all over her body. "And you've hurt a lot of people. Including people I care about." I look over at Dom. "You took his family. HIS ENTIRE FAMILY!"

"Stop it!" She screams. "Just stop it."

"I want to know where Rose is, Yelana."

My grin spreads across my face as I cut away her shirt, slicing it down the middle until it sways on either side of her body.

I lean my back against Dom, his lips dancing across my shoulder.

"Damn, little rabbit. Keep this up and I'm going to fucking cum right now." He murmurs in my ear.

I turn toward him, our lips meeting with the softness of a whisper. The taste of his kiss and the smell of his skin overwhelm me with desire, my body aching to be pressed against his.

"Get a fucking room you're making me sick." Yelana groans, turning her head away from our little scene.

"What a killjoy," Dom whispers in my ear, pulling away slowly. "Maybe you can make her a little less grouchy."

My answer is a simple cocked eyebrow.

I bite my lip and turn back toward Yelana.

She's mine.

"Is that all you have in you? A couple of shallow cuts?" She questions, her eyes panning down my body to the knife I hold in my hand. "How pathetic."

Oh, love. That's the furthest thing from the truth and you're about to find out how wrong you really are.

I shove the tip of the knife into the soft roundness of her left tit, slicing through the muscle and fatty tissue as her screams resound throughout the blood-stained room.

It dangles from a sliver of skin so I grab it, twisting it and yanking as hard as I can ripping it away from her chest and tossing it to the ground.

She watches in disbelief as the blood pours down her chest and onto her stomach, her eyes wide with horror.

Her screams turn into pleas for me to stop, but I pay her no attention. She almost passes out but Dom brushes more of the magic liquid on her lips, forcing her mouth open with her fingers to make sure the healing potion gets on her tongue.

It's barely enough to keep her conscious but it does the trick, so I continue, grabbing the right breast and plunging the blade into that one now too.

She screams louder this time, her hands and legs struggling against her restraints "Fucking stop! Please!" She cries.

I stop before I cut all the way through, "Are you ready to tell me where she is?"

"I'll tell you." She gasps. "I'll tell you. Just plea—please stop."

"Where?" Dom's voice rumbles from beside me.

I got so caught up in causing her pain that I almost forgot he was there.

She struggles for air, the pain becoming too much. The blood from both her tits drips down her body to collect in an ever-growing puddle around her feet.

"The Pink Flamingo. She's in a prison beneath the Pink Flamingo Country Club." She mumbles right before she passes out.

We got Rose's location.

I hug Dom, satisfaction and pride beaming on his face. "You did good." He smiles, squeezing me to his chest. "Let's go tell the others."

I nod and follow him back up the stairs.

Soon.

I just need you to hang in there a little bit longer, princess.

Chapter Thirty-Eight

Dom

The scent of aged paper and leather bindings overwhelms me as I stare at the pile of books on the table in front of us.

Dean is unrolling a set of blueprints that look older than me, stretching them out across the table.

I peer over Alice's shoulder at the faded lines and sketches detailing the layout of the Pink Flamingo Country Club.

"Hard to believe that Hatter's father designed this place," I murmur. "He was the King's favorite architect before—"

I don't need to finish. They both know the bloody tale of how his services were ultimately paid—no thanks to the Queen.

Dean nods, "These are before the addition of the prison. Nothing has changed on the property itself, only the ground beneath it has been altered."

"Too bad we don't have blueprints of the castle too." I frown.

"We have something better, or should I say—someone." Alice grins. "Rose has lived in the castle her entire life. Not only does she know what to expect inside the castle, but she also knows all of its secrets. She was a mere servant to the Queen--someone the Queen could abuse and control, but she was privy to all sorts of information, and she saw and heard everything that went on behind closed doors. She's the key to our plan."

"How do we know we can trust her?"

"I wish I knew the answer to that." Alice answers. "But I trust her."

"Well, I may not trust her, but I do trust you, Little rabbit. And that's good enough for me."

She smiles and it sends a shiver of warmth down my spine. She's remarkable—her unwavering determination and fearless attitude always leave me in awe.

This small little heathen of a woman has somehow managed to capture my heart.

She's a tempest, a wildflower in a sea of orderly gardens—her energy untamed and unpredictable, but always captivating, leaving me breathless and longing for more.

"Here is the best place for us to enter, and we can then have a few small groups of rebels posted in the woods near these entryways." He points to the very back of the castle and its sides.

"But then that would leave the member's only entrance unguarded." I counter.

"Shit!" Dean nods in agreement. "You're right. We'll need people there too. Me, you, and Hatter will take care of Absinthe's high-security detail and then him. Alice, once all the guards have left their posts to join in the fight, you will slip in and rescue Rose and the other prisoners."

My little rabbit's eyes gleam with excitement as she listens to the plan. "I'm ready," She says, determination etched on her face.

Of course, she is.

She's an indomitable spirit that never backs down from a challenge—a force to be reckoned with.

Hatter strides in, his coat tails flapping behind him like the wings of a midnight bird. His eyes sparkle with a hint of mischief, but there is also a sense of urgency in his voice as he addresses Dean.

"Dean, the last batch of pixie dust has been refined and it's ready for production," Hatter announces, the excitement of his progress rippling through his words.

That's a good thing. That means there will be plenty of magic for the rebel army when we begin our recruitment for people to fight at the incursion.

Dean is completely absorbed in the blueprints of the clubhouse, so he blinks in mild surprise when Hatter breaks his concentration.

He responds with a smile, "That's fantastic news, brother. The sooner we can distribute these, the better."

"Indeed. And how are the plans coming along?" Hatter asks, turning his gaze to me.

"Still a work in progress," I reply.

In my mind, I can almost see the intricate web of possible strategies and contingencies unfolding, each decision teetering on the brink of success or being a total catastrophe.

The rescue operation and invasion plan will require a delicate equilibrium, demanding precision and unwavering focus. We can't fuck this up.

As we sit down to review our progress—which isn't very substantial, I can feel the pressure of our mission weighing heavily on me. This moment has been a long time coming, and the weight of all those who are counting on us for success is almost too much to bear.

But I can't afford to crumble under the weight of expectation. Not now, not when we've come so far and sacrificed so much. The fate of Rose and the prisoners, as well as the future of Wonderland itself, rests on our shoulders. We cannot afford to falter or succumb to doubt.

Hatter places a hand on my shoulder, shaking it roughly, "We'll get it figured out." He assures me "By the end of tomorrow we should know how many fighters we have. The final number will dictate our next move."

"I'm heading down to the warehouse to finish up the final batches. Fill me in later." Dean says, excusing himself.

I nod, "Will do."

"Here," Hatter says abruptly to Alice, reaching into his pocket and pulling out a small bottle filled with a shimmering, silvery liquid and handing it to her.

"What is it?" Alice asks, her curiosity piqued as she takes the bottle from him, her fingers closing gently around the small glass vial.

"Something to keep you safe," He replies. "Remember, only use it if you're in danger, Trouble. And be *cautious* with it. A little goes a long way."

She nods, thanking him as she shoves the vial between her breasts.

"You didn't get me a gift?" I offer my appalled, feigned shock.

"You turn into a three-hundred-pound mutt, you don't need a gift."

"Mannnn. . .It's the thought that counts."

Alice giggles at our banter, a bright sound that lights up the dull, musty room we're in.

We turn our attention back to planning and a couple of hours pass.

Alice's head dips as she nods off, almost banging off the table, and she stifles a yawn.

"We have a long day tomorrow. You should go and try to get some rest, Little rabbit."

She rubs her eyes, "Oh, I'm fine."

I shake my head, a small smile on my face. "No, you're not," I say. "You're exhausted."

"You need to rest," Hatter urges, standing up from his seat. "We can finish this tomorrow."

I stand up from the table and walk over to Alice. "Come on, I'll walk you to your room."

She stands up, stretching her arms above her head as she lets out a deep sigh. "Oh, alright. But I'm only going because we have an important mission tomorrow—not because the two of you told me to."

"Understood." I laugh.

Hatter bids us both a goodnight and I lead Alice out of the room. Once we get to her door, I turn to her, my heart racing.

I know I shouldn't, but I can't help myself.

I lean in, capturing her lips in a feverish kiss, and she responds eagerly, her hands tangling in my hair as she presses herself against me.

As our kiss ends and I pull away, I notice the haze in her eyes, a mix of desire and exhaustion."

Taking Alice's hand, I lead her into her room, my heart pounding in my chest, but I'm not going to stay. I guide Alice to her bed, the soft moonlight spilling through the window, casting a gentle glow upon her delicate features. Her breath hitches and she gazes up at me with lustful eyes.

The desire that ignited between us begs for me to give in, but I hold back, understanding that she needs time to rest.

Rather, she crawls beneath the sheets, and I tuck her in before shutting off the lights.

She's out quickly, the light sound of her snores filling the room. I linger for a moment, watching her sleep, before quietly turning to slip out the bedroom door.

I get about two steps away from the door, and I hear her calling out to me, "Dom?" Sleep crusts her voice as she speaks. "Stay with me?"

I freeze in my tracks, my heart pounding even faster than before. I turn back to her, unsure of what to do.

Part of me wants to stay—to crawl into bed with her and forget about everything else, but the other part of me knows that it wouldn't be a good idea.

My mind races with reckless thoughts, searching for a way out of this impossible situation. But as I meet her desperate gaze, filled with longing and vulnerability, my resolve crumbles like a house of cards in a hurricane. Against all reason and self-preservation, I give in to her innocent plea without hesitation.

"Of course, little rabbit. I'll stay."

CHAPTER THIRTY-NINE

Dean

Coming up with an elaborate plan and one that could actually work, made the next couple of days breeze by.

We have been visiting some of the surrounding towns, gathering rebels to fight with us, in between coming up with our plans to rescue Rose and overthrow the Queen.

Hatter found out that a rival of Chester's had put a hit out on me and my brothers, and he's pretty certain he's the one responsible for the missing pixie dust too.

Chester and his cats will be paying the guy a visit this afternoon, so that problem is about to be solved too.

Everything seems to be coming together now, and we plan to make our move tonight. The plan is to wait until the night is at its stillest before we attack.

One group of rebels will assist us at the Pink Flamingo in Rose's rescue, while the other group surrounds the castle, waiting for our signal.

Having Rose on our side and her knowing the inside of the castle is an advantage we didn't have before so once she and Alice make it inside the underground tunnels of the castle, the rebels will attack.

Dom and I will be taking our vengeance against the Queen's executioners. We intend to make them suffer as they deserve. I will not warrant them with a quick death.

I want it to be deliberate, slow, and agonizing.

A light breeze floods the cab of the car. We're visiting the last of the towns before we lose the rest of the daylight.

Alice is laid back against her door, her feet kicked up in Dom's lap as he lazily strokes her ankle and calf.

We've come a long way with her since we first met, and she doesn't try to kill us anymore so that's a plus.

"I can't believe how many people have agreed to fight," Alice says.

"It's not surprising," I reply, "It's because they're tired of living in fear and they're tired of living under the Queen's oppressive rule. They want change, and we're going to give it to them."

Alice nods her agreement. "I just hope we can pull this off."

"We will, little rabbit," Dom says, giving her leg a light squeeze.

I can see how she's doubting herself, but I don't. She's strong-willed, intelligent, and benevolent—with a little dash of crazy mixed in.

If anyone can put an end to the Queen, it's her.

She took out Yelana like she was nothing.

Doubt shouldn't stain her mind with its dark toxicity. She's capable of so much more than she realizes.

Her small stature belies her strength; like an angry lion, she is ready to fight tooth and nail. She stands tall and proud, radiating a fierce determination that refuses to be silenced.

As we come around a large hill, I can see tendrils of smoke rising from the town ahead, and the townspeople are gathered near the bend where the road turns.

The scent of ash and burnt flesh fills my nostrils with an overbearing smell of death.

Alice gags in the backseat, "What the hell is going on? What is that smell?"

I can see it all clearly, but we're still too far away for her human eyes to see all the devastation yet.

"The work of the Absinthe and the Jabberwocky," I say, grabbing Hatter's pocket napkin out of the front breast pocket, and offering it to her to cover her nose.

My heart clenches as we get closer, the annihilation that has been wrought upon this town is sickening.

What was once a thriving and prosperous town is now reduced to a state of utter destruction. The sight is overwhelming, flooding me with horrific memories of my own.

Shattered buildings with a few walls still standing jut out from the ground like broken teeth and debris is scattered all around. Children cling to their parents, tear-streaked faces covered in dirt, their eyes vacant with shock. The sound of anguish and grief reverberates off the streets, echoing through the air, a mournful melody for lost loved ones.

I can feel anger bubbling up within me, and I clench my fists tightly.

These were innocent people, living their lives in peace until the Queen's minions descended upon them. It's sickening.

Alice's breath catches in her throat as she takes in the scene before her. "This is terrible," she whispers, her voice choked with emotion.

"This is why we fight, why we started making illegal magic. To finally put an end to all of this." Hatter's solemn voice speaks out from the driver's seat.

I glance over at Hatter, noticing the tears gathering at the corners of his eyes, and turn my attention back to Alice.

Her eyes are fixed on the destruction before her, and for a moment, I see the same fury that burns within me reflected in her gaze.

The car comes to a stop in the center of the town, and Hatter pops the trunk, hopping out of the car.

Alice, Dom, and I follow suit, stepping out of the car and taking in the devastation once more as I butt out my cigar. The air is thick with sorrow and loss, and I can feel it seeping into my bones, weighing me down.

I see a group of survivors huddled together, their faces filled with fear and desperation. One woman catches my eye: she's holding a small child, her face etched with exhaustion but there is a need for revenge in her eyes.

When I approach them, I see the woman's grip on the child tighten, her eyes following my every move. I stop in front of them, feeling the heaviness of their gazes on me.

"We have resources to help you all out." I grab my wallet out of my back pocket, flip it open, and grab one of Henry's cards, handing it to her. "Here. He'll have whatever you need. Food, shelter, water, anything that may help you get back on your feet."

She timidly takes the card from my hand, "Tha—Thank you." Tears roll down her cheeks.

"PEOPLE OF WONDERLAND!" Hatter shouts as loudly as he can. "THE TIME TO TAKE BACK OUR LAND, OUR MAGIC, AND OUR FREEDOM IS NOW! NO LONGER WILL WE STAND IDLE WHILE THE QUEEN CONTINUES TO DESTROY EVERYTHING WE'VE EVER KNOWN. OUR CITIES, OUR HOMES, OUR FAMILIES—THIS ENDS TONIGHT!"

The crowd begins to murmur, their eyes flickering with a newfound hope.

"WE HAVE ENOUGH ILLEGAL MAGIC TO GO AROUND FOR WHOEVER WANTS TO JOIN THE FIGHT. WE HAVE THE OPPORTUNITY TO STOP THE QUEEN AND HER ARMY ONCE AND FOR ALL. BUT WE CAN'T DO IT ALONE, WE NEED YOUR HELP!" Hatter continues to shout, his voice booming across the town square.

The crowd of survivors grows, as more and more people join in on Hatter's call to arms. I can feel the electricity in the air, the excitement of adrenaline coursing through my veins.

This is it.

This is what we've been waiting for.

Alice steps next to Hatter, taking his hand in hers, "COME WITH US, IF YOU WANT TO TAKE BACK WHAT IS RIGHTFULLY YOURS! WHY LOSE ANY MORE OF YOUR LOVED ONES TO HER TYRANNY? YOU HAVE THE POWER TO MAKE SURE YOUR CHILDREN DON'T HAVE TO GROW UP WITHOUT YOU, YOU HAVE THE POWER TO RECLAIM YOUR FREEDOM! ARE YOU WITH US?"

The crowd erupts into cheers, their fists pumping in the air. I can feel my heart racing faster and faster as I watch them, the fire of revolution burning bright in their eyes.

Alice turns to me, a fierce determination etched on her face.

She's a natural-born leader.

In the short amount of time she's been here she's been able to not only bring us closer together, but she has also made the rebellion more than just an idle thought, but a tangible reality.

Alice is the spark our world needs, and she has no idea of the flames she has evoked in my heart. Every day, I find myself wanting to be closer to her, to feel her warmth and hear the beauty of her laughter. I can't get enough of her and the way she looks at me, as if she sees something in me that no one else ever has before. She makes me feel a sense of accomplishment like I've done something right for once in my life.

So much has changed since she came into our lives, she took us all by surprise and shattered the delicate balance we had carefully maintained. But I can't bring myself to regret her presence, no matter how twisted our situation has become.

I was drawn to her; I couldn't get her out of my mind. The second I saw her smile and our eyes met, I was hooked.

For so long, darkness has crushed down on me, and I've struggled to find a means of escape. I've gone through the meaningless motions and had superficial encounters with random girls because I couldn't find anything in the abyss of blackness to hold on to. Then Alice came along and took my hand, those ocean eyes pulling me out of the darkness.

She could have stayed away or kept running, but she returned to us and watched the fire burn brightly, unafraid of the dark. She became a sea of possibilities swarming around me, pulling me under until I could no longer breathe--until the only thing I needed to survive was her.

As we stand here, surrounded by the fervent crowd, I watch Alice's expression change. The determination fades, replaced with something softer, more vulnerable.

I can tell by the way her lips part slightly and her eyes lose their focus that she's lost in thought. I can only imagine what she's thinking about, what demons she's fighting in her own mind.

But I'll be there to fight them with her.

Whatever it takes to make her feel safe, to make her feel worthy, and loved.

Alice is a warrior in her own right, but even warriors need someone to lean on sometimes. And as long as I'm still breathing, she'll never have to face her battles alone.

Chapter Forty

Rose

Alarms screech in every direction, and guards are practically falling over each other running to get to wherever all the chaos is unfolding.

Absinthe's voice rings out over a loudspeaker, *"All guards report to the main floor. Your only priority is to protect me at all costs."*

The prison guards are never pulled away from their duties. Not with all the assassins and private security protecting this place.

I tug at a broken shard of the tiny mirror hanging in my cell, putting it through the bars to try to see what's happening but I can't see anything through the horde of red uniforms.

My heart races as I wonder what could be happening.

Absinthe runs this place and always seems to have everything well-managed.

If something was causing this kind of chaos, then it must be something pretty big and if he needs that much protection, then perhaps my father has attacked.

It's been a few days since I was captured by Absinthe. From what I gathered when he was beating me senseless, Yelana didn't return with him.

Perhaps Alice managed to escape after all. A smile tugs at my swollen mouth, but I quickly suppress it. Even if Alice escaped, I'm still trapped in this hellhole. The guards are ruthless, and Absinthe is a sadistic man. I don't know how long I can hold on.

I can hear growls and shrieks coming from the mansion above the prison, gunshots echoing as hundreds of rounds are shot consecutively one after another.

What is going on up there?

I hear footsteps approaching my cell. I quickly hide the shard of the glass behind my back.

The guards must be coming back.

"Princess? Are you down here?" A woman whispers.

I quickly turn around, trying to get a good look at the woman. She's dressed in all black, and there's a mask covering her face. It's hard to make out her features, but something about her voice sounds familiar.

And when she makes it over to my cell and I'm met with blazing blue eyes, I know who it is instantly.

Alice.

She came for me.

"Yes! I'm over here!" I jump waving my arm through the bars so she can see where I am.

"Rose!" She cries out when she reaches my cell, her hand instantly grabbing mine.

Her eyes darken and I can feel the anger seeping off of her, her eyes narrowing as she takes in my appearance.

"Rose," She growls. "Who the fuck did this to you?"

"That's not important right now. The only thing that's important is you being here. How did you make it down here?" I ask her, squeezing her hand, my heart still pounding in my chest as the screaming and gunshots continue to sound overhead.

She nods but doesn't push on it. We both know who did it and they are going to die for their sins either way.

"Let's just say I have some help." She examines the cell door. "Do you know how to open the cells?"

"Fingerprints. You need one of the guard's fingerprints."

"Easy enough." She says, turning to walk away.

I watch as she quickly disappears from my sight, her footsteps echoing down the chilly corridor before coming back a few minutes later with a severed bloody hand.

"Which finger?" She asks.

"Try the thumb."

It works and the door to my cell creaks open.

She wraps her arms around my neck, "I told you I'd come for you." She murmurs.

I stare at her in astonishment, unable to comprehend how she managed to get down here to get me out of this living hell. "Thank you," I whisper, tears streaming down my cheeks as I clasp her tightly. "I thought I'd never see you again."

"As many times as you've saved my ass, it's the least I could do," she grins, pulling away from our embrace. "Do you know if there's a way to open all the cells at once?"

"There." I point to a door that leads to the control room that overlooks the second floor of the prison.

We quickly make our way towards the door, carefully avoiding puddles of blood and bodies strewn across the hallway. The smell of death fills my nose and I try not to gag.

I attempt to keep my gaze fixed on the door, but my attention is unavoidably drawn to the horrific scene surrounding me.

"Did the rebellion go through with an incursion?" I ask.

"I am the rebellion, Princess." She winks, busting out the small glass in the door, reaching inside, and unlocking it.

My face warms and I can feel my cheeks change from pink to red, my heart doing summersaults in my chest.

She looks back at me, her nose crinkling as she grins, "But, yes. We are overthrowing the kingdom." She says. "Tonight."

It's really fucking happening. The kingdom will be free of the Queen's reign once more and we can finally heal our dying land.

"Alice, you're incredible." I smile, ignoring the pain in my cheeks, and grab her face, kissing her quickly.

"No, princess. That would be you."

She swings open the door and there are security cameras playing above our heads, each screen focused on a different part of the country club, each showing the chaos and destruction that has taken place.

Most of the guards have been slaughtered. The scene is gruesome: blood covers everything in sight, limbs are strewn across the property, and two massive wolves are tearing one of the guards apart as a swarm of rebels power through the group of about twenty guards a few yards left of us.

"Holy fucking shit." My eyes widen into saucers.

"Focus!" Alice snaps. "We need to get these people out of here"

She's right.

"Do you know how to work this thing?" She asks before she begins to press random buttons.

There are a lot of different controls, but I know exactly which one to press. After all, I helped lock some of these people up. Of course, I'd know how it works.

My people will never forgive all my deceptions, all my betrayals. They won't understand what she did to me, what she put me through.

Guilt gnaws in my gut, but I push it aside and focus on the task at hand. I quickly scan the panel and locate the button that will release all of the cells at once. With a shaky hand, I press the button.

There's a loud rumbling sound as the locks disengage and the doors of the cells swing open.

Success.

"We have to hurry," Alice says, grabbing my hand and pulling me back out the door.

Prisoners—no—families, begin to timidly filter out of their cells, flooding the floors.

"EVERYONE, TRY TO STAY CALM AND GET OUT OF THE EXIT SAFELY AND SLOWLY. YOU ALL ARE GOING TO BE OKAY. YOU'RE FREE! THERE ARE PEOPLE OUTSIDE WAITING TO HELP YOU AND SHOW YOU WHERE TO GO. WE HAVE SHELTER AND FOOD IN PLACE FOR ANYONE WHO WANTS IT. YOU'RE FREE TO GO BACK TO YOUR HOMES OR STAY HERE AND FIGHT. THE CHOICE IS YOURS. THE QUEEN'S REIGN OF TERROR ENDS TONIGHT!" Alice shouts, the vast space amplifying her voice for everyone to hear.

Loud whispers buzz like electricity around the prison as people question the legitimacy of her claims. They've been locked up for so long, it's difficult for them to believe that they're finally free.

As the last of the prisoners trickle out of their cells, Alice turns to me with a mix of exhaustion and triumph etched on her face. The weight of what we've accomplished tonight finally seems to be settling in.

"You did it," I whisper.

She takes my hand and presses it to her lips, "No, princess. *We* did it."

We make sure everyone makes it out before we check over all the cells, ensuring they're empty before we make our way upstairs with everybody else.

The two wolves I saw earlier on the monitor are circling Absinthe, their jaws snapping viciously at his legs.

Serves the bastard right! I hope they shred him to fucking bits.

Yelana is on the ground next to him, her body still and lifeless.

He swings his axe, but the wolves jump out of the way, not skipping a beat as he thrashes wildly. They dodge him with ease, nipping and drawing blood from his heels.

The golden wolf lunges forward, its teeth wrapping around Absinthe's calf, a sickening crack resounds as the bone snaps and Absinthe falls to the ground screaming in pain.

The bone protrudes from the skin as blood gushes out of the wound. And the black wolf does the same to his other leg.

The wolves continue to tear at him, ripping chunks of flesh from his body. It's a gruesome sight, but I can't look away. Absinthe deserves every bit of this punishment.

He's covered in blood and his legs are bent in ways they shouldn't be, he drags Yelana's lifeless body in his arms, cradling her against his chest. Mournful wails pour from his mouth as he weeps into the curve of her neck, grieving his one true love.

The lighter wolf shifts into a man with weird eyes and blond hair, "Fucking hurts, doesn't it?" He asks, getting right up in Absinthe's face, the black wolf howling next to him. "Tell me how it fucking feels to have everything you ever loved taken from you while all you can do is watch as they take their last breath. HOW DOES IT FUCKING FEEL?!" He screams, spits flying from his mouth and into Absinthe's face.

"Just kill me," Absinthe begs. "I have no reason to live anymore." He strokes Yelana's bludgeoned face. "Please."

"Death is too easy for you." The blond tells him. "No. I want you to suffer like me and my brothers have suffered. I want you to live knowing that you're nothing, knowing that you'll never walk again-- knowing that you'll never love again." He laughs. "I want your heart to always ache with the constant reminder that something is missing, and I want you to know that you'll forever be alone."

"This is your help?" I look at Alice and she giggles.

"Yep."

"Ok, then." My heart pounds in my chest as a mixture of fear and exhilaration courses through my veins.

I'm questioning every moral of my being right now as my core heats and my body hums with desire.

It may be twisted and taboo, but I can't help but feel a surge of arousal as I watch him systematically dismantle a man who has left a trail of destruction in his wake.

His sharp words cut through the air like daggers, leaving the other man defenseless and exposed. The raw power emanating from him is intoxicating, drawing me in and making my heart race with a mix of fear and desire.

It's an odd sensation, to be both repulsed and entranced by such a sight, but I can't look away as he stands there--triumphant and unscathed, and it occurs to me that this is the epitome of true strength.

Alice's brows knit together, her demeanor taking a more serious note, "We have one last thing we need to do before all of this can be over with and I'm going to need your help. You know the castle better than anyone and I need you to get me in so I can kill the Queen. There's already an army of rebels there waiting to attack."

I nod, "Whatever I can do to free my people. I'll get us in. The quickest way to get in will be to cross the pond. It leads into the back of the castle, it's the way Absinthe and Yelana traveled there. The back of the castle isn't as guarded so we should be able to sneak in without alerting anyone."

Alice shares a look with Hatter as he guides the rest of the people to where they can go to seek refuge.

He nods, removing his hat as he excuses himself for a moment before the black wolf shifts into a man who looks exactly like the blond guy, and takes over guiding the refugees.

Hatter runs up to us, grasping Alice around the waist, pulling her in close, "Be careful, Trouble. Watch your back, and if anything feels off, wait for us. I'll see you soon." He says, then kisses her deeply.

I find myself growing hot and I squeeze my thighs together trying to subdue the sudden ache in my pussy, averting my gaze.

As Hatter breaks the kiss, Alice's lips glisten with a mix of passion and determination.

She looks at him, her eyes filled with an unmistakable hunger, and whispers, "I promise, I'll be careful, but I won't let anything stop me from ending this nightmare." She says.

"Do you have that thing I gave you?"

She pats her breast, "Yep. I thought I might need it."

Afterwards, the blond guy switches places with him and then his twin follows suit; they all take turns saying goodbye to Alice and kissing her.

At last, she meets my gaze and reaches out to hold my hand, our fingers intertwining. "Okay, Princess, ready to go?" She asks.

I nod, my grip tightening on hers.

"Good," Alice replies. "Because we have a date with the devil herself."

AMBER BUNCH

Chapter Forty-One

Hatter

I can't shake the feeling that something is off.

As we check over the property one last time before making our way to the castle, I can't help but feel like we're being watched. The hairs on the back of my neck stand on end, and my heart beats faster with each passing second.

I try to calm my nerves and reassure myself that it's just my imagination. But deep down, I know something isn't right.

An icy chill creeps down my back, the sensation of something sinister winding its way through me like a venomous snake.

Dom's body suddenly contorts, as he shifts into his wolf form. His fur stands on end, ears perking up while his lips curl back to reveal sharp fangs and a menacing growl rumbles deep in his chest.

All of a sudden, out of nowhere, Henry appears, his white hair messily standing out around his distraught face.

"Henry, did something happen? Are the refugees ok? Did they make it to town?" Dean asks.

"Of course, they're fine." He smiles widely. "Why wouldn't they be?

"Are you ok, Henry?" I ask him, stepping closer to the old man.

"Oh, I'm fine." He waves. "Just a little winded. I wanted to come out and check to see if you boys were okay and if there is anything I can help out with.

I look at Henry skeptically, something about his behavior seems off, or maybe I'm just jumpy given the circumstances.

"We're all good here," I say. "We were just about to leave and meet Alice and the other rebels at the castle."

His nose twitches beneath his mustache, and he looks to the sky, his eyes gleaming, and says, "It's a good night for an exchange of power, isn't it?"

Okay...The old man has always been a bit off but he's entirely bonkers tonight.

"Hatter. I think Alice is in trouble." Dom breaks through my thoughts.

"I have a feeling we are too," Dean says next.

My gaze shifts to Dean's and I give him a subtle nod to show him I'm in agreement.

We all feel it.

"Indeed, old friend," I finally respond to Henry, my hand clasping tightly around the sleek black cane in my hand with a silver upside-down spade adorning its handle. "And by the end of the night when the Queen no longer reigns over Wonderland, that's exactly what will happen."

"I sure hope those poor girls don't get caught. It'd be an absolute shame if the Queen found out about their whereabouts." Henry's smile shifts into something sinister, his lips forming a cruel line as his eyes glint with dark intentions. "Tell me boys. . .Have you been drinking your tea?" He smiles deviously, the moon highlighting the insanity in his eyes.

"I'm afraid not," I answer. It's been a little bitter lately. I think I'm becoming partial to a robust coffee with a bit of light cream these days."

Every one of the muscles in my body tightens, and paranoia sinks its razor-sharp claws into me. I take a step backward, not sure what to make of the old man's sudden change in demeanor.

Dom's lip curls, his mouth turns into a snarl, and foam starts to gather at the edges as he lets out a guttural growl at Henry.

The old man's smile broadens, and he lets out a cackle that echoes through the night, "I see. That's no mind, I only needed you each to take a sip of it anyway for it to work. Now I'll only have to kill one of you for all of you to die."

I flick my cane, a flash of sharp metal reflects in the moonlight, and I step in front of Dean and Dom, "I'll admit. . .You had me." I say to Henry. "I never even suspected it."

Henry's eyes narrow, his grin growing even more twisted. "Oh, my dear boy. You always were the brightest of the bunch, but not even you can outsmart me."

I grip my cane tighter, my heart pounding in my chest.

The bastard fucking tricked me!

It's been him all along calling the shots.

"Who has been working for you? Chester? Is he who killed our guy and Alex Frost?"

"I gave you too much credit, Hatter. Try again." Henry laughs. "You're getting warmer." His eyes flash red.

No fucking way.

It's him!

"But how?" I question.

"Funny you should ask that," Henry growls, his voice becoming inhuman. "Unlike my wife, I wasn't born with physical magic, which is why I spent the last year and a half altering your formula, making it my own. Making myself into this."

He starts to convulse, his body cracking and twisting, growing incredibly larger, and white hair sprouts from his body. His teeth and ears elongate, and he lets out a guttural ear-deafening roar. His fingers morph into sharp claws, and at the end of his conversion, he pillars about five feet above us.

He's a giant man and rabbit-like creature, his eyes glow a bright red, slicing through the darkness. His talons are dangerously sharp and his fangs glimmer in the light as a low rumble of rage rises from the depths of his throat.

I stare up at his demented form, "My only question is why, Henry? What do you gain from all this?"

"Your death, along with everyone else's that you love." His voice no longer belongs to the man I knew and loved—it's rough and animalistic now. "I spent forty years taking care of you and your father," He begins. "And when the Queen began to terrorize the kingdom, I took care of all the people who needed sanctuary. But do you think anyone thought about me? What I needed?" His voice rasps as he lowers himself on all four paws, so he can look into my eyes. "No. No one did. Not even your father when the guards came and killed my, Molly. I needed him to hide her just until I could get a boat for us to leave Wonderland, but when the guards showed up to take her in for using magic, he refused to shift, too worried about being taken away from his pregnant wife who was sleeping soundly at my shop that night per our agreement. He could have saved Molly; you know what he was capable of, you know about the demon inside of him—inside of you. Yet, he didn't let it out, didn't change—he let them get to her and she was executed on the spot." His chest heaves as if he's crying, though no tears fall. "I was three minutes away. Three minutes away when they killed her! If he had held them off for only a few minutes longer, my Molly would still be here." He croaks.

My eyes fixate on the colossal being standing before me, my brain struggling to make sense of his words.

"My father almost died that night protecting her!" I snarl, disgusted by his foul use of my father's memory.

"Your father almost died because he was a coward!" His voice rises again. "And because of his cowardliness, your mother had to die too. He had to feel the loss of his wife—had to understand my pain."

"You killed my mother?" My hands are shaking and the demon inside me is trying to force its way out.

"She must have gotten a bad batch of tea." He sneers.

I take a deep breath, trying to control the fury that's boiling inside of me. I can feel Dom and Dean tensing, ready to pounce at a moment's notice.

"And you call me and my father's monsters? You call us the cowards, but you were too much of a pussy to kill her yourself. You had to poison her?" My resolve is slipping, and I feel my hands curl into tight fists, my nails digging into my palms, as the urge to unleash my wrath upon this despicable creature intensifies.

"And it still wasn't enough!" He snaps. "Because her face was all I could see when I looked at you. He still got to keep a part of her, and I couldn't have that. It wasn't fair. So, you can only imagine my excitement when he approached me, desperate for me to protect you after the Queen demanded that he either turn himself in for the assassination of the King or risk losing his only son. I was delighted to oblige your father and of course, I promised him that I would take care of you. He then chose to turn himself in, even though he knew he wasn't guilty. The plan was always to kill you too, but then you ran away—a coward just like your father. I waited for years for you to return to Wonderland so I could finally be rid of you, but when you came back with magic that the Queen's seeker couldn't trace, it changed. My plan was set in motion, and I bided my time when I realized I could hold power of my own." He leans back and sits hunched on his back legs.

I stare at him, my mind buzzing with a whirlwind of emotions. The revelation of my mother's murder sends a surge of anger through my veins, mingling with the darkness that resides within me. The demon claws at the edges of my consciousness, hungry for vengeance.

A dark laugh erupts from my chest, "You're a weak man, Henry. You were supposed to help Wonderland—bring it to its former glory."

Henry scoffs, "Wonderland can't be helped. It's a twisted, corrupted place, just like the souls that inhabit it." His voice drips with bitterness as he glares at me through narrowed eyes. "I had no interest in saving it. My only goal was to destroy everything your father held dear and now everything you do as well." He laughs. "On that note, how do you think Alice is faring off?"

Dom and Dean snarl, their teeth dripping with saliva. They circle him, snapping at his legs, though he doesn't flinch, he just looks straight ahead at me, daring me to make a move.

I take a step forward, my heart pounding in my chest. The devilry inside me churns, fueled by the hatred that burns deep within my core. Henry's words echo in my mind, taunting me, pushing me to the brink of madness, awakening a primal rage, and a thirst for retribution that I can no longer ignore.

I take off my hat and carelessly drop it to the ground. My cane and gloves follow suit as I turn to my brothers. "Go help Alice and Rose. The guards need to be taken care of, so they only have to worry about finding the Queen. I'll take care of this...Mess."

"What about you?" Dom's thoughts rush into my mind.

"I'll be fine," I answer, my flashing red eyes flickering as I struggle to contain the beast inside me *"Look out for one another and, most importantly, keep the girls safe, my brothers. Alice needs Rose just as much as she needs us."*

Dom and Dean nod their wolfish heads in understanding.

"You know we will," They commit.

I pull up my sleeves, twisting my toes in the dirt, readying myself for the fight that's about to come.

My only worry is that when this is all over, I won't be able to take control back, and I could lose myself to the darkness forever.

My brothers let out a mournful cry as they bid their farewells and sprint towards the castle, unsure of what awaits them upon arrival.

Shifting my focus to Henry, I give in to my inner demon, and a rush of power fills me as it takes control and comes out to play.

My skin is an inky black, my face more bone and spiky little horns protruding from my head now than it is skin and I can feel my eyes glowing, burning, as I lock them onto Henry's, determined to take him down.

He may have thought he had the upper hand, but he has clearly underestimated me. I take a step forward, growling low in my throat as I do.

"Let's dance, old man."

I leap into the air, letting out a roar as I lunge at him with my claws ready to swipe his head off.

He does the only thing he can do.

He dodges and twists out of the way, flying through the air faster than I imagined he'd be able to move for an old man.

I land with a thud, my claws sinking into the ground, creating deep gashes in the earth beneath me.

Henry smirks, his eyes glinting with a wicked amusement, "Missed me."

I growl, the sound reverberating through the air. The beast inside me craves blood, and Henry's taunting only fuels its hunger.

I crouch low, feeling the muscles in my legs coil like springs, ready to launch myself again. With a snarl, I charge towards him, my feral instincts taking over. The air crackles with energy as I move, my movements fluid, yet powerful. Henry's eyes widen in surprise not expecting me to attack again so quickly.

But he's quick to react, ducking and weaving as my claws slash through the empty air. He dances around me effortlessly, his movements almost graceful. It's infuriating how easily he evades me it's as if he's toying with me.

My frustration grows with each failed attempt to strike him, and he takes notice. Suddenly, he changes his approach and it's me on the defense. His attacks are quick, his large hind legs giving him an advantage.

He lunges at me, claws extended, aiming for my throat. I barely manage to duck in time, feeling the rush of air as he grazes my skin. Adrenaline courses through my veins, heightening my senses and sharpening my reflexes.

"You know, it's one thing to manage to be a little bitch, it's another to make me look like I'm moving in slow motion," I mock avoiding his attacks in a hopeful attempt to wear him down.

"I'm going to enjoy ripping you apart limb from limb and feasting on your flesh," Henry retorts, his voice tinged with a sinister edge.

"Well, that's a bit grim, don't you think?" I say though he doesn't seem amused.

His leaps, soaring sideways at me and his hindlegs connect with my chest sending me flying through the air, my back crashing against a large tree trunk.

Fuck.

He possesses far more strength than I had anticipated.

I never imagined he would be so challenging to defeat and truthfully, I'm starting to fear that I may be outmatched and in over my head.

But fear has never been an option for me. It only urges me to fight harder.

My adrenaline surges, my heart pounding in my chest as I focus on Henry's every move. I analyze his patterns, searching for a weakness amidst his agility and power.

Deciding to go on the offensive once more, I slash at his face, but he dodges every time.

My fangs are dripping with venom, a potent concoction that can paralyze even the strongest of adversaries. I know that one bite from me could turn the tide in this battle.

But Henry is no fool; he's aware of the danger that lurks within my jaws. He keeps his distance, avoiding any close encounters that might allow me to sink my teeth into his flesh.

"You truly believe you can defeat me?" Henry's voice resonates, carrying a hint of amusement despite the intensity of our fight.

"I do, and I will," I growl.

The longer I allow the demon to control me, the more of myself I lose, slowly becoming a mindless creature with an insatiable taste for blood.

I want to be in control, but I also want to win.

I hurl myself once more at him, hitting him as hard as I can and letting the force of the impact lift me up into the air. He tumbles down to the ground and I land on top of him. I sink my fangs in his neck and his eyes widen, his body stilling beneath me.

My claws dig into his chest, and a feral grin spreads across my face as I feel the warm blood seeping through my fingers.

A guttural roar escapes from his lips as the panic sets in and he begs for me to show him mercy, to let him go.

But I refuse to let go.

With every ounce of strength in my body, I tighten my grip, feeling his bones crack beneath my claws.

The taste of victory is so close, I can practically savor it on my tongue.

The scent of blood fills the air, seeping through the white fur that covers Henry's body. It's intoxicating and invigorating, fueling the savage hunger within me, igniting a primal fire that consumes all reason and control.

Although the wound I inflicted isn't particularly severe, the blood that flows from it sends me into a frenzy, my mind growing hazy as I lose the fight and the darkness begins to take me over.

Henry's pleas for mercy fall on deaf ears as I revel in the power coursing through my veins. The demon within me, once imprisoned, has been unleashed, and there is no turning back.

I begin to laugh, there's nothing I can do to stop it now. No one can.

I have to kill him.

I *want* to kill him.

"This is going to be so much fun," I hiss out.

"Please, Hatter! Have mercy on an old man! I only did this for Molly. It was all for her." He weeps.

"Time for us to say goodbye, old friend," I say with absolution before plunging my claws deep into his chest, tearing away chunks of skin and bone with merciless abandon.

The sounds of ripping flesh and cracking bones echo through the dark forest, Henry's agonized screams slicing through the air until all signs of life drain from his eyes and he's nothing more than a hollowed-out carcass.

As the lifeless body of Henry lay sprawled on the forest floor, a gruesome testament to my own descent into darkness, I stand over him, panting heavily.

Fuck.

I lost.

I've lost control, and I've lost myself.

I'm nothing more than a mindless monster now—a beast who will now kill anything and anyone who gets in my way.

CHAPTER FORTY-TWO

Rose

As we enter the tunnels, I can feel my heart racing. Damp air fills my lungs with each breath. The sound of water dropping echoes off the walls and it's almost deafening, making it virtually too hard to hear myself think.

The hair on the back of my neck stands up, goosebumps rising on my chilled flesh as we creep through the darkness.

I was quite surprised to see that there weren't any guards in sight when we arrived.

This feels way too easy. I think my gut is trying to tell me we're walking right into a trap, but if we are, it's too late to turn back now.

As we proceed further down the winding passageways, a feeling of apprehension begins to overtake me. The silence is deafening and the darkness is all-consuming.

Our footsteps are amplified by the empty halls, bouncing off the walls and distorting any other noises present. We can't discern if we're alone or if anything is trailing us in these reverberating chambers.

Suddenly, a soft breeze brushes against my neck, making me shiver. I turn around to see if someone is breathing down my neck but there's no one there. My heart is racing, and my hands are shaking.

"Are you okay?" Alice asks as she stops walking and turns to face me.

I shake my head, trying to shake off the feeling of unease that's settling in my chest. "Yeah, just a little spooked," I say, forcing a smile.

She takes my hand, pulling me in close and an inferno builds in my core, my pussy clenching around nothing, "It's alright." She winks. "I'll keep you safe, princess." Her words are a gentle kiss on my neck, teasing, almost daring me to react.

"We'll keep each other safe," I whisper back.

She pulls out her phone from one of the leg pockets of her black cargo pants and types rapidly, the light of the phone illuminating the hollow of her cheeks and the seductive curve of her bottom lip, that's poked out in concentration.

"Okay," She whispers. "The rebels should be attacking soon. We have to keep moving."

I nod, squeezing her hand and I lead the way down the corridor.

The empty passageways didn't seem as scary as a child when I would run through them, pretending that I was in a world of my own. One where pain, heartache, and the Queen didn't exist.

As we round the next corner there is a small, vented metal square on the wall that leads directly to the throne room.

All we have to do is pop it out and we're in.

I peek through the slots but I don't see the Queen anywhere in sight. She might be in her chambers by now, it is rather late. Either way, we can get to it by going through the throne room, out the door on the other side of the room, and into the study that leads straight into her room.

My mother created the open design so she could easily come and go as she pleased without having to excuse herself to hundreds of people.

Alice leans in close, her warm breath tickling my ear. "I can hear your heart beating. It's fast." She whispers, wrapping her arm around my waist. "Are you scared?"

"A little," I admit. It's not like I haven't survived her abuse for years but I just—I don't know.

Maybe it's because I have a reason to survive, a reason to want to live and I wonder if Alice realizes that one of my reasons is her, that my fear isn't just for myself, but also for her.

I'm not sure what I would do if something happened to her—if I lost her—and I hate thinking of the possibility of never seeing that beautiful smile again, those perfect dimples that dent her cheeks, or never experiencing the soft touch of her fingertips on my skin.

"Don't be scared, princess. Fear doesn't suit you."

"You're right," I say, holding my head up, then pushing away the urge to kiss her.

My fingers fumble as I reach up and pry the metal square from the wall. It comes off with a loud screeching sound, making us both wince. We freeze for a moment, waiting for any sign of alarm, but there is none.

With a deep breath, I crawl through the open vent, Alice following directly behind me.

All the lights in the throne room are off, and the curtains are drawn. The only source of light is from the slit in the ceiling that lets a small amount of moonlight filter through.

Alice and I tiptoe across the room. We almost made it to the door on the other side before out of the corner of my eye, a movement in the shadows catches my attention.

"What the fuck was that?" Alice gasps, and I hear the heavy flap of wings.

"That would be my father." I grin, sighing a breath of relief. "Dad!" I yell, running over to the center of the room.

He emerges from the darkness, a massive chain hanging around his neck but something about him seems different.

He snarls, clawing and tugging at the chains holding him, trying to attack us. He opens his mouth and the back of his throat has an orangish glow.

Oh fuck.

"Alice, we need to go. We need to get out of here. NOW!" I yell, grabbing her by the hand and running back to the door that will lead us to the Queen.

"Your dad seems a bit grumpy," She comments, her footsteps pounding off the floor behind me.

"Just a little," I reply, giving a shaky laugh.

We tumble through the door right as his fiery breath explodes the door behind us, blasting it into a million little pieces.

The floor trembles as he fights against his restraints, his roars reverberating down my spine, rattling the teeth in my skull.

What the hell did she do to him?

He seems to have been taken over by something darker and more sinister. It is almost as if he has become a host for some kind of malevolent force.

A loud crash behind us makes us both jump.

"Follow me," I instruct Alice, as I weave through the long aisles of bookshelves that make up the enormous library of the study.

We're almost to the Queen's room.

A roar thunders through the walls and it sounds like my father has broken free.

"Shit! Shit! Shit!" We push ourselves to go faster, flying past shelf after shelf until we finally make it to the door that holds the Queen's room on the other side.

I turn to Alice, breathless with tears welling in my eyes, "I'm so sorry I got you into all of this. You shouldn't have come to save me. If you hadn't come for me, you'd be safe with those men you were with instead of with someone who has nothing but fear to offer." I shake my head, tears falling to the floor below.

I'm not strong like she is, or fearless. I'm everything Alice isn't. I'm not a fighter or a killer.

I'm weak and pathetic.

With this necklace holding back my power—I'm nothing.

"Rose, stop," Alice says, running her fingers through my unruly red locks before pressing her lips against mine.

She tastes so good, like sweet honey mixed with a hint of cinnamon and danger, an addictive combination I can't resist.

My heart races as she pulls away, her eyes locked onto mine. "I'm here because I want to be. I don't *need* anything from you. I just need you. Yes, I could be with those guys right now and they could take down the Queen with ease, but here, doing this with you after everything this bitch has taken from us, that's what feels right."

My knees go weak and for a moment I forget about the danger, there's nothing else but me and her, and this moment.

"I'm selfish, Rose." She admits, looking away. "I want to have it all. I want revenge. I want closure. I want Hatter and the twins, but I also want you too."

"I want you too," I lean into her, my lips finding hers again.

Our tongues waltz, dancing together as the sparks between us fly like stars shooting across the galaxy.

Suddenly, the room shakes again, and we both pull away, panting. "We have to go," I say, my voice shaking slightly.

She nods and turns to open the door to the Queen's room.

When it pushes open the Queen is sitting on the edge of her massive round bed, her legs crossed, and she has her fingers wrapped around a stone exactly like the one she implanted in my father's chest.

"Ah, there you are," she says, a wicked gleam in her cold ruthless eyes. "I was wondering if you'd be eaten or if you'd actually make it this far."

The Queen's eyes find mine, and I swallow the lump in my throat. She knew we were coming.

"Come on in, girls." Her voice is sweet and innocent, too innocent to be coming from her.

Alice takes my hand, a sense of dread filling me as we step closer to the Queen. The Jabberwocky growls from somewhere behind us, closing in the distance, and trapping us so we have nowhere to run.

The Queen stands up from her bed, walks over to the large ivory mantle on the left wall, intricately carved with immaculate detail, and picks up an expensive-looking vase.

She reaches her hand inside and when she pulls it back out, it's coated in blackish-grey ash, "How precious." She laughs, sprinkling the ash to the ground. "It's a family reunion."

It's Alice's father's remains.

"You fucking cunt!" Alice seethes, lunging at her and tackling her to the ground.

The Queen laughs, wiping blood from her mouth, and the vase rolls beneath the wooden console table nearby.

"You're still nothing more than a hot-headed little girl. Always so impulsive." The Queen chuckles.

Alice is straddling her, trying to get her hands around her throat, "I am going to make you suffer before I rip your fucking head from your shoulders." She screams.

The Queen brings the gemstone to her lips and speaks into it, "Kill them." She says, and the Jabberwocky busts through the wall, wood and rubble flying everywhere.

She's using the fucking stone to control him.

"Alice!" I shriek, "Grab the stone!"

I grab the nearest thing I can use for a weapon—an iron poker from the stand near the fireplace, and wave it at the beast.

The Queen bucks up off the floor, disorienting Alice. She tumbles from the loss off balance, and the Queen takes the opportunity to roll away.

Alice grabs at her ankle, missing, and the Queen's foot connects with Alice's face. I hear a loud *crunch* and see the blood pouring down from Alice's nose.

I'm unsure of what to do.

I freeze, holding the iron poker in front of me, as the Jabberwocky roars, charging towards me.

The size of the beast is impressive, easily towering over me and his eyes seem to look right into my soul, stirring up dread like an icy wind that sweeps through me from head to toe.

I pelt back against the wall, fear coursing through every cell of my being ripping me apart like a tornado.

The Jabberwocky swipes at me, claws barely missing my shoulder.

I can't kill my father. I can't do it.

I spring off the wall and slash the iron poker into his paw, "I'm so sorry, dad!" I wail, tears flooding my eyes.

I hate that I hurt him, but I can't let him kill us either.

He roars, getting me in his sights, raising his paw to strike me down. I pivot on my toes, and spring away, narrowly dodging the attack.

Alice now has the Queen in a chokehold, her one forearm beneath her chin, pressing into her throat while the other wraps behind her head, pushing down, cutting off her air supply.

I dodge yet another attack, running over to the Queen, and struggle to get the stone from her. She's still fighting back, and she's much stronger than I expected. Alice tightens her grip, and she loosens her hold on the gemstone, allowing me to pry it from her hands.

The Jabberwocky is right above us, his jaws open wide as he edges closer and closer, as he prepares to make us his next meal.

I raise the stone to my mouth, "Stop!" I scream. "Dad, please!" Tears are raining down from my eyes, and it feels like time freezes.

He looks at me, an intelligence and recognition coming back into his eyes. Slowly, he begins to come down from the rage high the Queen had him on, and backs away.

He prances, pressing his head to mine, and I know he's trying to say sorry.

"It's okay. You couldn't help what you were doing. I don't blame you." I whisper.

"Can you go make sure none of the guards get to us?" I ask.

He nods and turns, walking out through the pile of rubble he caused.

I turn back to where Alice has the Queen, "I want you to break the curse on my father."

Alice keeps her in a firm grasp but allows her just enough air for her to answer me, "There is no way to break it." She coldly chokes out a hoarse laugh.

"Then there is no reason left for you to survive," I growl.

I walk over to her and slap the Queen in the face as hard as I can like she has me so many times before, "Take it off."

"I'd rather die than allow you such freedom." She spits.

I shove my thumb in her eye, pressing it into the socket as she screams, her face twisting in agony from the pain.

"TAKE IT OFF!" I scream, giving her one last warning.

"I should have killed the both of you when I had the chance." She snaps. "*Poor little daddy's girls.* You make me fucking sick. Always vying for attention that you didn't deserve. You're worthless. Both of you. And no one will mourn the loss of you. *No one.*"

"That's where you're fucking wrong," I strike her across the face again.

Alice's grip loosens and the Queen falls to the ground at my feet. I grab her by the chin, blood oozing from the eye I damaged.

"You are the one who won't be mourned. Your time is over. You will never terrorize my kingdom again. Now, bow to your fucking Queen, bitch." My knee comes up, crashing into her face and she falls over.

"Go to hell."

"I've been living there ever since my father met you," I say my voice filled with disgust.

"My guards are—"

"Dead," Alice says. "Your guards are dead."

The Queen moans as I stand above her and dig the heel of my shoe into her face, pressing it into the hard floor, "Tell me something," I begin. "Did you ever even love my father or hers? Or was it all just a power trip?" I ask.

Her voice is muffled by the floor and blood, but I can still make out her words, "Yes, I loved them. That's why I kept them around."

"Then why kill my father and curse hers to live as a creature?" Alice demands.

She lets out a weak laugh, her eyes flashing with something eerily close to sadness, "Because they loved you more. They were supposed to choose me—*love me*."

And it's in this moment, that I finally know the truth.

The Queen's heart was consumed by a seething, insatiable jealousy towards our father's love for us. Her icy demeanor and callous actions were born from a deep-seated fear of not being loved in return. The bitterness and resentment she held towards us only amplified her own feelings of inadequacy and loneliness.

In her jealousy and loneliness, she made us suffer all because she couldn't stand the fact that they loved their children more.

Anger boils inside me, but I keep my composure—for now.

I step off of her and give her a gentle kick with my foot, rolling her onto her back.

I want to watch as the light fades from her cold dead eyes.

Kneeling down next to her, I pull her up by the collar of her dress, "Take. The. Fucking. Necklace. Off. Me." I growl.

The Queen's eyes widen, fear and defeat flickering in their depths. She knows that her reign of terror is finally coming to an end. With trembling fingers, she reaches for the necklace that has bound me for far too long. The cursed artifact, pulsating with dark magic, represents her control over my fate.

When her feeble hands finally unclasp the thin chain, I instantly feel a surge of power flowing through me, and my neck tingles from where the necklace had been.

I'm free!

I'm finally fucking free...We're all free.

The weight of the curse lifts from my shoulders, and a sense of liberation floods my entire being. The Queen's hold on me has been shattered, and I can feel the shackles of her control falling away.

Alice finds a gold letter opener on the nightstand, grabs it, and offers me her hand, "We do this together?" She asks.

I grasp her hand, loving the way her skin feels against mine, "Together."

Chapter Forty-Three

Rose

There is something erotic about the way she pulls me down next to her and hands me the blade.

She wraps my hand around the handle, keeping her hand enclosed around mine the entire time. My breath hitches, my nipples going hard beneath the soft material of the ragged and torn shirt that I'm wearing. However, she doesn't seem to mind my current appearance at all.

I can feel the heat emanating from Alice's touch, and I can smell the sweet, floral scent of her skin.

It's driving me fucking wild.

The Queen is struggling, and screaming, begging for her life, but I could care less for her pleas.

I glance over at Alice, whose eyes are bright and mischievous. She's enjoying this too.

I can feel my heart racing, and my body trembling with adrenaline and desire.

I've never felt so alive before.

Alice's grip tightens around mine on the sharp blade as we plunge it into the Queen's chest together.

Her scream pierces through the room as it slices through her flesh, causing a pool of dark red blood to swiftly spread on the ground.

I feel a strange rush of pleasure wash over me as blood splatters on my face, and I instantly know this is what we both need.

We're both monsters, slaves to the darkness of our own warped and masochistic desires.

Alice guides me in front of her and places my back against her stomach, reaching around me with both hands as we plunge the blade into her again.

The excitement sends thrills to my already wet pussy, and I moan as our hands descend down together.

Over, and over, and over.

We keep plunging the cold steel into her, each time more satisfying than the last.

I can feel Alice trembling behind me, our muscles burning from the resistance of the Queen's flesh and bone.

Blood coats us both when we're finally done, and I gasp as I try to catch my breath.

My entire body trembles with exhaustion, but it's over.

It's finally over.

I look up at Alice and she's breathing just as hard as I am. She turns me around so she can see my face, seeming to be looking for something when she gazes into my eyes.

"Are you ok?" She asks.

"I-I think so. Is she—?"

"She's dead," Alice confirms.

She takes me back into her arms and I bury my head in her chest.

"It's ok." She purrs.

I pull back away from her, a smile on my lips, "Thank you." I whisper before my lips crash into hers, my hungry hands roaming her body.

As my lips move from her mouth down to her neck, she pulls off her shirt, and even though the fight has left us both covered in blood, neither of us cares.

She places her hands under my ass and lifts me up.

Her strength is unexpected for her size, so it catches me off guard at first.

She tosses me on top of the round bed, leaving the Queen to bleed out on the floor.

She claws at my shirt, tearing it over my shoulders in a quick swift movement. Then she leans forward, kissing me deeply before she moves her way down my neck and chest, her tongue tracing its way down until her lips and teeth attach themselves to my hard nipple.

She sucks it into her mouth, causing me to pant, and she begins to unbuckle my pants as she nibbles and sucks.

I crave her presence and my body aches for her touch.

Without much effort, she removes my bottoms and her hand drifts down my body and under my underwear until she finds the slit of my pussy, groaning when she feels how wet I am.

She makes trails up and down my slick opening, sending fireworks to my brain.

I moan as her fingers dance around my clit, my legs trembling when she hits that sensitive spot that makes my knees weak.

Taking off my panties, her blood-soaked fingers slide through my folds, lubricating me even more. She slips them inside of me, the sensation makes my head spin, and I grasp at the sheets.

Her tongue curls around my nipple as she grinds her palm against my clit.

I moan, desperately reaching out and grabbing onto her shoulders, panting as I feel her fingers move faster inside of me, curving up to hit the soft flesh of my g-spot.

"You're so wet, princess." She growls.

I can barely reply. All I can do is moan her name.

My body trembles beneath her touch and the world begins to fall apart all around me. My mind goes blank and my body falls limp, my consciousness vacating its physical form.

Her mouth makes a trail of wet kisses down my torso and a symphony of bliss cascades through my veins as her fingers start to thrust harder and faster inside of me.

My legs quake and my knees tremble, threatening to give out at any moment.

"I'm so close!" I say in a breathless voice.

She knows exactly what my body needs and she's hitting all the right places.

She rubs circles along my clit with her dainty fingers, adding more pressure with each pass until I'm on the brink of climax.

My back arches, lifting from the bed, my head slamming left and right, as my fingers strangle her arms.

She increases her speed, alternating her movements.

"Alice!" I scream out her name, biting my lip, my eyes fluttering shut, as my whole body shakes while I come undone, the sensitive walls of my pussy convulsing and clenching around her.

When she pulls her fingers out of me, my body is left shivering from the feeling of my release.

She licks her fingers clean and looks down at me with hooded eyes, "You taste so fucking good." She smiles this cute wicked little smile and it melts me before she finishes with, "The next time I taste you I want it to be with my face buried between your legs while my tongue is flooded with the sweet taste of your pussy."

"That sounds amazing." I breath. "Fuck. I don't think I've ever came that hard before."

"There's more where that came from, princess." Alice grins, kissing the back of my hand.

"Well, shit. Looks like you two have things covered here." A naked blond man grins as he enters the room, his twin right behind him.

Judging from how hard their dicks are, they must have been standing there for a minute watching us.

"Dom! Dean! Are you okay?" Alice, jumps up. "Where's Hatter?" She asks.

They make their way over to the bed, stepping over the Queens body, "He had some business to finish. He'll be here soon." The dark-haired twin replies.

Alice nods, embracing them both in hugs before she kisses them both, my cum still fresh on her lips.

"Is it too late for us to join the celebration?" Dom asks and my cheeks grow hot. "I mean, now is as good as time as any to start getting along with each other." He grins.

Alice laughs when Dean elbows him in the side, "Well. . .I guess it's ever too late for that." She looks at me. "Are you okay with—?"

"Yes," I reply with a nervous squeak.

My mind fills with a million thoughts, my heart racing, my stomach clenching with need.

I've never done anything like this before. I've barely had sex, let alone with this many people at once. It's like nothing I've ever experienced before—and I fucking love the idea of it.

Dom climbs into the bed on Alice's right, already hard, while Dean lowers himself onto my left.

My heart is racing with nervousness and with excitement, looking through them at Alice for reassurance and she nods, encouraging me to continue.

She holds my hand and maneuvers me onto my back so I'm laying between all of them.

I keep my eyes locked on Alice as she climbs on top of me, watching her as she raises her pussy to my face sinking down on my waiting tongue.

I lick at her pink folds, matching her moans with my own as she grinds against me. Alice's body trembles and I know this is giving her just as much pleasure as it's giving me.

Dom moves to the front of her, stroking himself as he stands up and rubs his cock on her lips while Dean nestles between my legs, tracing circles around my hypersensitive pussy.

Every pass he makes with the rough pad of his thumb causes my legs to spasm as it nears the pleasure epicenter of my flesh.

Alice moans as Dom slides his cock into her mouth and Dean lowers his finger inside of me.

My eyes roll back at how amazing it feels, a breathy moan escaping as I lap and suck at Alice, taking her clit between my lips and sucking on it gently.

Her head rocks up and down as Dom fucks her face, her moans echoing through the room.

Dean continues to swirl his finger over my clit, matching the pace of Alice's hips grinding on my mouth.

I moan against her pussy as my body erupts with another orgasm and my juices flow freely from my weeping cunt.

Our moans increase in volume and Alice begins to writhe on my face.

She's almost there.

I flatten my tongue sliding it up and down her center at a quickened pace.

Dean is lining his cock up at my entrance guiding it towards my dripping slit as I continue to feast on her.

He plunges his cock all the way to the hilt inside me and a scream gets lodged in the back of my throat.

"Oh, fuck. You're so tight." He growls, his brows knitted tightly together.

He pulls back out then drives into me again—forcing another scream from me, though, it's drowned out by Alice's pussy.

He picks up his pace and begins to pound into me relentlessly, pulling my hips up so my ass is in his hands and I'm being lifted into the air with each thrust.

I wrap my arms around Alice's thighs to hold on for the ride.

"Fuck, fuck, fuck!" I moan around her. "Ohhh, yes!" I groan as Dean fills me.

Dom wraps his hand in Alice's hair and drives his cock into the back of her throat, and her gags turn me on even more.

"Show me how much you can take, Alice. I want to see you swallow all of him." I tell her before resuming my place between her legs.

Alice swirls her tongue around Dom's tip before slamming his dick into her throat, her head bobbing up and down as she gags on him, releasing just enough of his cock each time thats she doesn't suffocate.

He thrusts into her a few more times before he pulls out of her mouth and hand fucks his cock as fast as he can in front of her face.

"Look at me, Alice." He orders and she opens her eyes, gazing up at him and gasping as his cum sprays across her gorgeous face.

Dean has ignited my body with pure ecstasy, driving me over the edge and I'm soon lost in a whirlwind of bliss as I'm flooded with a tsunami of sensations.

My pussy clenches around his cock and I ride out my climax, my orgasm washing over me.

At the same time Alice loses it, coming with me as she reaches around my head and pulls my face closer to her cunt, her cum dripping down my chin.

Dean thrust into me one last time before he roars his release and we all fall into a panting, tangled heap of hot, sweaty flesh.

There's a comfortable silence for a few moments, the only thing that can be heard is our heavy breathing.

Dom is the first to break the silence, "Ready to get out here?" He asks. "I'm hungry."

"I could eat," I reply, laughing at how nonchalant and carefree he is.

I can't remember the last time I felt this happy.

"Same." Alice and Dean agree.

I could definitely get used to something like this.

The boys help clean us up and grab us clothes out of the Queen's closet to put on.

We get dressed and head out only to make it to the main foyer just to run into a demonic type of beast with glowing red eyes chewing on one of the guards' arms.

Seriously?

When does this shit fucking end?

Chapter Forty-Four

Alice

The beast in front of me is vicious, ripping three guards to shreds in a matter of seconds. It stares at me from across the foyer, only yards away from where Rose and I stand.

Obsidian skin glints under the pale light of the moon, its red eyes like eerie beacons in the night.

My heart races as the beast locks eyes with me, its stare sending shivers down my spine. I try to stay still, to not draw its attention, but it's too late. The beast takes a few steps towards me, its claws scraping the marble floor, and I feel Rose's grip on my arm tighten.

"Alice. Rose. Don't move!" Dom yells, and the creature turns its attention to them.

"Brother, stop!" Dean yells and only then do I put it all together. It's Hatter.

"What's going on?" I yell out to the twins.

"It's Hatter. He—He's gone."

"What happened? Why did he change?" I ask, confused.

"He found out it was Henry who betrayed him. Henry had been the one stealing from us all along and he admitted to killing Hatter's mother and that's when Hatter lost it. He was afraid he wouldn't be able to come out of it this time. Looks like he was right."

"Hatter?" I call out, hoping that he'll recognize me.

However, the creature side of him seems more focused on the slaughter than anything else.

"Alice, please don't. He's not the person you knew anymore."

"Nonsense. You just need to look a bit closer."

Rose tries to pull me back, but I shake her off.

The darkness inside of him might have been festering for years, a miasma of fear and pain that looms over him like a cloud but he's still the same person.

He needs someone to break through the walls he's built around his heart and soul, to understand his inner turmoil, and to banish the shadows that have taken up residence inside of him. He needs someone to accept him and share the burden of his tainted past.

I grab the small vial from my bra, popping off the small cork, and bring it to my lips.

"A little goes a long way." Hatter's voice repeats in my head, ensuring I only take a small sip.

My feet slip in the puddles of blood as I make my way over to him, and I can feel my body changing—stretching until I'm standing three times taller than normal.

I'm a fucking giant.

"Hatter?" I say again as I get closer, and I can see the pain in his eyes, the struggle between his human side and the beast that has taken him over.

His head jerks to the sound of my voice, and he charges toward me closing the small gap left between us. My gaze meets his, and I see a spark light up in the depths of his eyes.

His feet thunder the ground as he charges forward, mouth agape, showing sharp pointed teeth that are tinted red from blood.

I tense up, preparing for the impact, or for him to rip me apart, but instead, he stops just before me, his warm breath tickling my skin.

I open my eyes and see the wildness inside his. I can imagine the pain and betrayal he must be feeling from the deceitfulness of Henry, someone he saw as a close friend and ally.

My fingers stretch out to trace the contours of his face, and he lashes out, his long talon-like claws slicing through my face before he shies away from my touch.

"ALICE!" I hear Rose and the twins scream from behind me, but I silence them with a wave of my hand.

"I'm fine," I say, wiping my cheek with the back of my hand.

Hatter's teeth are still bared, and his eyes are ablaze with fury, but I can see a flicker of recognition in them. They're fixated on me as if he's searching for something way down in the depths of my soul.

I raise my hands to grasp his face and this time he lets me. "Come back to us," I whisper. "Your brothers need you. . .I need you."

His growl reverberates through the air, his fangs dangerously close to my face. I allow my fingers to trace the sharp angles of his jawline, and I can feel him relax slightly under my touch.

Inch by inch, I press closer to him, ignoring the pain from the deep gashes on my cheek when I lay my head against his chest.

"Trouble?" His voice is rough, but there's a hint of something softer in it now.

I lift my head, smiling as I see him starting to transform back into his normal state, "You came back."

"I'll always come back to you."

His eyes soften as he looks at me, and I know that he is still struggling to contain the darkness inside him.

"But, how?"

He takes a step back, his hands still holding onto my arms, his eyes locked onto mine with an intensity that sends shivers down my spine, "I guess somehow in all of this chaos, you became my calm."

I stare into his piercing eyes, unable to tear my gaze away. The connection between us feels tangible, like an invisible thread binding us together.

"Don't say that," I whisper softly. "I'm really nothing more than destruction itself."

I can feel his breath on my lips as he leans in slowly, his eyes never leaving mine, "Oh, but you are so much more than that, dear Alice. You are the warmth that melts the ice in my veins, you're the flicker of light that cuts through the void in my soul. Without you, I am lost in the darkness. You make everything better—You make me better."

His words wrap around me like a comforting embrace, and for a moment, all the chaos in Wonderland fades away when his lips brush against mine.

Our kiss deepens and his hands become prison bars, trapping me in a cage of desperation and yearning.

I can sense his longing for someone to confide in and share his struggles with, and I am more than willing to fill that role.

Because the truth is, I need someone like him just as much as he needs me.

Where I may be his calm, he is my chaos and together, we are a storm of passion and desire, an unrelenting force that cannot be tamed.

As we pull away from each other, I take a deep breath and look into his eyes, "So now what?"

Hatter runs a hand through his hair, throwing his arm around me as we walk back over to the twins and Rose, "Now we rebuild, Trouble. Now we rebuild."

"IT'S HER!" Someone screams. "IT'S THE KING'S DAUGHTER. THE ONE WHO BETRAYED US ALL!"

"GET HER!"

"YEA, GRAB THE GIRL!"

The courtyard echoes with calls for Rose's capture, as angry villagers and rebels seek revenge for the destruction that she inadvertently played a part in.

The whispers of betrayal hang heavy in the air, blending with the shouts of anger and desperation.

Hatter's grip tightens around my waist, pulling me closer to him as we navigate through the chaotic crowd, and the twins walk on either side of Rose, keeping her in the center of us all.

"Stop." Rose pleads. "They're right. I should be punished for what I have done."

"Princess, it wasn't your fault." I console her, but she shakes her head.

"No, it was, and I know that just as much as they do." She gestures to the growing crowd. "I should have died protecting my people and instead, I betrayed them and helped bring Wonderland to its knees."

Rose, listen to me," I say, my voice firm but gentle. "We all make mistakes. What matters now is how we move forward and make amends."

"We can't change the past, Rose. But we can fight for a better future. Together." Dean says, wrapping his arm around her waist. "Talk to them, I bet if they know the truth, they just might forgive you."

Rose's eyes fill with tears as she looks at each of us, "Do you really think they would forgive me? After Everything?"

"We did," Dom assures her. "And that's saying a lot." He smirks, caressing her cheek with his thumb.

She nods, turning to the angry horde of people, and takes a deep breath, her voice quivering with fear and hope when she speaks.

"People of Wonderland," She calls out, her words cutting through the mayhem and noise. "**I stand before you today, not as a princess seeking forgiveness, but as a woman ready to face the consequences of her actions.**"

The crowd falls silent, their eyes fixated on Rose, anticipation and judgment etched across their faces.

"I am not here to excuse what I have done," Rose continues, her voice steady and resolute. I know that my choices have brought pain and suffering upon this land, and for that, I am truly sorry. But I want you to know the truth. The truth about how I was forced as a young child to hunt those that used magic. I understand that while I may have not taken any lives with my own hands, I know it is because of me that many of our people were captured and killed. I—I was scared, the Queen took away my father, and my ability to use all of my magic. The truth is, I didn't know what to do. I felt so alone, and I—I didn't want to die." She confesses, tears streaming down her beautiful face. "But I have come to realize that my fear and betrayal only perpetuated the cycle of violence and suffering and I can see the consequences of my terror and ignorance. I see the pain and suffering that I have caused, and I can no longer ignore it. I am at your mercy. Do as you please with me—behead me, incarcerate me, choose whatever punishment you deem appropriate, but please know, I love Wonderland. I love my people and I hope that one day in the distant future you will find it in your hearts to forgive me."

The crowd is silent, the weight of Rose's words hanging in the air. I watch as emotions flicker across the faces of the people, their judgment slowly transforming into empathy.

Slowly, they start to recognize the fragile young woman standing in front of them, her pain evident in every line on her face, and every tear staining her cheeks.

"LONG LIVE QUEEN ROSE!" A child's voice yells from the crowd.

The child's voice cuts through the tense silence, and in that moment, something shifts within the throng of onlookers.

It starts as a murmur, a soft whisper that carries on the wind, but soon it grows into a chorus of voices echoing through the streets of Wonderland, until the entire crowd is echoing the sentiments of forgiveness and compassion.

The people of Wonderland, once so consumed by anger and resentment, begin to see Rose for who she truly is—a broken soul desperately in need of redemption.

As the crowd's collective voice grows stronger, Rose's knees buckle beneath her, and she collapses to the ground, tears falling freely down her face.

I rush forward, my heart aching for her, and I kneel beside her, gently cradling her trembling form in my arms, "See?" I whisper. "You don't have to bear this burden alone anymore."

Hatter offers her his hand, "Let us help you heal and rebuild. Wonderland needs its Queen."

Rose looks up at Hatter, her swollen eyes filled with gratitude and disbelief. Slowly, she reaches out and takes his hand, allowing him to pull her back to her feet, and a smile spreads across her face.

"Thank you. Thank you all." She says, and together, we stand before the crowd, hand in hand, a united front.

The people of Wonderland, once divided, now watch us with eyes full of hope.

A few days later, we're sitting around the table at Hatter's mansion, the smell of roasted vegetables and sweet red wine filling my nose.

Rose has easily fit in, and luckily for me, the boys have taken up nicely with her.

Dean is just happy to have someone else who knows how to cook.

"Uh, Alice," Dean says, tapping my shoulder.

"Hmm?"

He pulls a worn leather book from behind his back.

It's an original copy of my favorite book.

I jump up from the table, startling everyone else and jump in his arms covering his mouth with mine, drinking in his seductive moans.

"Thank you!" I squeal. "How did you get this? It must have cost a fortune."

"I made a few calls." He grins, rubbing the back of his neck. "I hope you like it."

"It's perfect. Better than perfect." I gleam.

"Not as perfect as you are, little rabbit." Dom chimes in from across the table.

"I can second that!" Rose smiles, kissing me as she passes my chair on her way out of the dining room.

I laugh, so full of contentment and happiness.

"I have a lot of damage control to do so I'll be in the study if anyone needs me," Hatter announces, already business as usual.

I watch him go, my heart aching as he disappears from view. He presents himself as someone who's never troubled, but I know there are hidden depths of worry beneath his exterior.

And yet, he trusts me with his darkest secrets, the weight of his pain becoming my own, so of course I follow him to get to the bottom of his restlessness.

"You okay?" I ask, leaning against the frame of his office door.

"I'm always okay."

"You're always a liar too."

He smiles, getting up from his desk and I walk over to him.

His hand reaches out and tucks a stray strand of hair behind my ear and his eyes lock onto mine.

"Maybe I'm not okay," he admits, his voice low and serious. "Maybe I'm terrified of what's to come."

"Talk to me," I plead, my heart aching for him.

"This is all I've ever known. Without the Queen and her executioners, anyone can use their magic. What good am I now?"

"Just because it's not illegal doesn't mean you can't still make and sell your magic drugs," I say, swirling my finger on his chest.

"They're magical confectionaries, not drugs." He laughs.

"Aren't there still people who don't have natural magic?"

"There is. Good point. I guess I'm having issues adjusting."

"So, then we'll just have to adjust together."

He takes my hand and pulls me into his arms, holding me close in a way that makes my heart skip a beat. "What am I going to do with you, Alice?" He murmurs, his lips hovering over mine.

I tilt my head back, capturing his gaze with my own. "Whatever you want," I whisper, feeling the heat rising within me. His eyes darken with desire, and he kisses me with a fierce passion that leaves me breathless, knocking me into his desk, and sending it screeching across the floor a good foot or two.

From the sudden jolt to the desk, the bottom of one of the drawers falls to the floor from beneath the desk making a loud *thud* when it hits the floor.

"I'm sorry," Hatter apologizes, offering me his hand to steady me as I regain my footing.

I notice an old envelope on the floor that must have fallen out and pick it up, reading the front.

It's addressed to a Jaxon.

"Do you know a Jaxon?" I ask, flipping the envelope around to show Hatter.

His face is void of color as he takes it from my hand, "I am him." His voice is barely audible.

"What?"

I'm confused.

"Hatter is just my father's name. I started using it to—I don't know—carry on his legacy or something." He shrugs.

He opens up the envelope, takes out an old, folded piece of parchment, and begins to unravel it, his gloved hands shaking slightly as he does.

The paper cracks with every fold he undoes and his eyes are fixed on the words, his mouth moving along as he silently reads to himself.

I watch him with bated breath, wondering what the letter could contain. Hatter's face, usually collected and enigmatic, reveals a rare vulnerability as he reads the letter. I can see his hands shaking slightly.

"It—It's from him...My dad." He croaks.

After a few more moments he finally, looks up with a mix of emotions twisted on his face, a single tear falling from his eye as he folds it back up, places it in his pocket, and sits down in his chair.

"Are you ok?" I ask, sitting on his lap.

He smiles, kissing the back of my hand, "Actually, I couldn't be better."

Jaxon,

I know growing up without a mother has been difficult and there's so many things that she would have been better at, when it came to raising you properly. I know I'm not around as much as we both would like due to my work, but please know that I would like nothing more than to be able to spend every second of every day with you. Your mother would be so proud of you, Son.

I'm proud of you.

You are the greatest gift in life that I have ever received which is why I must do what I have to do in order to keep you safe. It will be hard at first without me, but you are so strong and you will get through the loss. Just know that your mother and I will be together again and we will be watching over you. You're going to do so many great things, Jaxon. You'll be a better man than I ever could be.

I love you, Son.

Epilogue

ALICE

Two Months Later

"You look divinely delicious this morning, My Queen." I grin, rolling over on my side to face her.

Her red hair is frizzed and her cheeks are flushed. I can still taste her sweetness on my lips.

"And you are being quite naughty." She laughs.

"Did someone say they wanted to get naughty?" Dom asks from the other side of her as he stretches.

Rose giggles and tries to get up from our bed, 'Ah,ah,ah." I push her back down.

"I have duties to attend to!" She squeals.

"Mmm," that you do."

As she stands up, her long legs stretch out from beneath the covers. Her white nightgown clings to her curves, teasing me with glimpses of her voluptuous body beneath. I reach out to pull her back into the bed, but she slips out of my grasp with a laugh.

As Rose gets up to get dressed, I sit up, propping myself on my elbow and watch her every movement.

I can't get enough of her. She is the epitome of grace and beauty, the perfect Queen for Wonderland. And even with all of her duties, I know that she is still mine. And I am hers. And that the five of us belong together.

Hatter walks out of the bathroom with nothing but a towel around his waist and my pussy pulses with need.

He's still in the magic business but it's more legit now. He provides healing potions and medicines to the hospital that was built from the rubble of Absinthe's country club, but he still sells his normal product on the side.

Though, he's upped his security since what happened with Henry. Can't say I blame him there.

I help wherever I'm needed. Whether it be at the castle with Rose, at the hospital, or having a little fun in Dom's room downstairs.

"I can't let you leave just yet if Alice doesn't want you to," Hatter growls, grabbing Rose and pulling her into him.

She gasps.

Dean and Dom are on either side of me, their dicks already hard.

"What do you want, Little rabbit?" Dom whispers as he peppers kisses along my shoulder.

I think for a moment, my cunt growing wetter and wetter as scenarios run through my head.

I look at Hatter and smile, "On your knees, Princess." I demand and she listens, dropping to her knees. "Open your mouth. I want to see you choking on his cock."

She looks up at Hatter through her thick lashes, obeying me once again, and opens her mouth.

He grunts as she takes him deep into her mouth, "Fuck." He curses as she bobs her head, her cheeks hollowing as she takes all of him in. "So fucking hot."

Dom and I stand up on either side of her, watching him enjoy the way her tongue swirls around the head, his cock twitching as she teased the tip.

Dean moves beside her, his fingers going to the ties of her nightgown. She doesn't protest as he pulls it over her head, tossing it aside.

I watch her tits bounce as she sucks Hatter's dick harder, her hands moving in smooth circular motions as she strokes him.

I reach up and take Dean's cock in my hand, stroking it gently.

He lets out a low moan as I squeeze him, wrapping my fingers all the way around him.

His head falls back and his eyes flutter shut for a second as I move my hand up and down his shaft.

Hatter groans as Rose pulls him deeper in her mouth, and he wraps his hands in her hair, gently pulling himself out of her mouth. "Keep your mouth open." He growls, then thrusts hard, hitting the back of her throat.

She gags, tears flooding her eyes instantly as Hatter mercilessly pounds into her throat, stealing the air from her lungs, leaving her gasping as spit flies out of her mouth and down her perfect tits.

I'm so turned on, so fucking wet. I need to be filled. I need to be stretched so fully I can't fucking breath.

She drops her hands to his thighs, gripping them weakly, tears rolling down her cheeks.

Hatter pulls out of her mouth and steps away, stroking his hand down her cheek. "That a good girl." He praises her, his voice rough and low. "I knew you could take it."

"You want more Princess?" I ask her.

"Yes, please. More," She moans.

"You want him to fuck your tight little cunt?

"Yes!" She pleas.

Hatter flips her around pressing her pretty face in the floor, lining up with her entrance and he slams into her.

Her screams are almost enough to make me cum on the spot as he drives into her hard and slow, spreading her ass apart so I can see every hard thrust of his cock.

Dom and Dean lift me up between them, and Dean leans in and flicks his tongue over one of my nipples, lightly biting and sucking, then moves to the other, repeating the process.

Rose's screams grow louder as she chases release, and she reaches between her thighs rubbing hard desperate circles on her clit.

Dom and Dean thrust into me at the same time. Dean in my pussy and Dom in my ass.

They both grab a fist full of my hair and breathlessly Dom asks, "Ready to be ruined, Little rabbit?"

"Destroy me."

My screams are harsh and raspy, as their cocks stretch me impossibly wide.

The pressure burns slightly but I'm too turned on to fucking care.

I scream out as they drive into me, my nerve endings on fire as they suck on my tits, biting and gently nipping at the skin.

Rose raises her gaze to watch me take them both in, her pupils widening as she revels in the moment.

She trembles as her orgasm pulses through her.

The feeling of watching her cum and being stretched so full and by the twins is just too much, it overloads my senses.

My release washes over me, as the twins grip me harder, slamming me down harder on their dicks.

And just like that, Hatter is coming as well. He buries his cock inside Rose's tight pussy, balls deep, squeezing her throat as he releases himself into her.

"Fuck." I hiss as I cum again, my pussy and ass pulsing around the twins' cocks.

"That's right, little rabbit. I want your pussy to weep for us." Dom growls.

"Yes!" My legs twitch and I can taste blood from how hard I'm biting my bottom lip.

Rose pants, cum dripping down her thighs as she walks over to where Dean and Dom are pounding into me.

"You take them so well." She purrs, reaching between my legs and rubbing her fingers over my clit, gently, making me scream as yet another orgasm crashes over me.

"Look at me." She orders, her eyes flashing and her teeth bared.

I look up at her, my mouth dropped in an *O*.

Her gaze travels over my body, taking in everything.

"You're so beautiful baby," She says, her voice a dark and sensual promise.

I can't respond as the pleasure is still rushing through me and I'm weak. She begins to circle my clit, her fingers gently rubbing.

"Does it feel good? My fingers on your pussy?"

"Yes." I breathe.

"Yes, what?" She demands.

I love it when she takes control.

"Yes, My Queen." And I'm floating in the clouds once more, my hot juices squirting out around Dean's cock.

Dom and Dean roar at the same time, thrusting into me all the way and I can feel them filling me with their release.

As they pull out, my pussy clenches around the air, feeling the absence of their presence before they carefully stand me up, holding onto me since my legs are still wobbly.

Rose grabs my face, squeezing it hard, and kisses me. "Good girl. I am your Queen. It would do you good to remember that the next time you make me late again." She winks, grabbing fresh clothes out of her dresser. "Now, I'm going to get ready for work.

"If you could have anything in the universe what would it be?" I ask, my hand brushing over the curves of Dom's chest as we stare at the waves crashing against dead trees in the distance.

Dean and Hatter are underground in the warehouse working and Rose left earlier for the castle, which Dom and I will be heading for here soon.

"It can be anything?" He replies.

"Anything."

He pauses for a moment, lost in thought before his curious eyes lock onto mine, "I would ask for nothing." He shrugs.

"There must be something," I say, dumbfounded by his answer.

He strokes his fingers through my hair, "How could I ever wish for something more when I already have the best thing to ever exist?"

My head lifts from his shoulder, tilting slightly, "What do you mean?"

He lifts my chin and then he softly presses his lips to mine, his hand curling around the back of my neck as he pulls me closer before whispering against my lips, "I mean you, Little rabbit. You were always the missing piece to my puzzle and with you, I want for nothing because you gave me everything I could ever ask for. You filled the void in my life and made me whole again, and there is *nothing* in this entire universe that could ever compare to you."

"I know of something," I say.

"What's that?" He asks, surprised.

"Us. All of us."

"I can agree with you there, Little rabbit." He laughs, kicking back on the sand, and pulls me back into his embrace.

My eyes close as the cool evening breeze blows in, the sound of the ocean crashing against the beach is a soothing melody that lulls us into a peaceful silence.

The weight of the world seems to dissolve, replaced by the warmth of Dom's touch and the steady rhythm of his breath against my skin.

I didn't think happiness would ever be mine again, but everything is perfect, almost too perfect. And I'm not sure what I did to deserve it, but I'm thankful for it every fucking day.

I'm thankful for this. For us.

We may be a beautiful, messy, chaotic family, but it's us.

And I wouldn't have it any other way.

Also By

AMBER BUNCH

The Goddess of Death Series:

Invitation To Hell
Bound By Flames
Tempted By Fate (TBD)

A Twisted Princess Collection:

A Pursuit of Madness
A Taste of Revenge (May 2024)

Charity Anthologies

A Wicked Taste of Fate (All proceeds go to St. Justine Mother and Child Hospital in Quebec, Canada)
Twisted Desires (All proceeds go to Cincinnati Children's Hospital in Cincinnati, Ohio)

A PURSUIT OF MADNESS

Acknowledgements

Wow.

Where do I even begin?

Firstly, I want to thank you...my readers. Y'all are the real GOATS. I absolutely couldn't do this without your support. You guys are amazing.

I'm still so fucking astonished to this day that you guys read the shit shows I decide to publish.

Seriously, thank you.

To my cover designer, my PA, and everyone else who helped make this book a reality, thank you.

To my family and friends who listen to me complain and talk to the characters in my head, a special fucking thanks to you. I love you guys so much.

And lastly, thank you to myself. For not giving up, for continuing even when times got hard, and even when some tears may have been shed. You deserve to be called a good girl, and you should go ahead and buy that second coffee.

You deserve that too.

About the Author

Amber is the author of Spicy Romance with a twist... She isn't committed to any one genre. She lives in Ohio with her family and her dogs. When she's not writing or working, she is hanging out with her family and dog, playing guitar, baking, and of course, reading. Her favorite novel is Lewis Carol's Alice in Wonderland. She loves to travel and adores the beach and mountains. As a child, she was fascinated with magic, vampires, werewolves, mythology, ect. and she still is as an adult.

Keep up to date on all books, events, and other information, or contact me on my website: https://www.amberbunchauthor.com

Made in the USA
Columbia, SC
27 September 2024